CONFIRMED SIGHTINGS

For Bill, who made us a squad.

Contents

Foreword 11

A Piasa for Christmas 17

eyeofmoth.exe 73

Once Upon a Time in Turu 177

Acknowledgments 257

Authors 259

Salt Heart Press 263

Foreword

Cryptids change lives.

Maybe not every life. Some people wander this earth their allotted years without giving them much thought. There's a bit of a stigma to belief in them, isn't there? A convention of Sasquatch hunters or Nessie lovers might give the broader populace a bit of a giggle. Who are these people who give up their time and money, not to mention their dignity, to run through the underbrush on backwoods deserted farms? Who spend their days and nights with a camera trained on a single shot, their eyes aching with the desire to *see*, to *know*, once and for all. Don't they know how silly it all is?

But that's "people" as a homogeneous mass. We have a tendency to laugh off the things we can't explain, and dismiss those who believe, with or without proof. No one wants to be seen as a pitiable weirdo, so they shrug it off in front of others. Start talking to individuals, though, and you'll be surprised how many people have a story to tell.

Giant swooping bird-creatures taking pot shots at passing vehicles. Glowing eyes hidden in the darkness around an isolated camp site. A howling sound unlike any other, one that only comes when the moon is full. Unexplained footprints, exsanguinated cattle, crop circles that shouldn't be. Maybe there's an explanation—there certainly always seems to be some glib excuse, but at what point do the mental gymnastics required to *not* believe become more ridiculous than what's staring us in the face?

Myself, I'm a ghostie girl. Seen them, believe in them, though I'm open to explanations and don't have fixed ideas of what, exactly, they are. There are plenty of folks ready to scoff at ghosts, as well, but somehow there's less derision aimed at spirit hunters. Maybe it's because shades tend to wander dilapidated Gothic castles and Victorian era houses instead of swamps and isolated mountain tops. Seems a little classist to go rating the unknown by zip code. So while I wasn't really a cryptid person, I understood the belief, the desire to follow these things caught only in glimpses and blurry photos, that promise something new, an adventure. Maybe even magic.

Even so, I never anticipated writing a creature feature, much less one starring one of the more enigmatic cryptids I'm aware of. But Mothman interested me, so I read up on the lore, and when I found a chance, I wove him into a plot and called it done. It didn't occur to me I'd stepped into a world I was unprepared for. Since the publication of BELOW I've been on cryptid panels at every convention, regularly quizzed about them on podcasts, and given written interviews that delve into my knowledge (or lack thereof). Honestly, I feel a bit of a fraud. There are people who've devoted significant portions of their lives to studying, following, and writing about these unknowable creatures. I'm just the chick who bought the band t-shirt because I liked the way it fit—don't ask me my favorite songs.

But when I say cryptids change lives, I'm speaking from experience. About a year ago, in May of 2022, I attended a charity event at The Stanley Hotel and sold copies of BELOW, my Mothman novella. It was a wonderful night, with over three-hundred attendees there to buy books, hear stories, watch a special live-performance of the No Sleep Podcast, all to benefit the Glen Haven Area Volunteer Fire Department, who saved the hotel from the 2020 wildfires. We chose The Stanley as a location in part because of its own creepy history. There are lots of tales of hauntings wandering the halls and grounds of the hotel. What a delicious little thrill, to think we might see something beyond the realms of the known world, and I believe we felt bonded by the atmosphere and location as much as anything else.

At one point three charming and mischievous women approached to buy books, chat writing, and tell me about their own cryptid project, which immediately piqued my interest. They planned a three-novella collection that would run the gamut of critters, tone, and style. They asked if I'd consider writing the introduction to it, and I accepted, the only reluctance I felt stemming from that nagging feeling of being an impostor. Ryan, P.L. and Bridget knew what the hell they were talking about. They mentioned cryptids I'd never even heard of, but part of the reason I tamped down that feeling of inadequacy was, these stories sounded damn good. A Hallmark romance cryptid? Mothman in space? Murder mystery with Bigfoot as the detective? They jokingly took a picture to memorialize my agreement, but frankly, you couldn't have kept me from pouncing on this baby, even if we hadn't all become friends over the intervening year.

Whatever expectations might have arisen based on the above thumbnails, go ahead and double them. CONFIRMED SIGHTINGS is every bit as wonderful as I'd hoped. Delving into Bridget D. Brave's opener, *A Piasa For Christmas* (an unbeatable title), I laughed until my stomach hurt, then sobered quickly as things took a darker turn. (I also had the pleasure of hearing Bridget read from this novella at the Ghoulish Book Fest, and it was amazing.) Flipping quickly through my Kindle, I moved on to P.L. McMillan's *eyeofmoth.exe*, a space adventure reminiscent of all the best parts of Star Trek, Aliens, and Starship Troopers, but very much its own thing. McMillan has a knack for creating characters you immediately bond with, and even those you don't like, she makes sure you understand them. A harrowing tale that went places I never expected, and never once pulled a punch. By the time I got to the last in the collection, Ryan Ketterer's *Once Upon a Time in Turu*, I'd thrown all preconceived notions out the window. This collection was nothing like I expected—it delivered so much more. Ketterer's murder mystery, set in a city where every monster and cryptid comes out to play, had notes of Star Wars meets Law & Order plus a hearty dose of X-Files. Lots of fun and fantasy with plenty of gore and suspense—it's a great one to end the collection with.

As I'd suspected, this crew of talented authors were far more expert in the realm of cryptids than I. I learned of plenty I'd never heard of before, read their lore melded into a larger story line, and dug the way Brave, Ketterer, and McMillan made each legend their own. Ultimately I came away with the realization that *this* is what it's all about. Taking something with whispers of authenticity, tantalizing breaths of a trail to follow, and bending it to your will. The cryptids, the real ones, out there hiding and likely hoping we don't find them, in a way they belong to all of us. By casting them in roles unseen and previously unimagined—a romantic lead (sort of), a tortured, vengeful creature given new life in space with disastrous consequences, a Bigfoot gumshoe protagonist—we drag them into the future with us, and in the process, we give them new life. It's part of the tradition, isn't it? Oral and written histories, whispered tales and bellowed attestations. We add to the lore, and in so doing, we make ourselves part of a bigger community.

For what, after all, are we, the horror readers of the world? We're the same as our cryptid (and ghost) hunting compatriots. We're all seeking something beyond the borders of the known world. Maybe it's part of a desire to feel part of something bigger than ourselves, to feel there's a grander plan, more stars in more skies than we can know and see. Maybe it's a quest for camaraderie, for friends to join us on thrilling paths, any hope for which likely died at the end of childhood. Maybe for some it's even a way to connect with ourselves, with the darkest corners and furthest reaches that are as unknowable as our own psyches.

The nice thing is, it doesn't really matter why. What does matter is the open door, the standing invitation to come be part of a community. Whether you take it seriously or look at it solely as entertainment, it doesn't matter. CONFIRMED SIGHTINGS opens the door and beckons you close, offering humor and terror and human connection. Maybe you'll reach the last page unchanged, but for the undeniable enjoyment of damn good storytelling. But maybe, like me, you'll reach the end and discover there are no impostors in the land of the impossible. You belong here, with us, expert or not.

Welcome to the farthest reaches, friends. We're glad you're here.

Laurel Hightower
Lexington, KY
May 9, 2023

A Piasa for Christmas

directed by Bridget D. Brave

A Piasa for Christmas

Bridget D. Brave

The following entries are compiled from the online journal of Kaycie Cooley, a makeup blogger from the Midwest: facethedaywithkaycie.blogtacular.com

A Note to My Readers
From Kaycie Elizabeth Cooley
May 12, 2022

There is something you have to understand about me, if you want to know the *real* Kaycie Cooley: I am *not* like the other girls. I don't mean this in an edgy, terminally-online way, I'm just being honest about the very real situation I'm in. There're things about me that are dark, things that no one knows, not even my best friend, who is currently Jana McRenna, and I swear I tell her just about everything.

I currently live in the same small town where I was born; right where hitting the water means Illinois stops and Missouri begins. There's a hundred small towns just like mine: still trying to lure in tourists with steamboats, tales of Mark Twain, and promises of haunted hotels. My hometown wasn't different, just smaller and in an area where the waters of the Mississippi and the Missouri mix into a muddy froth. It's a place they call "The Riverbend."

Isn't that name just fucking romantic? I mean it. I say "The Riverbend" and an image is *evoked:* tiny brick storefronts and adorable shuttered houses, sleepy riverside restaurants where the locals will fry you up a catfish for cheap and spin you a big fish story for free. I'll tell you that image is not at all incorrect. My area, especially the little pocket my parents settled down in, is Picturesque. As. Fuck. It's like a Hallmark movie, but real. There's a post office that actually has a legit cafe that serves pie and cute little salads made and served by sisters who are eight generations deep in this area. You can also have brunch there and totally get wasted on mimosas and everything. We even have a local legendary monster, born from stories about a cliff painting discovered by the first white explorers in this area. It's called the Piasa Bird and even though we're not entirely sure who painted it or when, it's become the unofficial mascot of this sleepy little burg. I expected to be bored when I moved back, but it turns out this place is actually better than I remember it, and I will admit my memories of the place always border on completely nostalgic when I am asked to talk about "home."

When I left my job as a busy marketing assistant in New York and moved back to this place, I felt like this was a new era for me. I would get back to my roots, find myself again, learn to live my best life. Finally get that influencer gig going with this makeup and lifestyle blog, maybe rekindle with an old flame, if he was still around.

I guess I always thought I'd end up like a Hallmark movie, too.

I'm sure my parents had also hoped for that.

But I had to go and disappoint them.

You see, I recently got into a relationship with a… minor deity from a civilization so ancient I am apparently incapable of saying their name without going insane, so yeah. *That* happened.

I told you: I'm not like the other girls.

I'm in love with the Piasa Bird.

On Love's Golden Wings
Kaycie Loves Piasa
June 3, 2022

Back when I started *Face the Day with Kaycie*, I simply wanted to share my sparkle with the world. I was coming off a five year post-grad stint in New York with little to show for it. I'd graduated from my college business program full of hopes and promises and thought that the big city would hold all the answers, would provide me with a lifetime full of happiness. Instead I ended up spending all my fancy new salary on rent and food, hardly ever enjoying the nightlife I'd been promised. New York might be the city that never sleeps, but that was nearly all I had time for after an hour-and-a-half train ride, fighting my way up 54th, and then enduring my six-flight climb to my studio apartment full of roaches and not much else.

Worse yet, the love I was absolutely yearning for was nowhere to be found. Divey bars and dating apps didn't bring me any closer to the metropolitan Prince Charming I'd been dreaming of. I was lucky if I didn't worry I was going to get stabbed fifteen seconds after meeting a guy. There are some real sleazebags out there, and even if they aren't totally creepy, they barely know how to treat a girl. I was feeling doomed. I started to regret my decision to dump my high school sweetheart even after he stuck with me all through those four long years of undergrad. I just always believed that when I found The One, I would KNOW, you know? I thought that there would be sparks and music and magic and we'd fall into one another's arms and promise to never be apart ever again. Robbie Cartwright, while ruggedly handsome in that very corn-fed Midwestern way, was never my fate. Sure he was the hottest guy in high school and he definitely made my prom pictures pop, but I couldn't end up with him. It seemed too trite and overdone... too *comfortable* to end up with my high school boyfriend, especially after all those years dreaming of a big city life. I thought I was destined for a far greater romance, something for the story books.

Little did I know that love would be found in my hometown, with someone I had actually known *of* my entire life, and was certainly something out of the storybooks - in fact, it's a book you would have found right on my childhood bedroom shelf. This romance wasn't how I hoped, or where I planned, but it is perfect, nonetheless.

Of course, I was nervous about bringing my unconventional love life out into the open. When I first considered moving away from makeup tutorials and scarf-tying guides, I worried I would lose the few followers I already had. I never could have dreamed that my little romance would cause such a stir, or that posting about it would bring in such a HUGE audience, but here we are! Thank you so much for the likes, the subscriptions, and the sweet comments!

Additionally, thank you to everyone who submitted questions after my last post. Now that we've got the "why" out of the way, I'm happy to announce a rebrand! Face the Day with Kaycie is now officially Kaycie Loves Piasa!

As promised, here's Kaycie Loves Piasa's first-ever Q&A.

Q1 (from Stacee in Sarasota): How did you even meet an ancient deity in a town of less than 800?

Oh man, we get asked this *all the time*. I've been joking that I should really just put up an FAQ with that being the only question, hahahah! The fact is that I thought I was *helping,* doing my court-ordered community service for that tiny traffic ticket I got on St. Patrick's Day. I know some of you heard about that, and I want to tell you that the events of that evening were *greatly* exaggerated. I wasn't actually naked, for one.

So anyway, I was pressure cleaning the park signs at Three Ridges Bluff and I noticed that there was a ton of paint on the front of the bluff. I turned the sprayer toward it, started blasting, and the cop who was supervising shouted at me, "Hey, stop that!" Apparently it was some rare piece of cliff that had the original version of the larger Piasa Bird cliff painting, was a site of "historical significance," and it was ultra-protected.

Turns out it wasn't just protected, it was a literal magical prison. I know, I was also in shock. Removing it before it fades away naturally over time could free him from his captivity before his sentence was served and his eternal soul could be collected. I mean, who knew, right? They were always telling us that huge rock painting was something one of the local tribes in this area painted of a huge monster of legend, but it turns out that some white guy just made that shit up in the early 1900s. Don't misread, the painting concept was very real. But we have no idea what the painting was or what it was supposed to represent, whoever painted it wasn't around to explain it, and so we just kept copying it and selling it on t-shirts and finally putting a more colorful version in a more tourist friendly location.

So I stop spraying and there was this rumble and a loud crack and I'm thinking, "holy shit, it's an earthquake, we're all doomed." But instead of the earth splitting open there's a dazzling beam of electric hot light and I'm knocked fifteen feet back *straight* onto my ass, destroying my favorite cut-offs. Then this voice sort of starts thundering, only I realize I'm the only one who can hear it and I cannot understand a single thing it's saying because it's speaking in some guttural language with way too many "ou" and "ch" sounds and then I just *knew*. It's hard to explain, but it's like I was suddenly struck with this awesome weight of knowing that I have somehow released a supernatural, all-powerful being that was now bound to me forever.

Talk about a sign, am I right?

There I am, feeling like a total asshole, having just freed a literal ancient god. And I mean, it was a rough go at first. Piasa did kill that cop, and really roughed up some of the other community service prisoner dudes while trying to free them from their leg irons. They didn't quite understand they were being freed. I mean, this is a preternatural being from a time and place we cannot fathom. Piasa didn't exactly speak English.

Q2 (from Meeghan, no city given): Was it love at first sight?

I mean, no? Hahaha. I won't lie, I actually peed my pants. Fully vacated my bladder. I was fucking terrified! The moment my vision cleared, I saw Piasa in the flesh (so to speak) for the first time and just froze. I thought it was going to eat me, which I now admit was a dangerous preconception I had based on a lie told by a colonizer who was just trying to turn profit off a history that wasn't his to tell. It's pretty fucked up how we just decide that all indigenous practices automatically involve human sacrifice, right? That's why I started this blog. I want to get the real story out there and help people across this nation recognize the very real implicit racism that most of our folklore is based on.

Stop leaving comments telling me this is woke bullshit and that I'm being manipulated into thinking Piasa is a literal benevolent being who was wrongfully imprisoned by a mystic priest as part of an arcane ritual in a religious ceremony from a long-lost civilization we no longer have a word for. YOU DON'T EVEN FUCKING KNOW PIASA.

Q3 (from Mashlynn, Longview): How do you hang out? Isn't he like, gigantic?

This is a common misconception because of the size of the painting's *you've* seen at various tourist attractions. When they decided to repaint the Piasa further up river, they didn't copy the original as well as they thought. They missed the inscription at the bottom, mainly because it's not in a language we can completely perceive or read. Apparently it reads, "Actual size." Isn't that hilarious? I laughed *so* hard when he told me that.

PS. I'm actually taller than him when I'm in heels!

Q4 (from Bryce, Minneapolis): How do you two communicate?

Oh that took work! Piasa not only spoke a collection of languages I'd never heard of, but his primary method of communication is to directly place his thoughts inside my head. Imagine if you will a thousand voices speaking languages you can't comprehend, all at once inside your brain. I had a constant headache until we learned better methods, although I still get the regular nosebleeds and dilated pupils.

After I'd overcome my initial panic response and settled down, I realized that he was trying his hardest to talk to me. Just to talk to me. I felt my heart warm in response. I started slowly, the way you would with a child, pointing at various things and repeating the word until I saw that first glimmer of recognition spark in his eyes. Soon he was placing those same words in my head as he lifted each item. Rock, twig, leaf, grass, can, paper. The first time he understood and said my name, it was like the blood was singing in my veins. I couldn't wait for him to say it again.

Now we have full conversations and I'm even picking up some of his known languages.

Q5 (submitted anonymously): Can you even have sex with that?

I'll keep telling you: this is a very personal and rude question, and the phrasing is even more insulting. First of all, Piasa is from an ancient race of celestial beings that has evolved beyond the idea of a binary. There are actually twenty-seven distinct universal genders, anyway. Please stop calling Piasa a "that." While he is from a realm beyond gender, Piasa prefers he/him.

But you should know that I have ZERO complaints about the physical aspects of our relationship. I have never felt so fulfilled.

Q6 (from Jaycyeelynn, Memphis): Where is this relationship going?

I don't know! We're taking things slow right now. I just started that new job at the hospital and Piasa is adjusting to a world he no longer recognizes nor understands. We want to keep it casual!

Q7 (from Breanna, St. Louis): What do your parents think?

Oh my gosh, they want to meet him but I am NOT ready for that. I worry they'll just ask him questions about what happened with the people who were here before us and he is so tired of that. We stopped double dating entirely because of it. Every question just leads to a dozen more. It's always, "where did they go?" then "why did you make an entire civilization disappear?" and "did you actually kill them?" or "what do you mean by 'an endless river of suffering blood that awaits us all'?" Ugh. That's in the past, and should stay in the past. He wants people to be curious about who he is *now*.

Q8 (from Mike, Tempe): If the Piasa Bird thing is made up, why do you refer to him as that?

While I recognize that the name given to the creature painted on the rock is problematic, Piasa and I had to come to some sort of understanding that he needed to have something I could use to refer to him and I needed to both be able to speak his name aloud without flaying actual flesh off someone's arm (I'll tell that story sometime) and to sort of explain who and what he is. People know "Piasa" here, so that works.

Q9 (Candy, Placentia): Aren't you worried he's going to eat you?

You know, this is a really hurtful question. Piasa, to my knowledge, has never eaten ANYONE. The police officer's death, while tragic, was self-defense. He was being *shot* at. The municipal authorities are still not sure how to deal with this, since he's not exactly a citizen beholden to our laws but also not classified as any of the dangerous animals they're allowed to euthanize in case of rogue attacks. I don't think Piasa can be euthanized, anyway. He's an immortal interdimensional being. He doesn't even respond to ibuprofen.

Q10 (Teena, Killeen): What makes him so special?

This is always difficult to answer because Piasa came to me with a lot of internalized hatred and some serious self-esteem issues. He first learned that people thought he was ugly when he saw the way he was displayed in that frankly rude caricature everyone wears on t-shirts and prints on drink coasters. We won't even talk about his reaction to photos of my high school mascot. It's a lot to absorb for anyone. Now imagine you're trying to do that and understand how highways and debit cards work all at the same time.

But also, regardless of how he looks, he is really beautiful inside. He has this soul of just pure poetry. He loves music and movies! We just started binging *Friends*. He really likes Joey. And he's just so kind. I'd want to spend time with him, even if I wasn't attracted to him. He makes me feel so special, like I'm the only thing in the entire universe that matters to him. If you could understand how much of our universe he's able to actively perceive at any given time, you'd know just how very unique that is. I am the only girl in existence, in his eyes. It's incredibly romantic.

That's all I have time for tonight! Leave comments with more questions, or your thoughts on any of my answers!

We had a bit of an, uh, *experience* at this dining establishment. Recently my partner, Piasa, and I made our relationship officially official. After a few months of dating, I think we were both ready to admit that we had fallen in love. I wanted to do something special to commemorate this milestone in the Story of Us.

When we planned our first official "date" as a committed monogamous couple, I could think of no better location than the Rialto Bistro. I have celebrated many birthdays, my parents' anniversary, my high school graduation, and countless other occasions there and therefore it was a place that was actually special to me and my family. I wanted it to be special for Piasa too.

I made a reservation for Friday night, asked for a special table in one of the alcoves so that we could enjoy a bit of privacy, I even bought a new dress for the occasion. I should have known something was off when we arrived. The hostess seemed terrified, for some reason, and it smacked of bigotry to me. She left in tears when I asked if there was a problem, and we ended up being seated by another member of the staff. From the outset, the waitstaff was stand-offish and almost skittish when they approached, addressing only me when they had a question or a suggestion and largely behaving as if they were too afraid to engage with my date. Meanwhile, I could tell from the general demeanor of the other diners that we were in for a bumpy night. We hadn't even received our complimentary bread before some local prude had to come up to our table and start raging about how there was only one true god and I can't be dating another one and blah, blah, blah Jesus, blah blah.

It isn't like Piasa is going around saying he's THE god. He's just saying that maybe there are more gods than our teeny tiny human brains could process and they are all around us but only visible when conditions are right and we would be surprised just how fucking crowded this planet is with gods and other interdimensional beings if we could just get out from up our own asses for a minute!

Anyway, I asked her to leave us alone and called for the waiter to assist. I could tell Piasa was getting angry, he had already levitated one of the wine glasses and smashed it into the wall.

Imagine my surprise when the owner comes up and asks US to leave! I was so astounded I couldn't speak. Luckily, Piasa tore our table in half and banished two busboys to the shadow realm, so our thoughts on being treated like this were *crystal* clear.

You know, I'm really getting tired of the attitudes around this place. Sure, it's fine to wear his likeness on a t-shirt or celebrate him in your ironic parades, but get to meet the actual being? Real and in as close an approximation to flesh as we are capable of comprehending as carbon-based life forms? I would think people would be a bit more grateful, maybe even impressed. Instead it's just one dramatic meltdown after another, screaming about the end of days while blood runs from their ears.

Fortunately, after our terrible experience at Rialto, we found a pub down the way that, while not quite as elegant a setting, was very warm and welcoming to us. I'll be suggesting Scooter's Pub to friends and family as an excellent alternative with a much less snooty and judgmental vibe in the future. Plus Wednesdays are half price wings and taps!

A New Home
September 1, 2022

As many of you know, the question of where Piasa is going to live has been up in the air. He's now bringing in income (I still am not entirely sure how), it's getting to be fall, and quite frankly he's outgrown that studio he's been renting month to month and the smell is causing some complaints from the other neighbors. Also he's somehow managed to collect so much STUFF already!

After reviewing the terms of his lease, we decided to find him something larger but still nearby. He loves the water views and I wanted his place to be walking distance from the Farmer's Market. We started apartment hunting in earnest about two weeks ago and this afternoon we found just the cutest spot. It's a swanky little three bedroom, fully renovated, right above the old general store with a great view of the valley. And it's in his price range - score!

It was a bit white and beige for his tastes, but I promised to help him make it feel more like his home. After reviewing some of his must-haves and going over the key concepts he'd like to incorporate into his space, I think we have a vision in mind. I'm going to post some photos and walkthroughs of the DIY solutions we're planning to incorporate to make this apartment feel more like the dank den of his dreams.

1. Kitchen - This room was the first priority, we agreed. Piasa doesn't cook, he's on more of a raw diet. It's honestly so adorably west coast of him, going full paleo caveman. So the stove wasn't as necessary as more fridge space and storage solutions. We found this stylish and functional ceramic stovetop cover to expand the counter surface area! Now we can add an additional mini fridge to the counter and hopefully keep him from continuing to store rotting meat in the dishwasher. Relationships are all about compromise.

2. Bathroom - I haven't seen him shower or brush his teeth once in the time I've known him, but he does manage to leave the bathroom absolutely coated in filth and excrement. Men, am I right? Fortunately, the dollar store was offering these amazing rubber bath mats. You can just hose them off! I also added some slide-out organizers with drawers under the cabinet, so I have a place to keep my toothbrush when I stay over. Plus - extra towel storage!

3. Bedroom - Piasa *hates* my mattress any time he's stayed over at my place. It's much too soft for him to get comfortable. To make sure he's always getting his best rest, I built him a custom king-sized nest using the traditional methods he'd mind-beamed into me. It was rough to bring up that much saliva and phlegm to thoroughly paste the news-papers to the cardboard shell, but after I had painted the exterior a rich mahogany brown and added in some decorative throw pillows and fun fuzzy blankets, I fell in love with the finished product. Totally worth the effort and the dehydration.

4. Office - This was a really tough one. He doesn't really need an office, in the traditional sense, but he did need a separate space to commune with the Universal All, spend his moments of quiet meditation so he can focus on astral projecting into nightmares, and check his email! We tore up the carpet to give his space more of a "man cave" feel and I found these wall appliques on Etsy! He seemed to get a real kick out of the "It's Beer Thirty" one. Also these lamps were repurposed; I bought them at an estate sale and rewired the bases so they could line the summoning circle. He didn't love them at first (he smashed a few in a blind rage), but now I think they're growing on him.

5. The extra bedroom - I'm still not sure what the purpose of this room is. He's kept it fairly empty and every once in a while goes in to burn incense. He said that I will know the purpose of the space in time. Is it weird that I still get butterfly flutters when he says mysterious weird stuff like that? Takes me back to that first week of raw awe and terror.

6. New patio furniture! I couldn't resist that Caribbean Blue striping. Feels like a little mini vacation every time I step outside.

What clever solutions have you developed in your home to make it work for both you and your partner? I'd love to see your suggestions and photos! Make sure to tag me when you post!

The Proposal
September 3, 2022

I hope you're sitting down. Piasa just asked me to MOVE IN WITH HIM. Well, asked in his way. We were halfway through our double-pie special from Jacko's Pizza when I saw him staring at me with those rheumy yellow eyes, his thick dark talons drumming impatiently on the formica table. I could tell he wanted to say something, or maybe show me another vision of one of my possible infinite deaths. So I set down my slice of pepperoni and banana pepper thin crust and said, "What is it, babe?"

He told me then that I would not be returning to my apartment ever again. He had removed all of my necessary belongings. He had disposed of my cat. He had burned the building to the ground. He told me that the pact of our covenant would be sealed in blood, forever, and that I belonged to him and would remain by his side until the end of my days.

I said, "Wait a minute here, bucko. I don't know what you heard about me, but I don't just move in with a guy after a few months. And unless you're planning on putting a ring on this finger, I don't belong to anyone."

Piasa then cut a sigil into the tablecloth with his talons and mumbled a deep incantation I could feel in my intestines. I then felt a sort of singey-type pain on the back of my head, and thought I could smell my hair burning.

That was when Piasa proposed.

Right there, in that cramped little booth in the back of Jacko's. Him getting down on all four knees while I recoiled in delight on the cracked leather seats. It was almost exactly how I'd imagined it, only I wasn't in a fancy restaurant with an ocean view and there wasn't a Tiffany's box or a Mariachi band. Also, my family wasn't there, and I wasn't dressed as nicely as I'd like, and I was more than a little worried about the burning at the base of my skull… but it was magical, nonetheless. He didn't understand my questions about the ring fully, but he did take half the ring finger of my left hand. Just *pop* and it was gone right above the second knuckle, cauterized and all with minimal pain. I thought he maybe ate it at first, but later I noticed him wearing my finger on a necklace around his shaggy neck.

There were three other fingers hanging there, on a roughshod leather strap he had fashioned into a necklace. I'm assuming they were people Piasa once held special, like me, but he doesn't like it when I ask him about his past relationships. It's like he always says, "OUR PASTS ARE IMMUTABLE AND VAPOROUS AND CANNOT BE REVISITED, SO LAY OFF ME, KAYCIE." I understand, of course, but I can't help but be curious! Why didn't those work out? Did he end the love affair, or did they? What were his major deal breakers? I know that understanding one another is something we constantly struggle with, what with my being a total Virgo and him being a godlike figure beyond comprehension. I just hope that his past heartbreaks have made him a stronger partner, the way mine have for me.

What do you think, readers? Do you think disclosure of past relationships and encounters is required for a happy coupledom?

Hey all, thank you so much to everyone who joined our Live last night, where we showed you how we prepped for our first dinner party. Wow, we were overwhelmed by the outpouring of love and support. And I think you're right, Steffi! His English is SO much stronger than it was last month! Piasa is loving life here and I am loving having him around. You know when you meet someone who just clicks with you and you are like "where did you even come from?" and they tell you, "I FEED ON THE TENDRILS OF YOUR UNREMEMBERED DREAMS," and it's just so… gah. I don't know where to begin with this. I know it's only been two months but I just think I have found my actual soulmate. Like a shitty tv drama except it's happening to me and even though I should cringe… I'm just so fucking happy.

I know, no one hates me more than me right now. I *swore* I would not be like my aunt Janice, all stupid over some dude. But, I don't know. This is something extra special and now I'm starting to feel like it was destiny. Like maybe all my failures led me here, just like in the Hallmark movie. Instead of my high school crush, it was my high school mascot.

Life is a TRIP.

Anyway, as promised, here is the recap of the menu for our wine and regional cuisine night, where Piasa showed all my viewers the *real* Riverbend experience. Share if you decide to host a ritual of your own. Please use #RiverbendRitual in your posts, so we can find them!

Course 1: Three lizard eggs served sunbaked, in a sauce of spring water and rancid berries, fermented.

This dish is the start to your evening feast. You are tired from a long day of accepting sacrifice along the great mountains that once stood here. You see the eggs lying unattended and seize your opportunity.

The first course of your meal should be enough to satiate a hungry beast, while still leaving room for a few delicacies as the night darkens.

We paired this dish with a 1997 *Chateau Ste. Marie* Chardonnay from the Feist Family Vineyard in Napa Valley.

Course 2: A small rodent, cliff dwelling. Served seared in a red wine reduction with leeks, fennel, and fresh wild grass.

The fact is, you're usually coming back from a good string of sacrificial offerings and ritual libation. This means that you are pretty drunk, for a Piasa. The first course took the edge off and now you're ready for some real meat. This will give you the energy you need to head back and collect any pieces of the various sacrifices you might have dropped.

We've paired this with a 2001 Red Zinfandel from our private cellar.

Course 3: A charcuterie board representing sacrificial snacks.

I thought we'd all get a kick out of this. I even folded the prosciutto to look like little livers. And we had a really great sheepsmilk cheese from the new Trader Joe's!

This course comes with a sampling of various honey wines from Piasa's travels.

Dessert: The last breath of a drowned child, served atop a sugar crisp

I added the sugar crisp, because the vapory ether was just so wispy and unattractive on the plate. I think it really adds something!

Vomiting is normal. We purchased buckets for the guests.

After the food is finished and the vomiting has subsided, allow guests to linger in their thoughts. Having several universal truths recognized and shared is common. If they need to make a big decision, like to quit their jobs or divorce a spouse, it's best to ask them to wait until they have fully come down (usually 7-12 hours). Sometimes these thoughts are mistakes, but not always. As strong as the urge is to immediately resolve situations in which you are unhappy, it's also important to honor the relationship you have with your job or your spouse enough not to deliver this news while visibly and audibly losing your mind whacked out on space god juice. You at least owe them that.

Updates and photos to come after the party! Wish us luck on hosting our first ever soiree as a couple!

The Dinner Party Aftermath
September 15, 2022

Well, faithful readers, the dinner party I planned hit a few speedbumps. I'm really the one to blame here. I hadn't fully considered how Piasa would react to that many people in my tiny apartment. I thought that a meet-and-greet evening where Piasa could reveal a little something about him and his history to a handful of my oldest and dearest friends would be a great way to dispel some of the fear and anxiety surrounding our relationship and perhaps give him some new local friends to spend time with.

He can't continue spending *all* his time with me, right?

I didn't expect Robbie to come up *at all*, but of course Meeghan Elroy had to bring up the Apple Festival, and how I was queen and Robbie was king when we were seniors, and asking if we're going to recreate the famous kiss photo that made the front page of the paper. Meeghan being Meeghan, she had two aperitif cocktails and started going on and on about it. I could feel Piasa bristling beside me, and I knew that things were about to go downhill.

Now, I won't call the evening a disaster, because I do believe that all of us went into this with the right intentions and I know that Piasa is truly trying to fit in. He still doesn't understand all the social cues and also - he's a large predatory proto-bird. It gets complicated. I didn't think he intended to hurt Meeghan, she just kept doing this fluttery thing with her fingers that caught his attention. Before I realized what was happening, he had pounced and then the screaming started. It was hard to keep things under control once panic had set in.

It was just the one bite, don't believe the people calling it a *mauling*. Meeghan received prompt medical attention, only required a dozen or so stitches, and everyone else was able to get home safely once Piasa had released them from the nether-realm prison he manifests in his mind when-ever he feels threatened by a group of people. I know some of those I once considered my dearest friends have described the experience as "hellish" and "brutal" and "something straight out of a 1970s Italian horror film," but I assure you that the mind-prison isn't that bad. It can actually be meditative, if you try. I've spent more than one evening in there after accidentally insulting him in a way I still don't fully get and it has had little-to-no impact on my regular life aside from a few spooky dreams.

Needless to say I think we'll try to keep our evenings at home just the two of us from now on. I'll still be able to see my friends, once they've calmed down and start returning my messages. For the rest of you, I'd like to remind you all that I am a real person on the other side of this screen and your comments can and do hurt. I get that people are afraid and uneasy, but I will ask everyone to remember that year we had the exchange student from Norway who ate pickled herring at lunch. We were also horrified by her behavior, but we all learned to appreciate her customs. Some of us even grew to enjoy the taste and smell of herring as a result!

I ask for patience and understanding as we all try to learn to co-exist, and try to think back to a time when you were an outsider to a new and strange experience. Would you have wanted people to call you a monster online and threaten mob behavior, or would you have appreciated a friendly face telling you that they want to understand and know you better?

On a final note, please stop using the #RiverbendRitual hashtag to post baseless conspiracy theories about my beau or his "true purpose" for returning to us. I am the reason Piasa is here, and I am the reason Piasa remains. There is no sinister ulterior motive. Try to have respect for me and keep your xenophobia under wraps. It's 2022, people.

Meet the Parents
September 17, 2022

So I couldn't put off the inevitable any longer. It was time for Piasa to meet my parents. We spent the first two weeks of our engagement sort of lost in one another, wanting to really soak in the new direction this love is taking. Then there was the whole issue with the dinner party and that extensive clean-up. Also, I needed to get my things sorted out in his home. I can now happily report that I am fully settled in, domestically-speaking. I've assumed all food prep duties (no easy task when you consider how monstrous his diet is... *so* much viscera), and he has agreed to help with some of the more difficult cleaning tasks that inevitably come alongside life with an apex predator. Once I called and told them about the engagement, their first reaction was complete stunned silence. I mean, I get it. Their baby girl is finally getting married. It's a big moment for us all. Then my father finally regained his composure and asked if this meant they would finally be able to meet him.

How could I deny that request? I know Dad is probably upset that Piasa didn't ask him before proposing to me, but Piasa is trying to live a more modern life and I'm sure he thought that was an outdated tradition that would only serve to upset me. He's really quite considerate.

Anyway, we decided a dinner at their house would be easiest, considering they wanted to have a quiet, comfortable place to get to know my new beau and Piasa is already banned from several dining establishments in town. I sent over some suggested dishes, and my father said he'd try his best to accommodate when menu planning. I thought their willingness was a good sign - clearly they were trying!

So I wore a new blue flowered dress, the one he helped me pick out. Piasa agreed to let me shower him off and shampoo and condition the furry parts. He looked wonderful and fluffy and it removed most of the strange burning smell he seems to be developing. I was feeling over the moon to see the family that raised me meet the reality-bending beast I was to marry.

Dear readers, it was not the dream meeting I'd hoped.

First there was the matter of my parents' dog. I have tried to prepare Piasa for interactions with animals smaller than him - which is basically everything in this town excepting horses and cows. I have to remember, however, that he is accustomed to hunting and anything small that makes sudden, unexpected darting movements is going to activate those instincts. I'm afraid he ate Pumpkin, wolfed him right down after cornering him behind the couch. My parents were horrified, but I think the look on my face kept them from reacting right away. I was positively shooting *daggers* with my eyes, afraid they'd start screaming and we'd have another evening ruined by behaviors beyond his control.

Then there's dinner itself. Piasa has still not quite mastered the art of silverware, and sometimes his eating can be a bit messy. That is to say he positively chows down, especially when he likes something, and my father's attempt at a porkpie was a huge hit. He devoured two and then started eyeing the picked-at pie in front of my mother. She shoved the plate at him so quickly I was worried he'd take offense, but he ate it and then began staring at my father. I tried to gently chide him, letting him know that it isn't proper dinner etiquette to demand the other diners share their food with you. He responded by eating my salad, bowl and all.

My father took this as some sort of threat upon my safety and started lecturing Piasa about the way his daughter (me) deserved to be treated. Piasa didn't care for Dad's tone and threw him straight across the dining room, through the entry, and into the formal living room. That caused Mom to get upset, because no one is technically allowed in the formal living room, except at the holidays. She started fussing over the carpet immediately and Piasa took offense at that, as well.

Now my parents are threatening to withhold the money they'd always promised for my wedding, and telling me that they don't think this marriage is a good idea. I don't know how to make them understand that it isn't his fault, he isn't from this place or this time and doesn't understand our customs and social rules. It is like dropping one of them in Medieval France and expecting them to immediately adjust without any education or direction.

They weren't having any of my excuses. They actually demanded I leave this relationship and move home to be with them. Like I'm still a child and need them to come to my rescue. They don't understand that I'm safe and fine. He would never do anything to intentionally hurt me, and the times he's hurt others have been misunderstandings or accidents. He isn't a bad person, he just sometimes does bad things. Piasa is deeply remorseful about what happened and offered to buy them a new dog. I didn't think that was a great idea. I can only imagine what it would be like for him in a store full of smaller animals. Ugh. I can't even think about it.

Have any of you had bad experiences when dating someone from a different culture? Did your family understand, or did they treat your partner like an alien invader? Feel free to sound off in the comments.

The Ex-Boyfriend
September 29, 2022

Today in *That's So Kaycie:* you will never believe who I ran into at the hardware store today!

Robbie Freaking Cartwright.

That's right. THE ex-boyfriend himself.

I was trying to figure out if there was a difference between the clear bathtub caulk and the bathtub caulk with the monkey on it when I heard a deep baritone behind me say, "Do you need assistance, little lady?" I couldn't believe it, even after I had spun around and found myself gazing deeply into those chocolate brown eyes. I must have been more surprised than I thought, because I completely lost my balance and slipped right there in the construction adhesive aisle!

Of course, he caught me. He was an All-State athlete, if I hadn't mentioned.

We shared a laugh about how I hadn't changed a bit. Still clumsy as hell and hopelessly confused about man-things like caulking a tub! I agreed to join him for a chai tea from the cute little coffee shop downtown so that we could catch up.

It turns out Robbie found a job in the lumber industry right after we broke up, and then got into woodworking. He's running a successful furniture store a few hours upstate. He tries to get home to see his family as often as he can, and has dreams of hiring a manager so that he can work full-time from his parents' farm. He hates being away now that they're getting older.

I asked about his love life and he blushed so deeply, it was adorable. He told me there had been a couple of girlfriends, but none lasted long. Then he looked at my ring finger and went pale.

"What happened?" he asked.

So I explained about Piasa and our proposal, the horrible party I'd tried to host, everything up and until the disastrous dinner at my childhood home. It all just sort of tumbled out of me, the panic I'd felt when Piasa lost it at the party, the fact that my parents were barely speaking to me, wedding planning stresses, even the issue I was having with bridesmaids when every girl I know is too terrified to be within fifty feet of my husband-to-be. It just felt so good to be able to share all my worries with someone who had known me that long.

When I finished, Robbie looked like he had a storm cloud hanging over him. He took my hand in his and asked me if I was in danger, if I needed a safe place to go. For goodness sakes, he even offered up the guest house on the Cartwright farmland to me, if I needed it. In his eyes, I had bound myself to a dangerous creature of unending power, and my life was in danger. I told him he was being absolutely ridiculous. I *knew* how Piasa felt about me. Every night, he invades my dreams with his mind-presence and ensures that every tale my sleepy brain tells is only of him. Who would do that, if not a man deeply in love? I have never felt threatened by him, nor do I believe his violent acts will ever be turned on me. He has been nothing but a consummate gentleman while we're together.

"But what about what he might do to everyone else?" Robbie pressed.

At that point, I could feel a deep pulsing in my brain, almost as if someone were probing through my thoughts. I had to tell Robbie that what happened to others didn't matter. All that mattered was Piasa and my future. The pulses stopped, and I knew I had said the right thing.

I hurried home, rattled by the things Robbie had said to me. It's upsetting when someone who once knew you so well questions decisions that you've made. As if he was trying to influence the direction of my life. Dear lord, do you think he still has feelings for me?

I'm not sure how, but Piasa just *knew* I had been with Robbie when I came home. I found him pacing a circle in the living room, a rage I'd not yet felt from him filling all the space until it was as if he'd sucked all the air from the room. I quietly set down my tote bag and immediately sat on the couch, waiting for him to tell me what he was so upset about.

"THERE IS AN INTERLOPER IN YOUR MIND AND YOUR HEART," he declared in the thundering voice I could only hear inside my head.

"There isn't!" I insisted. "Robbie is an old friend."

"AN OLD FRIEND WHO HAS KNOWN THE UNENDING DELIGHT OF YOUR FLESH."

Oh dear lord, readers. Yes, I had disclosed my (very limited) sexual history with him, as I thought was appropriate for two individuals embarking on a physical relationship together. So it isn't as if this was a new revelation. Piasa knew my longest-running relationship had started in high school and continued while I was away in college, and that yes, it had gotten physical starting our senior year in high school. But something in his tone showed that this had *clearly* bothered him. I was surprised. By Piasa's own admission, he had enjoyed hundreds of thousands of lovers in the eons he had been alive. That's why I was so upset when he was unable to obtain an STD screen initially - the clinic in town was simply unable to figure out how to get a sample from him, since his anatomy is so very different than ours and that whole thing where he bit the physician's assistant and she immediately developed weeping sores near the bite location.

"That was in the past," I reminded him. "You are my future."

"I NEED TO BE YOUR EVERYTHING."

It was one of those moments I so often have with Piasa, where he says something that would have made me swoon to the point of passing out, were it in a movie I was watching or a steamy romance novel I was enjoying. But something about hearing it there, in person, from the fanged mouth of a delirium-inducing monster made my blood run cold. I could already feel the poker-hot tendrils of him invading my mind, searching for the answer to the question he dared not ask. I raised my hand defensively, as if I could sever his connection with my own arm.

"I did NOT cheat on you!" I shouted, surprised by my own ferocity.

Piasa recoiled as if I'd slapped him, dropping his attempt to read my thoughts immediately.

In an instant he was on the floor before me, his head in my lap, begging for my forgiveness. His whispered promises seared my heart. He would always love me. He did not mean to frighten me. I was everything to him. Losing me would be like losing his soul.

Of course I forgave him. How often does your guy admit he's wrong, ladies? Probably best not to lose the one who does, and then apologizes to boot.

We made love in his nest that night, and I woke to find six silver bangles left on top of my folded clothes. I'm not sure where they came from, and one did have some strange rust-colored gunk on it that flaked off when I scratched at it. I know I shouldn't question this. That would just raise his ire and besides, aren't I the one who loves antique objects and thrift store finds? I should celebrate how well he knows me. I should not question the depths of his love. I should learn to be happy with my fate.

The Apple Festival Stampede
October 3, 2022

It's that time of year, Riverbenders! That's right, it's the APPLE FESTIVAL!! Those of you who have followed *Face the Day with Kaycie* for a while know this is by far my favorite part of living here. I just love the big carnival and parade and everyone at the orchard scrambling to get the best picks of the season. As a child, I kept a calendar countdown to the big kickoff fireworks, so of course I couldn't wait to share this with Piasa.

I'll start by saying it didn't go exactly as I'd hoped.

To be clear, while I acknowledge that the majority of the damage was directly caused by Piasa, I do not feel it is entirely fair to blame him exclusively for the events. He was most certainly provoked, and I think that trying to play this off as some sort of deliberate act is completely wrong and frankly pretty bigoted. I would like to remind everyone that we have been presented with a unique and incredible opportunity to get to know a species and a consciousness that is completely different and separate from anything we've ever known. Try to approach interactions with Piasa with a bit of grace and humility, please.

For those of you who aren't local to the area and perhaps missed the news, there was an incident and some people might have been critically injured, but so far there hasn't been a single reported death, and I think we need to focus on that! There is time for healing and forgiveness!

Although I'm trying not to focus on the bad, it is important to recognize that mistakes were made. I probably should have done something to prepare Piasa for the parade and the concept of fireworks. In hindsight, maybe watching a couple of videos online would have been a good idea.

Additionally, he was already behaving like a total buzzkill because he knew Robbie was going to be there. It's not like we were going to jump onto the finale float and make out for everyone, but *thanks a pantload* to Meeghan for putting that idea in his head.

In my defense, I had no idea he would feel so threatened by the entire spectacle. How was I to know that he would see an oncoming stream of cars and marching bands as some sort of attack? It took everything in my power to restrain him and get him calm, but then the fireworks started over the fairgrounds and he went completely ballistic. I guess he believed some mighty war was raging around us and when the press of friendly parade marchers drew closer, he thought he needed to stand his ground.

On behalf of Piasa, I want to apologize to all of those wounded in the resulting fracas. Although I will point out that several locals were trampled by their own friends and neighbors in the mad dash to get away from the terrifying visage of a long-forgotten god wreaking havoc on their loved ones and collector-worthy vehicles. Piasa was not the sole cause of the disaster.

Of course, when people started to run his natural hunting instincts kicked in. I watched in total cringey embarrassment as he lifted the father of my high school boyfriend high into the air and dropped him. The man I'd long known as Mr. Cartwright crumpled to the ground in front of me, and rose chanting in a deep voice I'd never believed he was capable of. Mr. Cartwright was speaking absolute nonsense, words I'd never heard before. Then the blood began gushing from his nose and I instantly knew what was going on: a head injury. I'd learned to recognize the signs in my lifeguard training class in high school. So I tried speaking to him in a quiet, gentle voice.

That was when Piasa dropped the firetruck onto the Toncer Bros furniture store. My attention wandered and I lost Mr. Cartwright in the crowd. I was glad to hear that Robbie collected him and took him to Memorial Hospital.

The link to the GoFundMe to help repair damage to community buildings and facilities and to contribute to the hospital fees for those injured in the Apple Festival Stampede (as the local news is calling it) is below. Please consider helping if you can. Yes, I am aware that Piasa is a powerful being, but that doesn't mean he's naturally a wealthy one. His hoard of gold and trinkets was lost ages ago, and he still struggles with the fundamentals of our currency and banking system. We're contributing what we can of our own funds.

I'd appreciate it if you try to keep the comments civil. I am still working on finding sufficient moderation software, but I remind you that any attack on Piasa is a direct attack on me. Please think of my feelings when you're commenting.

Halloween
November 1, 2022

Apologies for the delay in updates, all. Piasa and I have been spending most of our time alone together in the apartment, really focusing on making *us* work. He's begun to fix up the third bedroom and won't yet let me inside, he wants it to be a surprise. I think it's a space for me to focus on my hobbies and interests, since I have mentioned the lack of space I feel I have in this apartment over and over again. It's really the only thing we argue about. Not that we argue much, readers. Please don't feel you need to be concerned about my well-being. I have read your thoughtful messages and understand your concerns, but I can only tell you again that it's hard for you to understand the good in this relationship if you're just looking in from the outside.

Yes, I miss my friends and family. Yes, I hate not having a job and not knowing where the money is coming from. Yes, it scares me sometimes when I wake in the night and find him in the corner of the bedroom, glowering at me. But these are things I will work through in order to be with him. A guy like Piasa doesn't come around often - in fact I think I can confidently say that this is probably the only time I ever could have met someone like him in a thousand lifetimes. I feel like it's in my best interest to try to make this work.

No one has ever claimed that relationships are easy, right? You sometimes have to struggle, to make the happiness more worth it in the end. At least, that's what I've always been led to believe. How often did my mother remind me of everything she put up with just by virtue of being married to Dad? Not to mention my friends! The stories of bathroom disasters, dirty laundry piled up beside the bed, lack of any effort on the part of their partners to do even the basics when it came to housekeeping or child rearing. I cannot believe that I'm the first one to struggle with their chosen life partner.

I just didn't expect it to be this much of a struggle. I'm certain that the headaches I've been experiencing can be directly linked to the sheer amount of interpersonal stress I'm under on a daily basis. They come on so suddenly now, like a loud thunderclap that starts right at the base of my skull. No one seems to appreciate that I'm trying to maintain this relationship, plan the perfect New Year's Eve wedding, ensure there's food on the table, deal with the anger and resentment from friends and family, and the nonstop aggression I am feeling from my fellow townspeople.

I had hoped to make some sort of grand re-entrance to society at Halloween. It's long been my favorite holiday, probably because I love doing makeup so much. Did you know that in high school I was in theater? It's true! I love doing special effects makeup in addition to a perfect smokey eye, so any excuse to show off my skills is a welcome one.

Of course, I had to account for how such a holiday may affect Piasa. He was not a fan of large crowds, loud noises, unexpected music, flashing lights, or small children. Unfortunately, there wasn't a single Halloween festivity that didn't include at least one of those things, and most had more than one. I knew it would be a total mistake to try to take him out and risk another front page news night, so we agreed to watch movies at home and I told him I'd make dinner. I thought that a relaxing evening, snuggled together under a blanket, would be exactly what we needed to reset everything.

I planned out a full meal featuring some of my favorite things, grabbed a few bottles of wine, and an apple pie for dessert. I guess that in all the activity, getting things ready and running to the grocery store and picking out a movie I thought he'd like, I forgot to turn off our outer light. I hadn't anticipated kids, especially not at our apartment door.

We were just getting to my favorite scene in the movie I'd chosen. If you've been following my blog longer than a year, you *know* which movie I'm talking about. So they're starting to sing in the restaurant and it's just such an outpouring of absolute joy and I steal a look at Piasa to see if he's enjoying this and that's when I hear it....

A low knock.

I had just a moment of confusion before I realized what was happening. I had completely forgotten about trick-or-treaters. Piasa was already growling, his hackles rising up along his back and he slowly pivoted his head toward the door. I felt the now familiar knot form in my stomach. He turned his venomous stare toward me then and I rose quickly.

"DID YOU INVITE SOMEONE TO OUR HOME?" the voice in my head put my teeth on edge.

"Of course not," I responded. I knew how much Piasa hates unexpected guests, or even expected guests, if I'm being honest. I wouldn't dream of doing something like that. I know how he reacts when he's surprised, and I can't go through that again.

I opened the door and there was a whole little squad of kids, couldn't have been a single one older than seven. There was a little cowboy, he was the youngest. Two ghosts, a fireman, a clown. But one of them, a little girl, was dressed as Piasa. She had the whole cartoony look you see on the tshirts, big wide googly eyes stuck to her forehead, the curved horns, a lion's mane and a gigantic tail she'd hooked over one shoulder.

Any other year, I would have found this the most adorable thing. Now it just sent a cold chill running down my spine. I could feel Piasa's eyes boring into the back of my head, raising the familiar itch at the base of my skull. I stuttered through my explanation, my apologies, my assurances that they were very cute, but that I didn't have any candy. I shooed them away as gently as I could before pushing the door back closed.

I could hear them giggling in the hall. I turned back toward Piasa, who was already silently slipping from the room, into his den. I hit the mute button on the TV and prepared myself for what would inevitably come next. I want you to know that I absolutely don't blame those kids for what they did, they're just kids, and this is a traditional area. We had failed to provide treats on Halloween. What did we expect would happen?

And so we became the victims of tricks. News had clearly spread fast in the streets that our place wasn't providing the requested candy, and worse yet we were doing it all under the false pretense of a friendly-lit front door. The older kids learned of our transgression from the younger ones. Those older kids had come prepared with the accouterments: eggs, toilet paper rolls, soap bubbles in balloons and, of course, chalk crayons.

I heard the first balloon hit our window a little before midnight. I woke with a start on the couch, where I must have dozed off while waiting for Piasa to re-emerge. I ran to the window and looked out in muted horror as a group of children began pelting our building with eggs and balloons. One boy ran around whooping loudly as he threw rolls of toilet paper over the awnings and street lamps. Another was writing something on the sidewalk I couldn't quite make out from this angle. Behind me, I heard a sound like a great bomb had hit the side of our building. I ran for Piasa's office. The door was locked, and he wasn't responding as I shouted and beat my palms against the door. I rushed into the bedroom, looking out the side windows to see if I could discover what made the loud sound. Below me, the children were scrambling.

Then the screaming began.

I tried not to watch. I turned from the window. I grabbed one of the foul-smelling blankets from the nest we shared and made my way back into the living room. I wrapped myself in the blanket like a cocoon and turned my movie back on. I didn't want to know, readers. I couldn't know.

When I woke up again, it was sunny outside and the door to Piasa's office was open. There was a pleasant breeze blowing through the apartment, ruffling the paper napkins that stood on the kitchen island. When I rose to see if he was in his office, I discovered it was empty, a large hole now torn in the wall where the window once allowed us to look down over the parking lot below.

I found him peacefully asleep in the nest, his thick wooly chest rising and falling in regular rhythm. I gently laid my blanket over him and went to close the door.

That's when I saw the small, bloodied cowboy hat.

Readers, I didn't know how to react. I didn't want to believe the worst had happened. I wanted to think that perhaps he'd found it outside and brought it back, a curiosity more than evidence of a crime.

I realized his breathing had quickened, and turned to find him staring at me. He didn't speak a word, just lifted the blanket, inviting me into his embrace. I curled up against him, trying to suppress a shiver. His fur smelled of soot and blood as he pulled me close.

Sometimes I feel as if I don't know who I am. Almost as if I'm losing myself to whatever madness this love brings.

Giving Thanks
November 23, 2022

I never fully understood why our new year begins in the coldest part of winter, the time when it's so cold that your eyelashes freeze and it physically hurts your face to be outside. A friend of mine once agreed, saying that she always wanted to begin again in the spring, when the flowers first come to bud. That was her time for renewal, for change.

For me, it was always the fall. Something about the smell of bonfire in the air and the soft crunch of freshly fallen leaves underfoot. That was the time I always felt my life needed a reset. Maybe it's some leftover echo from my school days, expecting a new re-invention of myself, complete with fresh colored pencils and a new notebook.

I broke up with Robbie right before every Thanksgiving break. That's something I never admitted to anyone. He would usually just spend the holiday in quiet sadness before I would inevitably get back together with him, sad and lonely and desperately wanting the drama of a reconciliation. I think it was part of this "new year, new me" philosophy, exercised in the autumn.

When I was in college, a boy offered me a joint in a dorm room and I proposed this theory to him. He laughed and said, "You think you're so fucking deep, but really you're just a secret Led Zepplin fan. Season's changing, time for Kaycie to move along."

Maybe that was the first hint that men didn't take me entirely seriously. I used to blame it on my petite height, my golden honey blonde hair, my light and airy voice that made my IQ sound thirty points lower than it is. Or maybe it's because I always put the effort in on my hair, my nails, my curated capsule wardrobe. I always liked people thinking I was pretty, thinking I was a catch.

And so I played the part, pretending to be this fun-loving and quirky girl. I wasn't going to make too much trouble, I wasn't going to cause you any pain. I was just here with my ballerina pink nails to hold your hand and show you all the fun you're missing in life. Even this dumb fucking blog, thinking that videos showcasing the perfect winged eyeliner and skincare dupes was some way to make my life meaningful or worthwhile.

The fact is, readers: I'm a fraud. I'm such a failure. I lost my job in New York and it was a *blessing*, because I was barely hacking it there. For all my posturing about being perfect and unique, I barely made a ripple in that city. There were a thousand girls just like me, and even more who were better at being the me I wanted to be. I realized just how small and insignificant I was.

I think that's why I took up with Piasa so quickly, so thoughtlessly. I wanted to be special. I wanted to *matter*. And to be the girl who married the monster that had presided over every piece of merchandise this town has produced since the 20s? Who would pass that up? I would be like royalty, or so I believed.

Now I'm worried that I pushed him into this, pushed him into being part of this society, pushed him into being with me. I should have stopped before it was too late.

Readers: it is much, much too late.

I went to see my doctor, despite Piasa disapproving of most Western medicine. I had to find the cause of these headaches and see if there was something they could prescribe. There are days when the pain is so bad I can barely stand, like a sharp ice pick driving into the base of my skull. The ringing in my ears is so loud at times that it wakes me from my sleep. I read online that sometimes tinnitus can be so loud that other people can hear it *from* your ears. Did you know that? I wondered if my doctor would be able to hear it, it was so *loud*. So insistent.

She could not hear my ears ringing, but there was something on the back of my skull. It was hard for her to see, my hair is still pretty thick, but it looks like there's some sort of brand burned into my head, right above where my hairline begins on the nape of my neck. She said it feels raised, she wanted me to have a scan.

Nothing could have prepared me for what that scan found. It isn't a brand but some sort of implanted… *thing*. I had a follow-up MRI that showed it was organic, and the vasculature of the object is somehow threaded into my brain tissue. The two neurosurgeons she consulted with are still debating, but the fear is that an attempt to remove it will leave me brain damaged.

I am getting a third opinion from a specialist at the Mayo Clinic after the holidays. There weren't any appointments any earlier.

I tried to talk to Piasa about this, especially since this all started on the night we got engaged, but he only repeated the words "THE COVENANT IS IMMOVABLE." I don't know what this means. Is the covenant a thing he put in my head? Is this something that is lost in translation?

I'm ashamed to admit it, but I've been communicating with Robbie covertly. Piasa can read my thoughts when we're in the same room, but I've learned that if I replay scenes from the times we've had sex over and over in my mind, he focuses on that and ignores anything else I might be hiding. He seems to think I'm distracted with preparations for the wedding, which I have not given him any reason to doubt.

I feel guilty about lying to Piasa, but Robbie understands me in a way that no one else does, and he is so without judgment. Despite the fact that Piasa left his father partially paralyzed and I'm the direct reason Piasa is out in the world, Robbie doesn't blame me for any of it. He keeps telling me, "This is an ancient god. We don't know how much we can blame you for your own actions. You might be under his influence." Now that we found this thing in my head, I am starting to believe him. I have often felt as if I'm in a weird daze when around Piasa, overlooking things the old Kaycie would have never been down with.

I literally live in an apartment smeared with monster shit. Who is this person, and why is she okay with this life?

I lost my train of thought. I wanted to talk about Thanksgiving. This will be my first without my family, and this is hitting me harder than I thought it would. After the incident with the children, my parents have strictly forbidden me from bringing Piasa to the house. I was welcome to go alone, but my mom started referring to him again as "that thing."

Of course, Piasa didn't want me to go without him. He has been whispering to me in my dreams as of late, telling me that my family is against him and therefore against me, that I will never be understood by those I once held dear, that he is the only thing capable of loving me in this world.

For a few minutes after I wake, I believe it. And that *scares* me.

I don't know what to do. Most of the friends I still had here have turned their backs on me, the first after the party, some after the Apple Festival Stampede, the remaining few withdrew once the news started reporting on the dead children. He'd eaten their faces, reader. They'd still been alive when he did it. Then he took their little hands.

I only have Robbie now. Funny how life works out.

Wedding Planning
December 4, 2022

Hello again, readers. Sorry it's been another long gap. Two weeks feel like an eternity to me.

I tried on my wedding dress today. It's something I've dreamed about since I was a little girl. I even had the exact style chosen: ballgown with a corseted top, lace-up in the back. Tulle full skirt. Ivory because white-white makes my skin look sallow.

I had always imagined my mother would be there when I put it on for the first time, me emerging from the dressing room to her happy tears as she told me "oh yes, that's the one." But my mother isn't allowed to come here, isn't allowed to see me. Piasa thinks she is poisoning my mind against him. He believes something is interfering with my love for him, and my parents are the easiest target. I wish I could talk to them, but Piasa is anxious when I leave the apartment. I'm getting worried. They haven't tried to contact me in weeks. Robbie told me he'd check on them this weekend.

And so instead of my dream dress, chosen with my mother's blessing, I will wed in the gown my betrothed has chosen for me. One he knit himself out of thread I cannot stand to touch. The fabric is slick and rubbery against my skin, and smells of bitter copper and decay. He tells me he's been weaving this since the day we met, the robe I will wear when we are finally joined forever. Everything he's destroyed is sewn within these garments, with bits of hair and fur here and there. Lining the sleeves is something so soft to the touch I quiver when it brushes against me. *Kidskin sleeves.* Only I think that "kidskin" used to refer to goats.

This is not made of goat.

I stood in front of the bathroom mirror and stared at myself, my wan face peeking out from above the neckline, hollows in my throat and cheeks, my collarbone prominent. He is concerned about my weight, for he tells me I will have children shortly after the ceremony. He claims the seed has already been planted, and I must care for myself to make it grow.

The thought makes me want to tear at my own skin.

The thought makes me wish I could starve.

December 6, 2022

I don't know what to do, readers.

My parents are dead.

Robbie went to check on them, as he promised. The car was still in the driveway, and he said he could hear the television inside. But no one answered the door when he rang the bell, no one responded to his shouts. When he went around the back of the house, hoping to find my mother working in her garden, my father enjoying his newspaper on the deck, but all he saw was the rear door ripped off the hinges.

He won't tell me what he found inside, just that they were gone.

Robbie wants me to leave with him. He wants me to pack and be gone before the snow starts to fall.

It's going to be a White Christmas in the Riverbend.

Robbie doesn't understand that I can't leave. Piasa and I, this thing between us, the thing in my head, the unborn children inside me… we're all connected now. I can't walk away from it.

I think it would kill me if I tried.

It's Christmas Eve. Normally the downtown would be festooned with decoration and lights, but there isn't much reason to celebrate this year. People have stayed home, too afraid to wander close to Main Street, to our apartment above the old general store.

The Riverbend is like a ghost town, one where everyone keeps their curtains closed and their doors locked. They cower inside their homes, watching the skies for the now-familiar shadow, fearing it comes for them at last.

Tonight I received a gift from Piasa, although I'm still not certain he's aware of the impending holiday as anything that needs to be marked with gifts. He has stopped pretending to care about the social mores and traditions of this place.

Tonight, Piasa finally showed me the spare bedroom.

It's a nursery.

He has filled it with branches from trees along the bluffs, and lined the floor with animal skins. The thick feathers of his undercoat provide soft bedding for... for so many beds.

Too many beds.

In my panic, I ran. I didn't know how to react to seeing the evidence of what he had left inside me, what he wants me to birth into this world. So many, like him. So many that will kill and kill again. Me, complicit in their very existence.

How is that a life?

I went to the only place I thought I could feel safe: the Cartwright Farm. Robbie greeted me at the door, the sounds of his father's ventilator filling the foyer. He wrapped me in one of the warm plaid blankets they keep on the porch for chilly nights. I sobbed as he held me, then allowed myself to be led inside. His mother was so nice and sympathetic, in spite of me breaking her son's heart all those years ago.

In spite of me being responsible for the incident that caused her husband's injuries.

In spite of everything.

She made me a cup of hot apple cider, with a little cinnamon stick in it and everything. I had it near the Christmas tree, all warm and comforted in their cozy family room.

It was like life was normal again. It was Christmas Eve, I was with people who loved me. I was warm and safe.

I'd forgotten how nice she was. I'd forgotten how nice normal could feel.

I couldn't stop myself, I just started letting everything pour out of me— all that had happened since I accidentally awakened Piasa. The killings, the apartment, the thing in my head, the threat of new life growing inside me. I noticed the concerned looks they kept exchanging while I spoke, but I couldn't stop. It felt so damn *good* to finally tell someone all that had happened. I realized I should have told my parents, and I admitted this to Robbie and his mom. And then I cried while Robbie held me, his mom patting my foot and crying with me.

Mrs. Cartwright heated up some dinner for me and I had it in the kitchen nook, Robbie standing guard in the doorway. He told me he was going to put me in the guest cabin behind the house. Safer for me there, and he could keep an eye on me from his room on the second floor. I gratefully let him lead me to the cabin and secure me inside. After a hot shower, I collapsed into clean sheets and properly slept for the first time in months.

I dreamed of strange visions of death and destruction, as if I were the one perpetrating the crimes. I saw from the point of view of a giant flying predator, swooping down to lift someone on an evening bike ride, or to pick off a hiker and his dog. I could feel the shatter of their delicate bones in my talons, the bitter taste of their flesh against my tongue. The rest of the dream was red rage and the crunching noises, my mouth filling with the hot taste of blood, gristle between my teeth. Then I circled over the farm, noting the guest house but focusing instead on the main dwelling. Strangely, I did not rend the door from its hinges. Instead I stood outside it, my acrid breath fogging the glass of the transom windows until finally someone opened it for me.

Robbie, his face filled with determination, then regret. I felt a rush of sympathy from him as I turned uneasily in my sleep. All he'd ever wanted was to keep me safe, and happy.

How I've failed him.

How I've failed everyone.

Christmas morning dawned gray and cold, and I laid in bed for a long time, willing myself to get up. I had to figure out what to do, I needed to figure out who to go to. I couldn't stay here.

That's when I heard shouting. Robbie's older sister had arrived with her husband and children for Christmas Day, to open presents with the rest of the Cartwrights in that sprawling family room I had loved as a teen. I knew they'd have a roaring fire and peppermint mocha hot chocolate for the kids, with a nip of brandy for the adults.

I stumbled from the guest house and headed toward the loud voices. Then I heard one above the others, a woman shrieking to "get the kids out of here." I broke into a run.

At first I thought they had repainted that huge family room. It was a brilliant red, arterial. Then I noticed the same crimson running down the window glass, splattered on the fireplace stones, smeared in globs on the leather couch.

I think I threw up. I remember Robbie's sister, Felicia, swatting at me with her hands. She was frothing at the mouth with anger, calling me a monster and a whore, blaming me for what had happened, for what had happened to everyone. Her husband pulled her off of me and I fell out of the house onto the porch. I laid in the yard in a daze, staring at the sky, stomach curdling at the leathery sound of approaching wings. I accepted my fate as I felt myself lifted. We flew over the valley, the tiny dotted houses with their curling smoke below us. I wondered if any of them knew yet, if the word had gone out that the great beast of the Riverbend had killed once again, this time removing most of the Cartwright family.

Later that evening, I stood before my bathroom mirror once again, after Piasa had added the crowning veil to my wedding garb. Robbie's precious teeth, straightened a decade before by an orthodontist, now lined the headpiece, threads of his hair tangled in the delicate web of the trailing veil, wrapping me in its sorrow and loss.

Our wedding was held under the darkness of the night sky, the only decoration the dull glow of the fingernail moon, the only attendants the silent creatures of the forest who stared from their havens in their trees and their thickets. We did not consummate the marriage. He has lost all interest in such things, now he sees me only as a vessel. My betrayal has removed any other interest I might have held for him.

I have begun to feel the new life stirring inside me. At night they slither over one another in my gut, clawing at my ribs and shoving my intestines out of the way. A deep ache has settled in the lower left side of my stomach, some unknown wound they are causing from within. I did not understand how my womb could hold such a thing, until I understood they are not inside my womb at all. They are filling my torso, pushing into every space, where they will feed as they grow.

Until they inevitably chew their way out, spilling from my swollen split stomach, rushing out from the torn remnants of my mouth, bursting from my ribcage glistening red and wet with my lifeblood.

I know because this is the vision he shows me each night, as I lay locked in his clawed limbs.

This is how he reminds me of my covenant.

Of my duty.

Of my purpose.

I thought I would fear the idea of not surviving this birth, but instead it fills me with a sense of relief. I do not want to endure this any longer. I have no reason to want to endure it.

This is to be my fate. My only hope is that he will move on, once he has his brood. That he will find another place to inhabit and leave the poor people here alone.

I fear he will not.

If you are one of the few locals who once read this blog, please protect yourself. Move on. Leave this place.

I wish that I had that option.

I am sorry, please believe that.

I'm not like him. I'm just like you.

And I am so fucking sorry.

EYEOFMOTH.EXE
Directed by P.L. McMillan

eyeofmoth.exe

P.L. McMillan

I

"Space Station *Goremades* circles the Gorghast Star and houses over two hundred thousand Citizens." Captain Angiola Müller pointed at the holo-display behind her, where a small schematic of the space station slowly rotated. "As of sixty hours ago, all comms to the *Goremades* went down. But you all know this from the initial Company briefing. What you need to know now, as authorized, is that the Company detected an anomaly in the last communication they received from *Goremades* Command."

Executive Officer Vinn Pharo held his personal digipad, typing down keywords at random and tried to look riveted. The screen of the small device glitched for a moment, blacking out, then fading back. Annoyed, Pharo tapped the screen hard with the back of the stylus. He'd sent in a request to Engineering to have someone look at it, but so far been ignored.

Straighten up, boy. Pharo's dad's voice was a whip crack through his mind and he did as he was told. The Captain flicked her hand over the display and it switched to a report marked across the top with the word, "CLASSIFIED". She looked over at him and Pharo stifled the yawn he felt, instead smiling and giving a small nod. Captain Müller was a striking figure in her burgundy uniform and her black hair tied back in an intricate braid dotted with silver beads, he couldn't help but be intimidated by her.

Pharo looked over at the other four members that made up the crew of the CRS *Piasa*. They leaned in, narrowing their eyes as they tried to read the faintly vibrating holo-text.

"I'll sum it up for you," Müller said. "The last broadcast from SS *Goremades* Command read as follows: 'Virus aboard. Unable to stop spread. Confirm warning received. It wanted us to know. You must acknowledge. Send help'."

She flicked to the next screen. "There was also this."

On the screen flickered strings of symbols. Pharo made a note: 'should search up confidence speaking class in Academy alumni database and practice'.

First Engineering Officer Joel Duncan stepped closer to the holo-display, rubbing his chin with one hand. He was a short, stout man, with a clean shaven head and wild red beard. From the back of one of his ears to the other was a ring of tattooed runes, faded to gray over the years.

"Hm," Duncan said.

"Do you recognize it?" Müller asked.

Duncan shook his head. "Nah, it's a right mess. I can take a crack at identifying it, if ya want."

"Good. Report the results to me as soon as you have any," Müller said and returned the display back to the ship schematic, pointing to the schematic. "We'll be docking here and proceeding to the *Goremades* Command Center here."

Pharo drew a smiley face, topping it with a hat, then tapped his stylus against the edge of the tablet. *Something feels off.* His father had never lent any beliefs to hunches. His mother had though, she had believed in intuition, otherworldly guidance. That hadn't helped her in the end.

"Are we expecting casualties?" Pharo asked, forcing himself out of his own thoughts.

"We will go in expecting the worst," Müller said. "But hoping for the best."

"Are we going in armed then?" The CRS *Piasa*'s Security Officer was a tall, gaunt man named Zol Z'lomm. His dangling limbs, pale colourless eyes, and washed-out, yellow-tinged skin always reminded Pharo of an albino spider. He disliked the Security Officer at all but felt obligated to be respectful. It was well known within the Company that Z'lomm and the Captain had been friends since the Academy and she trusted him with her life.

"Yes, everyone should have lazguns," Müller said. "We'll be reaching *Goremades* in less than two days. Should the Company reach out with any more updates, I'll let you all know. Until then, rest up."

Dismissed, Müller's crew left the bridge with the exception of Navigational Officer Yui Suzuki and Pharo himself. He sighed, putting his digipad away and running a hand through his hair.

"I have a bad feeling about this mission," he said.

"You always have a bad feeling about our missions," Müller replied, shutting down the holo-display.

"I was right on Neo-Ythuni." Pharo slumped in the chair next to Officer Suzuki.

"You caused the issue on Neo-Ythuni," Suzuki replied, shrugging his head from her shoulder.

"You wound me!" Pharo moaned, turning around to face the touch screen at the station.

Despite his jovial response, Pharo's face burned in shame. *Don't show it, fake it til you make it.*

Captain Müller sat in her own chair, overseeing the main control console of the CRS *Piasa*. The *Piasa* was a Vulpes Company long-distance reconnaissance ship and Müller had been its captain for the last four years. Pharo glanced at her and she seemed calm, probably thinking of next steps. Pharo turned back around and stared at the screen in front of him, seeing nothing. *Something's definitely off.* The Company had been reticent with information, but that wasn't unusual.

It was something else. Something itching in the back of his brain, out of sight. His mother would have called it intuition. Pharo thought about the message again: *Virus aboard. Confirm warning received. It wanted us to know.*

A virus. The standard Company spacesuits would protect the crew from contagion and he was sure that Officer Bando's expertise and experience would carry them through whatever danger there was.

But what had *Goremades* Command meant with 'It wanted us to know'? What was 'it'? And what did the population of *Goremades* know?

Second Engineering Officer Lynn Thorne watched her superior, Officer Duncan, pecking at his keyboard with two thick fingers.

The two officers were in the Mech Room, a space buzzing with the electrical humming of the various workstations throughout and reeking of plastic and ozone. Lockers bolted to the plexicarb walls contained tools, replacement parts, and random supplies that didn't seem to have a home anywhere else on the ship.

"Are you sure you don't need my help with that?" Thorne asked.

"Off with you, buzzing skeeter that you are!" Duncan barked and Thorne shook her head with a smile.

Duncan was a genius with machinery and computers, but lacked any kind of delicacy or tact. Thorne, twenty years his younger, had always admired him and it had been her dream to apprentice under him. Duncan wasn't as renowned as other Engineers in the Company's fleet, nor did he boast any awards.

No. The moment that had caught Thorne's attention, her very first year in the Academy, was a news broadcast about the passenger ship CPS *Hera*. An asteroid had knocked into the *Hera*'s port-side thruster, sending it spinning downwards into the orbital pull of Planet Yorender.

She went over to the wall mounted beverage dispenser and activated it. The machinery behind the wall clunked and whirred.

Her whole class had held their breath, watching the grainy footage of the plummeting ship on the classroom's holo-display and with it, the thirty thousand souls aboard. Certain death.

Except it wasn't.

The *Hera* slowed, kept upright. No one understood what was happening, but the ship landed in the Kender Sea. No casualties. Minor injuries. The news called it a miracle of Company engineering. That hadn't satisfied Thorne and she had snuck into the Academy administration offices one night. Administrator Huit wasn't the most tech savvy and kept her password written on a piece of notepaper on her desk, allowing Thorne to log in and review the Company records on the *Hera* Incident.

Joel Duncan had been a Third Engineering Officer at that time. When the *Hera* began to fall, he'd tried to convince his superior officers to let him create a makeshift thruster using the ship's core. They'd said no. They hadn't trusted or believed in his idea, so he'd knocked them both out with a wrench and done it anyway.

This earned him a black mark on his file and exclusion from working on the majority of Company ships.

But he'd saved the *Hera*. And captured Thorne's respect.

With two cups of the steaming black liquid the Company's liquid dispensers' called coffee, Thorne mixed in powdered sweetener, and placed one on Duncan's desk.

With her own mug, she left Duncan to his work and went to the core's workstation to run her daily diagnostics report, checking on the core's stability levels and overall performance. Her inbox blinked, another request from Pharo to fix his stupid digipad. Thorne deleted it.

"What do you think it is?" she called to Duncan as the report continued to run.

The First Engineering Officer let out a gruff grunt as an answer and Thorne heard the sharp clack of the backspace key several times in a row.

"It could be a coded message," she said.

Clack, clack, clack went Duncan's keys. Thorne almost thought she could hear his brain ticking in time with his key taps.

"Of course, if it was standard Company encryption, we would have already translated it," Thorne added.

She waited, spinning in her chair, and listened to the rise and fall of the core's grumble. She loved that sound. Like the sleeping breaths of some massive beast.

 Finally the clacking stopped.

"Yegh," he muttered. "Blasted coffee's got sugar."

A wave of grief, old but still painful, rolled over Thorne's body. *Of course,* she thought, *Dad liked sugar, Duncan likes his black.* Duncan pushed the mug away and spat into the waste receptacle next to his desk.

"It's strange," he said.

Thorne stopped spinning and planted her feet on the floor.

"It's in an old coding language, Pre-Calamity." Duncan paused. "This might be... a program."

Thorne furrowed her eyebrows and stood, going to stand behind Duncan so she could look over his shoulder at the computer screen.

"If it's a program, it's nothing like I have ever seen," she said. "But why would *Goremades* Command send a Pre-Calamity coded program to the Company?"

III

The CRS *Piasa* exited FTL close enough to the Space Station *Goremades* that it could be seen by the ship's exterior optics. Captain Müller activated the *Piasa*'s bridge display to show the space station—the Company removed frontal view ports to prevent space madness from viewing open space during FTL..

"Looks intact," Pharo said, tapping through his screen display.

The SS *Goremades* was a massive colony structure made of a half dozen habitation towers connected by hundreds of bridges and orbiting around a massive cylindrical power core. In the far distance, lay an endless asteroid field. The Citizens of SS *Goremades* were miners and their families—a generational business going back decades—and those nearby asteroids were rich in valuable minerals and ore.

"Suzuki, open comms and try a hail," Müller said.

The Navigational Officer nodded and opened the *Piasa*'s external comms channel. "SS *Goremades*, this is the CRS *Piasa* sent on Company orders. Please respond."

Pharo waited, breath held. Static buzzed on the open line. Static and the strange susurrus of space.

"SS *Goremades*, we will be docking shortly. Please confirm."

Static and whispers. Suzuki closed the line and looked back at Captain Müller.

"Take us in, Suzuki."

The *Piasa*'s engines growled to life, Pharo could feel the very floor beneath his feet buzzing. It thrilled him, riding this leviathan of metal, polycarb, and pure power.

As the *Piasa* drew closer, the SS *Goremades* grew, a monstrous collection of towers whose thick walls were the only protection for its inhabitants against the unforgiving void of space.

"Looks like there's still power," Pharo said, tapping through his screen menus. "I'm picking up activity from the core. If we're lucky then gravity and life support will be on."

"Time to dock?" Müller said.

"An hour," Suzuki replied. "Still no response on comms. I'll input the override the Company gave us to open the loading bay doors."

Müller opened ship-wide comms. "An hour to dock. I'll need all hands ready to go in the cargo bay."

A chorus of confirmations responded and she closed comms again. Pharo stood and approached the Captain. He wanted a chance to shine, to finally get some proper experience. He knew he wasn't her first choice of XOs. Her previous Executive Officer had been head-hunted from her by a luxury space liner. Pharo couldn't blame the guy, being an Executive Officer on a cruise ship was far more luxurious than a common recon ship.

"Captain Müller," he started and tried to sound confident. "I think I should lead the team inside."

"Officer Pharo—" she started but he continued.

"I know I'm young, Captain," he said. "But I've been acting as your Second Officer for over a year now. I think this is a great chance for me to leverage that!"

"This is a highly sensitive Company mission, Officer Pharo," Müller replied with a sigh. "I doubt they'd appreciate me putting a rookie in charge."

Pharo's face burned and, unbidden, his father's face rose in his mind. "With all due respect, Captain, but it is your duty to guide and help your Executive Officer excel, isn't it?"

Müller opened her mouth, then paused.

"Officer Pharo." Müller stood, forcing her Second Officer to step back out of her way. "I agree. I think it is time for you to exercise your leadership."

Pharo struggled to smother the smile that wanted to burst into being.

"However," she continued and his smile faded a bit. "This is a sensitive mission. I will accompany the team as well. You will lead, but I will be taking this opportunity to evaluate you."

Pharo was overwhelmed with excitement and dread at those words. *An opportunity for both success and failure.* For a quick moment, Pharo felt as though he would be sick.

Müller went on. "Suzuki, I am trusting you in charge of the *Piasa* until the team returns. You will comms me with any updates and news, if any. Understood?"

"Heard, Captain," Suzuki said with a nod.

"I'll start prep," Pharo said, making an excuse to escape the bridge.

IV

Thorne gripped the locker in front of her, bracing her feet wide, as the *Piasa* shook, its stabilizer jets erupting in loud bursts as Navigational Officer Suzuki guided the ship in the SS *Goremades*'s docking bay. Thorne's teeth rattled in her skull and she counted backwards from a hundred, waiting for the *Piasa* to finally dock.

She hated take-offs and landings. The way the ship vibrated and trembled made her feel like her stomach would launch right up out of her mouth and her whole body would buzz for hours afterwards. Officer Duncan seemed unbothered, making his way past her with a laden toolbelt in his hand. Balancing through the *Piasa*'s protestations, the First Engineering Officer dropped the belt off next to Thorne's left foot, ignoring her obvious discomfort.

The CRS *Piasa* shook one last time and the sound of it touching down inside the SS *Goremades* echoed through the ship's hull. Thorne breathed a sigh of relief, finally letting go of the sharp locker frame. She'd gripped it so hard that there were indents in her palms.

Thorne had been born on a space station much like the *Goremades*, grew up on one or on ships. Her father had been military and was often transferred between the many stations located on the far reaches of the Company's territory.

Thorne never intended to be assigned to a ship. She preferred the consistency of being on a space station, preferred artificial gravity to planet-side.

But Duncan was on the *Piasa* so it was on the *Piasa* she would stay until she had learned everything she could from him—or convinced him to transfer to a swanky space station somewhere close to a beautiful planet like the Archimedes spa belt planets.

Thorne sucked in a few more breaths, waiting for her stomach to settle, then pulled her space suit from her locker. Each Officer had one specifically designed to fit their body and the Captain had let them know that they were expected to wear theirs at all times within SS *Goremades*.

After she'd zipped herself up, Duncan held out her tool belt.

"Keep yer lazgun on hand, lass," he said as she clipped it around her waist. "Better they be dead than you."

"What do you think happened there?" Thorne asked, touching each tool in the belt to assure herself it was there and properly clipped in.

Her superior officer shrugged. He was still in his normal ship-side jump-suit. He'd decided that she would go alone and he would stay behind. He'd said he was intrigued by the bit of code—he wanted to stay behind and try to crack it. Past him, Thorne could see his computer screen rapidly flicking through various programs as it tried to identify what exactly the code was.

"Will you let me know as soon as you figure that out?" she asked.

Duncan let out a grunt. His form of agreement. Then he bumped his rough knuckles against her right temple. "Be careful, lass."

Thorne bumped into Medical Officer Imani Bando as she exited the Mech Room into the hall. Bando's dark hair was cut just below her ears and stood out in ferocious curls. Her eyes were a striking shade of orange—a sign of ocular augments.

The officer was carrying a large med kit in one hand and she nodded at Thorne, smiling.

"Your first solo assignment, hm?" Bando said.

Thorne admired Bando's serene confidence and her careful hands. On her first week aboard the *Piasa*, Thorne had managed to drop a laser cutter while it was lit. It had fallen, slicing through the meat of her left thigh.

To this day, Thorne only remembered the moments after in fragments. Snapshots that she didn't feel any agency in.

The bright flare of the spinning laser cutter.

The quick wisp of smoke as the blade had burnt through the fabric of her jumpsuit.

The sharp, blinding pain as it slipped through her skin, her muscle, her arteries like butter.

The smell of cooked meat. The burnt red and black crispiness of the inner landscape that was her leg.

Beads of blood appeared. Grew to rivers. A flood. A raging tsunami.

Duncan's hands under her arms as he yanked her up. Threw her over her shoulder.

Her vision narrowed to a pinpoint.

The laser cutter had partially cauterized the wound, which is likely the only thing that saved her then. It had bought her valuable minutes. It had dammed up the wound long enough for Duncan to run with her on his shoulder.

She remembered Bando's soft voice a million lightyears away as she stared up into the bright light over the examination table. Her ears buzzing, her tongue coated with the sour taste of copper.

In recovery, she had sweet half memories of Duncan sitting at her bedside. Fragmented scenes of the man reading to her out loud from a core maintenance manual, him fussing over her blankets, refreshing her water. Memories had crossed like bad wiring. At times Duncan had looked like her Dad. She would drift back into fevered sleep, thinking of her father with Duncan's face, or that the two of them were friends, alive and well.

Thorne had woken up a week later, the savage wound on her leg merely a thin delicate line of stitches and a slight numbness through her right thigh to remind herself to always, always be careful.

Her other souvenir was a new admiration of her superior officer.

And maybe something else.

The loneliness of her father's sudden death was slightly eased. The pain dulled.

Thorne yanked herself back into the present. *Gotta concentrate on the mission and make him proud.*

Bando placed a hand on Thorne's shoulder. "Stick with me. We'll make a good team."

Though flattered by Bando's attention, Thorne also couldn't help but feel a bit of resentment. Was Bando treating her like a child that needed minding? Or did she actually think Thorne could help?

Either way, Thorne was determined to do whatever was needed on this mission. For Duncan, and for herself. Even if Bando thought her to be too young, Duncan was sending her alone. If Duncan trusted her to take on this mission then Thorne was confident she could handle it.

After all, Duncan was a hero. An acknowledged one or not. He saved lives. He had saved her life.

Ahead, the Second Engineering Officer caught sight of the others: Security Officer Z'lomm, Captain Müller, and—Thorne scowled—Second Officer Pharo.

The young XO looked down the hall at her and raised a hand in a half-salute. Thorne bit her lip in annoyance. *He's such an asshole.*

Z'lomm knelt and opened a small case at his feet to reveal six lazguns nestled in gray foam. Z'lomm took them out, one by one, checking their battery level and settings before handing one to each of the crewmembers. She attached it to her toolbelt and hoped she'd never need to use it.

"Remember," Captain Müller said. "We are here to investigate why *Goremades* has been cut off from the Company. You saw the message. There could be a contagion aboard, in which case, we need to observe all Company approved protocol."

The woman looked at each crew member individually. Thorne shivered when she locked eyes with the taller Captain. Müller was intimidating.

"I also want to make you all aware that Executive Officer Pharo will be managing this operation under my observation." Müller gestured at her XO. "Treat him with the same respect and obedience you would give me. Understood?"

Pharo beamed, tucking his shoulders back, puffing his chest out. He nodded at the captain as he stepped forward. Thorne allowed herself the privilege of rolling her eyes. *He's just as egotistical now as he was at the Academy. Once a bully, always a bully.* He'd put on the same act with teachers and just because his dad was some high-up general, Pharo had gotten away with everything. Unwanted, an intrusive memory of Pharo dumping week old leftovers over her textbooks rose in Thorne's mind. "Some charity food for the scholarship kid," he'd sneered, turning and puffing his chest out in the exact same manner for his snivelling friends.

"We will be proceeding straight to *Goremades* Command," he said, with a stupid smug smile. "If we encounter any Citizens, we will order them to submit to testing by Medical Officer Bando. If they are uncooperative, we will subdue them for our own safety."

Thorne frowned. Pharo sounded almost as if he would prefer the Citizens resisted. The way he ran his gloved hand over the butt of his lazgun unnerved her. The Officers all pulled on their helmets, sealing everything tight, and stepped into the *Piasa*'s small cargo bay. As the inner doors closed, Z'lomm activated the outer cargo bay doors and the pneumatic pistons hissed, gears groaning as the doors separated.

The *Goremades*' docking wing was dim, quiet. Pharo stepped forward first with the Captain close behind him. Thorne's nerves sparked with anticipation. This was the first time Duncan had let her leave the ship for a mission without him.

"Suzuki, lock the *Piasa*'s interior cargo bay doors," Pharo said over the crew's private comms channel. "Make sure we don't get any unexpected visitors."

Beside him, the Captain nodded with approval and pulled her lazgun from its holster. Seeing that, Pharo continued.

"Everyone, have your lazguns ready at all times," he said quickly, earning him another nod. "I'll lead."

The *Goremades'* docking bay was cavernous and the crew's footsteps echoed in a faint tempo against the metal grated floor. Thorne looked side to side, noting that—besides the guest docking section—all the stations were taken by the station's mining ships and common cargo ships. None seemed to be missing. The brighter overhead lights were off, meaning the crew only had the small strip lighting beneath the metal grated floor to guide them. Pharo took the lead, heading towards the ship-side end of the bay, where airlock doors would give the *Piasa* crew access to the interior of the station.

In the majority of cases, the docking bay was pressurized and the airlock doors were for emergencies only, but the crew were keeping their suits on regardless.

Thorne paused a moment. Several of the ships had been opened up, their inorganic guts splayed out, but no visible damage to indicate why they were being worked on. Thorne's left thigh ached a bit and she rubbed it through her suit.

At the airlock doors, Pharo swiped his hand over the lock pad. She jogged to catch up, not wanting to be left behind or—god forbid—give Pharo a chance to reprimand her. Seconds passed before the pad beeped and the doors opened. The crew passed into the intermediate chamber between the airlock doors, waiting as the exterior one closed and the interior opened with a pneumatic hiss.

Thorne shifted her lazgun from one hand to the other. The station beyond was quiet. Brightly lit. No one in sight.

Pharo and Captain Müller stepped out first, together. Security Officer Z'lomm and Medical Officer Bando followed, leaving Thorne last.

She didn't like the feeling of being left behind and hurried to follow.

The airlock doors opened into a large service hall, all shades of white polycarb and steel.

"Lights are on, gravity is on," Pharo said over the private team comms. "Let's head to the Command Center."

Based on the station schematic Thorne had studied, she knew that the *Piasa* crew would need to access the main elevator of the station block they were in. The elevator would take them straight up to the highest level, thanks to Müller's executive access codes.

Thorne kept to the back of the crew, trying to breathe shallowly so she could hear the slightest sounds. The hum of a far-away core, the hiss of air filtration, the click of heat through the vents that ran along the top of the halls. To her engineer ear, the systems sounded fine—as far as she could tell at least. In the same way, there were no visible flickers in the lights to indicate power fluctuations.

Down the hall from the airlock doors, the *Piasa* crew passed several doors with plaques that indicated these were storage rooms, workshops, and access to the station's maintenance tunnels. Passing one door, Thorne thought she heard the quiet sound of crying and she hesitated, faltering in her steps.

"Keep up, Officer Thorne." Pharo's voice snapped over comms, startling her, and she pulled herself away from the door.

But she couldn't pull her thoughts from the sound. Crying. *Why?*

Up ahead, she spotted the slick silver elevator doors that would take them to the Command Center of the station. Executive Officer Pharo jabbed his finger against the elevator button and the team waited in a tense silence until the elevator dinged, and its doors slid open.

Thorne was the last one in. *If there's cheerful elevator music, I'll scream,* she thought. But the ride up was silent and Thorne realized that was worse. When her comms crackled, she nearly jumped out her skin.

"Lass." Duncan's voice was a balm.

"Duncan, is something wrong?" Thorne lowered her voice, even though she knew the others couldn't hear her on the private engineering comms line.

"The program." He paused and there was something in his voice that made Thorne hyper-focused on what he was about to say. "It's nearly finished."

"Do you know what it does? Or why *Goremades* Command attached it to their message?"

"Lass, I canna see each step," he said.

"Duncan?"

"I shouldna know how to finish this, ye ken?" His voice was hushed, as if he were afraid someone—or something—was listening. "But I see it. I see it before I type it."

Thorne stared at the back of Bando's head. Her brain fuzzed as she tried to think of how she was supposed to respond.

"Almost finished." Duncan said, still hushed.

"Duncan—" Thorne started but the elevator door opened, revealing the hall leading to the Command Center. "We just reached Command. I'll call back straight after, okay?"

Nothing but silence on the line.

V

Pharo swallowed and heard his throat click, it was so dry. Captain Müller stayed one step behind him. She was actually letting him take charge and his heart swelled. He pulled his shoulders back, sucked in a deep breath of canned air. The elevator had dropped them off at the end of the long hall that took them out of the Block where officer Suzuki had docked the *Piasa*.

In space stations such as the *Goremades*, the Command Center was located in a separate structure, connected to the various station Blocks by access halls, and powered by its own miniature power core located just beneath it. So Pharo led the four others down the narrow hall to the Command Center. The curved hall had plexiglass windows set along the length of it, allowing him the view of the stars and asteroid field nearby. It was beautiful and lonely.

At the end of the hall, they'd walked the length of it in silence, was a thick security door that blocked their way in. Pharo looked back at the crew, trying not to show his nervousness. At the back, Second Engineering Officer Thorne seemed distracted. She was a short, slim woman, looking like she might break at any moment. Her blond hair was cut in a short bob, usually kept in check with a black bandana. *When is she ever gonna fix my digipad?* he couldn't help but think before turning back to the door.

The security scan to the right was lit red. Pharo swiped his palm over it, activating an override process. The Company had equipped him and Captain Müller with codes that would allow them access to any part of the *Goremades* station without fail.

The security pad blinked, processed, flashed green. He breathed a sigh of relief. A part of him had expected something to go wrong. For something to change or to prevent him from continuing. Then Müller would take over and he would lose his chance. Lose his moment to make his father regret everything.

This fear burned like an ember in his heart, an acidic degradation of his self as a whole. The lingering haunt of his father's overall disapproval. A bitter taste.

But the door slid open. Revealed the interior of the Space Station *Goremades'* Command Center for the crew of the CRS *Piasa*.

The Command Center was the hub of control for SS *Goremades* and was located between all the Blocks, above them all but connected.

And there, behind the central command station were four men. They wore no suits besides the Company-issued gray jumpsuits and Pharo spotted the Commander by the triple yellow chevrons with the black star above them on his lapel.

"Commander—" An icy wave rolled over Pharo's nerve-endings as, for a moment, he couldn't remember the briefing he'd spent so much time studying before. Then his memory kicked back in. The gears whirred. "Commander Wayt. I am Executive Officer Pharo, here on the orders of the Company. You are to relinquish control of the SS *Goremades* immediately."

Commander Wayt stared at him, his face blank. Pharo swallowed, and he desperately wished he had some water. He knew he was sweating. He could feel the humidity of his own anxiety on his forehead. He shot a glance at Captain Müller out of the corner of his eye. He could tell by the way her eyebrows were lowering, her eyes narrowing, that she was annoyed.

"We will not relinquish." For a numb moment, Pharo thought he'd misheard the Commander.

He looked back at the Commander, whose men had gathered behind him in a V formation, a defensive position.

The Commander was shaking his head, hands behind his back. "The Company has no power here. We know what they will do. We have *seen* it. We found the ship in the rocks out there. We found what they made and what it can do."

Pharo opened his mouth. Closed it. His gears had stuttered to a stop. What the Commander was saying sounded like gibberish. Utter alien syllables.

"We ran the Mothman program. We have seen the point of intersection. The horizon," Wayt said, calm, still, robotic even. "We watched how it unfolds and we won't allow it."

Pharo hadn't imagined any other outcomes than the Commander stepping aside, obedient. And now the Commander was standing in front of them spouting nonsense. Obviously affected by space sickness, lost to the darkness in his mind. Müller took over. Pharo didn't know whether to be grateful or resentful.

"Commander Wayt," she said, stepping forward. "This space station is not under your jurisdiction anymore."

Pharo only had half a second to wonder if he would regret asking to be brought on this mission when the Commander pulled an industrial boltgun from behind his back, aimed it at Müller's head, and pulled the trigger.

Pharo was only twenty-five. Fresh from the Academy.

He'd never seen anyone die.

Not until today.

The fist-sized bolt shattered his Captain's head, her skull cracked into a dozen shards. Blood bloomed out, a mushroom cloud of crimson droplets and pink-grey chunks. A spray striped across Pharo's chest.

Müller's head jerked backward, her body bent the same direction, for a moment defying gravity as she curved in a bizarre C shape. Then her knees went. Her body fell with a meaty thud to the plexicarb floor.

"This isn't supposed to happen," Pharo told himself in a whisper.

The Commander's men stepped forward, boltguns raised. Boltguns meant to repair drills and harvesters, for service of the Company.

"Put your guns on the floor," Wayt said, his voice calm, unaffected.

Pharo knelt, his vision losing focus, for which he was grateful. Grateful he couldn't see the Captain's body just next to him, as he laid his lazgun on the floor. Still, despite the shock, his blurred vision, he could see Müller's left foot stuttering on the floor, beating the faintest tempo of judgment as he didn't hesitate to surrender.

But behind him came an inhuman howl, jump-starting his vision into focus. He looked over his shoulder. Z'lomm jerked out of Thorne's grip, shoving her into the wall. Then the grotesquely proportioned man charged, lazrifle raised. The Security Officer's first shot was true and the brilliant pulse ammo zipped through the eye of the man standing to the left of Wayt. The man's mouth went slack and he dropped to the floor, his eye socket smoking.

Z'lomm was a crack shot, Pharo had to give him that.

One of Wayt's men fired his boltgun, the report of its chamber thunderous, but Z'lomm ducked and the bolt slammed into the Command Station's door.

Rifle still braced against his shoulder, Z'lomm took another shot as Wayt fired.

The man to Wayt's right howled, clutching his gut, falling to his knee. Z'lomm merely grunted as Wayt's bolt smashed against his sternum. His ribs collapsed like twigs and the momentum carrying the Security Officer to slam against the wall.

Despite his chest being a ruin of blood, bone, and leaking organs, Z'lomm jerked into a seated position, his arms trembling violently, as he raised his rifle again.

His shot went wild, singeing the ceiling. Wayt shook his head, aimed, and fired.

The second shot found the same spot as the first and blood fountained from Z'lomm's mouth as his spine broke with a wet crack. Finally, he went still, eyes open and accusing, staring straight at Pharo.

"I won't tell you again," Wayt said and his voice almost seemed remorseful. "Put your guns down."

Pharo pressed a fist to his chest as his throat burned with bile and he swallowed the sourness back down. Next to him, Bando tossed her gun down. Thorne's face was knotted up in a furious snarl and she only put her gun down when Bando gripped the Second Engineering Officer's shoulder with a trembling hand.

"This is for your own good," Wayt said, to them, or maybe himself. "We have to stop them before it all meets in the eye of the moth."

"Take them to the brig." Wayt was turned away, speaking to one of his men, who nodded and approached.

"Come on, son," the man said, stopping in front of where Pharo crouched, shivering.

"What are you going to do with us?" His voice cracked and he felt shame, more powerful than his fear, and twice as caustic.

The man reached down, as if to help Pharo to his feet, but the Executive Officer jumped up. Not wanting to be touched, not wanting to be seen as weak.

And still, he felt the absence of his captain, felt the eyes of her dead Security Officer following him as he and the others were escorted from the Command Center.

VI

The SS *Goremades*'s brig was a level below the Command Center, all brightly lit, sparsely furnished cells. Prisoners were kept contained by old fashioned bars of steel, locked with biometric pads keyed to the space station's command and security teams.

Thorne clenched her hands into tight, tight fists, her nails biting into her palms, bright crescents of pain. It was the only thing keeping her from throwing herself at the man escorting them down the brig hall, boltgun still in hand.

He'd forced them to take off their suits, leaving them in their thin inner jumpsuits only. He'd stripped Thorne of her belt, Bando of her medkit. Pharo was useless, sniffing constantly as though he were on the verge of tears and practically tearing off his suit, the Captain's blood a scarlet letter on its breast.

The station officer put the three of them in the same cell, the door locking with a final click, and he left without a word, leaving them in a humming quiet, shaken in the events that had just occurred.

When Thorne had caught her breath, she whirled on him, the coward, the one who had laid down his gun first, when he should have tried to do something, anything.

She caught the front of his jumpsuit in her fists, but he was taller than her, and when she wanted to shake him, she could barely make him sway, which made her furious. *Lucky bastard, if I still had my belt, he'd be dead on the floor by now, a lazcutter in his throat.*

"Thorne! We don't have time for this!" Bando reached out but Thorne was already flinching away from Pharo, disgusted at him and herself.

"Are you from the Company?" A voice drew Thorne's attention to the cell next to them.

She looked at the solid plexicarb wall that separated her cell from the other.

"Hello?" the person called again, forlorn.

"Yes, we are from the Company," Bando called, shrugging when she caught Thorne's stare.

"Ah," the person sighed. "We were hoping we'd be saved. But if you're in here…"

Pharo straightened back his shoulders, seemed to catch his second wind, though he avoided looking at Thorne.

"I'm Executive Officer Pharo. Can you tell us what's going on?" he said, his voice overly loud, edging on falsetto.

Thorne wondered where the confident boy had gone. The loud one in the halls, the one that demanded everyone's attention in the cafeteria, the one who'd pushed her around, laughed at her. The one that thought he was hot shit.

I guess all bullies are cowards in the end.

The other prisoner's voice grew louder or closer. "The Mothman program."

Thorne looked at Bando again. The Commander had mentioned the same thing right before shooting Müller in the head. Thorne thought of the fragmented program that had been sent out with the message to the Company.

"A team of miners found an old ship among the rocks. Pre-Calamity kind of old."

"A ship from Earth?" Thorne asked.

It wasn't unheard of, but it was exceedingly rare for an old Earth ship to be found, especially out this far and intact.

"And you found some kind of software onboard?" Bando prompted the prisoner.

"It was something the humans of Earth had made. Something they thought could do something miraculous, something unnatural, something that shouldn't be done." The prisoner's voice dropped to a whisper and Thorne had to strain to hear them. "The ship's black box indicated that its original destination was Jupiter. To a high security testing site there. The program… It was based on some kind of creature they captured. The humans of Earth called it Mothman and they thought it could predict calamities. That it had some ability to predict the future. They experimented on it, tried to map its brain—what was closest to a brain it had."

Thorne looked at Bando. The Medical Officer looked as lost as Thorne felt at this information.

"So you're saying it can predict the future?" Bando asked.

"I don't know," the prisoner said. "Commander Wayt and the leadership team were curious. They say something in it. In whatever it is the program showed them. It made them believe. They made the crew watch too. Wayt held an assembly in the mess hall, I was the only one not there. I was out with my team, repairing some minor damage on a section of the hull. When we came back…"

The pause that came next was unbearable. Pharo broke first.

"Spit it out!" His voice cracked.

There came a strange scratching sound from the other cell. The sound of nails on the wall, or teeth on metal.

"The knowledge changed them," the prisoner whined, their voice lower still. "The Commander asked us to see it too but I refused. I thought they were all infected with space sickness. They put me here."

"You're saying that this Mothman program gave the Citizens space sickness?" Bando shook her head. "Impossible."

"Not the sickness, no. No, no, no, no!" the prisoner shouted. "It showed it all to them! All lines of fate converged in the eye of the moth, they said. And Commander Wayt said something had to be done. They thought I might send out a comms, or I might try something to stop them. They put me here. But my wife—my wife was one of those infected. Whatever she saw, it was too much for her. And she went to the Mech Room and opened up her wrists with a laser cutter."

Thorne's whole body went cold, her skin numb, and her scalp prickled. She thought of Duncan, back on the *Piasa*, trying to rebuild the program and the words he'd used on their brief comms call when she'd been on the lift to Command Center: *I see it before I type.*

"Is it possible?" she said, reaching out and grabbing Bando's wrist. "Is it possible for a computer program to do something like this?"

"I—I have never heard of anything like it," the Medical Officer replied, rubbing her forehead with her long fingers.

"We need to escape. Duncan needs to be warned," Thorne whispered fiercely.

"Duncan? The *Company* needs to be alerted of this rebellion!" Pharo responded and she shot him a glare.

"There's no use arguing, we're trapped in here until they decide what to do with us," Bando snapped, crossing her arms.

"Not necessarily," Thorne said, looking up to the ceiling, three meters above them. "There, a service panel."

It was barely distinguishable from the white ceiling, but Thorne knew what to look for: the two thin tubes that covered the panel's hinges.

"Oh, helpful," Pharo hissed between clenched teeth. "Maybe you can adjust the climate control a few degrees in here to make us more comfortable."

Ah, here comes the bully I know so well. Thorne sneered at him as she knelt. The officer who had escorted them down had made them strip off their suits but let them keep their boots. Duncan always lectured her on keeping a small toolkit inside her left boot. *You canna know when you might get stuck in a tight spot.* She heard his voice echoing in her head. Now, looking at the small felt kit in her hand, Thorne's heart ached and she squeezed its case hard, once, before opening its zipper.

"Holy hell, Thorne!" Pharo said, the excitement clear in his voice and she shushed him.

Inside the small toolkit were mini wire cutters, a flash welder, zip ties, and two screwdrivers. It was the flathead screwdriver that she pulled out, before closing the kit up again and slipping it back into her boot.

"If I can reach the panel up there," Thorne whispered and pointed up, "I can open it and get into the maintenance tunnels."

"And from there?" Bando asked.

"Hopefully get to the brig control room to unlock these doors." Thorne thought about Duncan, pictured the large man hunched over his workstation, thick fingers pecking away at the keys.

Pharo nodded and knelt. "We need to get back to the *Piasa* as soon as possible. We need to warn the others. Who knows what these people are willing to do."

Thorne trusted Pharo as far as she could throw him at standard gravity, but he was the tallest of the three in the cell, so she set her foot in his cupped hands. She pinned the screwdriver handle between her teeth then nodded at the Executive Officer.

Pharo strained, hefting Thorne up. One foot in his hands, she braced a hand on the top of his head, awkwardly balancing herself. His thick, dark hair was absurdly soft, though Thorne could feel a faint greasiness from whatever hair product he used, could smell its floral fragrance. *Of course he would get all dressed up for this mission.* She couldn't help but be annoyed at his arrogance. His vanity.

And then feel self-conscious about her own hair, several days between washes.

Still, she re-centered herself to concentrate as Pharo straightened. Thorne stretched up, pressing her hands against the ceiling to steady herself. Once she was confident she wasn't about to topple over, Thorne took the screwdriver from her mouth.

"Take two steps back, Pharo," she said, keeping her free hand on the ceiling still.

The Executive Officer obeyed, his arms trembling a bit with her weight. Two more steps took her directly under the panel and she ran her fingers over the plexicarb until she located the first near-invisible seam.

Normally, the panels were accessed with a special tool known as a magkey, which deactivated the small lock that kept the panel closed. But Thorne had spent her internship on a rickety old cargo ship running scrap metal through the inner planet belt and that ship had been as janky as it got. More often than not, the ship's maintenance panels wouldn't recognize Thorne's magkey, so she would need to force it open instead.

And that's exactly what she planned on doing now.

Thorne put the tip of the screwdriver to the seam of the panel.

"Steady, Pharo." Thorne pulled her other hand back, open palm, fingers extended. "Don't drop me."

She didn't wait for him to reply, slamming the heel of her hand against the butt of the screwdriver. Pharo wavered a bit, stumbled, but recovered. Thorne examined the panel. The tip of the tool lodged into the seam, but not deep enough, so she pulled her hand back.

"Steady!" she said and slammed her hand against the butt of the tool again.

The plexicarb panel's edge bent with a groan as the screwdriver jammed deeper between the seam. Thorne twisted the tool, leveraging it against the panel. With a pop, the panel swung open on its hinges, nearly swiping the side of Thorne's head.

"Got it!" she said, staring up into the dark interior of the maintenance tunnel.

She reached, grabbed the edges, brought her foot up, braced it on Pharo's shoulder, and pulled herself into the tunnel.

The tunnel was larger than Thorne was used to, tunnels on a space station being more spacious than the narrower, claustrophobic tunnels aboard the *Piasa*. Here, Thorne could kneel rather than belly crawl. She looked down at Pharo and Bando, still in the cell and staring up at her.

"Be careful, Thorne," Bando said with a weak smile.

Nodding, Thorne turned and made her way down the tunnel towards where she knew the brig control room to be. The Company was consistent in its structure builds, every room had a panel to allow maintenance access so she knew she'd be able to get inside. What she couldn't predict was whether or not the room would be empty.

The tunnel was neat, all the wires and tubing pinned against the side with pristine brackets. As with the *Piasa*, small plaques above each access panel indicated the corresponding room's ship-based coordinates and label. As she stared into the pitch-dark tunnel ahead of her, her courage failed.

What wasn't included in her toolkit was a flashlight, which made Thorne nervous. The interior tunnels weren't lit and the light from the open panel would only reach so far. Thorne's heart was already starting to race, thinking about being enclosed in absolute darkness, the tunnels becoming endless coffins. The eternal intestines of a mechanical leviathan known as the *Goremades*.

Focus, Thorne. Think of Duncan. Any second now he'll finish that program and—knowing that loaf—he'll run it too. A shiver ran down her spine, but Thorne shook her head in annoyance at her own trepidation. Duncan needed her.

The light faded to a gray twilight, then to blackness. Thorne's eyes ached, straining to see despite being blind in the all-encompassing dark. The Second Engineering Officer reached out from time to time, feeling for minuscule seams and the small plaques that identified them. Thorne had counted the cells they'd passed on the way to theirs—four in total, and so she counted four plaques in the darkness. From there, she would need to be careful. Panels could be set in any location, be it corridors, closets, what have you. The last thing she needed was to pop out in the middle of a hall and be spotted.

So Thorne kept a hand on the side of the tunnel, feeling for plaques and spending time—what felt like millennia—feeling the letters and sounding out the labels: HALL, ELECTRICAL CLOSET, HALL.

She was concentrating so hard on finding the next plaque that her brain stuttered when her left knee, sliding along the plexicarb bottom of the maintenance tunnel, found a gap. Found a void.

Her brain struggled as she tipped forward and her heart jumped in her throat. *A service ladder*, her brain screamed as it shoved images of her broken body crumpled at the base of the rungs, blood steaming, bones shattered. Then her flailing hands found the opposite wall and she came to a stop, her left shin pressing painfully into the edge of the drop, screaming with pain. *The access ladder is narrow.* A moment of panic and relief and panic yet.

Thorne hovered, delicately balanced with hand and shin, pain shooting upwards through her body, and the hungry void beneath. She hoped she could recover, but a powerful fear, fantasies of a plummet, the echoing thunder her body would make on impact, haunted her.

Smarten up, lass. Duncan's phantom voice chastising her. Kind but brutal. She anchored into the present again. Thorne braced her other hand on the wall, pressed backward, sliding along the plexicarb surface, ignoring the brilliant ache. Fingertips only touching, but both knees were on solid ground. Safe.

Thorne sunk forward, over her teeth, her eyes prickling, her breath laboured. She stayed there, feeling the floor beneath her legs and arms, her forehead. Feeling the living thrum of the station's internal systems: the hum of air being pumped, the grinding of distant gears working some unseen mechanism, the buzz of electricity through wire. Steadily her breathing, her heart rate slowed, matched the life within the station. The sounds she found the most comfort in: the living grumble of working machinery.

After what could have been moments, minutes, millennia, Thorne sat up, back in control. All was still dark and she felt a strange disconnect with the event that had held her here, a disconnect with the world around her.

Now's not the time, Lynn Thorne! Come on! One hand out, she felt for the edge she'd nearly toppled over. Once found, Thorne inched forward, feeling, always feeling, her hands as her eyes.

She reached down and found the first rung of the ladder, which was bolted to the wall of the maintenance tunnel. Turning, she slipped one foot over, finding the rung. Then she descended.

The ladder was shorter than a standard level, indicating it was a half level descent. This was used in many Company stations to change the placement of access panels from ceiling to floor level, depending on what systems might be in use through the level.

The plaque identified the first panel from the access ladder as BRIG SYSTEMS. Thorne's heart kicked up a gear and she pressed her ear against the access panel.

Silence.

From the inside, the panels were easier to open. Thorne fumbled, located, then lifted a tiny latch, which deactivated the magnetic lock, allowing her to swing open the access panel.

The artificial light that poured in assaulted Thorne's retinas and she flinched away, blinking rapidly. Pressing against the side of the tunnel, Thorne wiped her arm against her watery eyes over and over again, trying to clear them. In the seconds it took her to adjust, she imagined someone spotting her, grabbing her, dragging her back to the cell.

Her vision cleared. She was alone. Thorne crawled through. As she'd thought, the panel was set at floor level. Looking around, Thorne recognized the room immediately as the same place where the station officer had forced her and the others to strip out of their suits. In fact, she could see them hanging in open lockers by the closed door.

She got to her feet, unsteady for just a moment, still reeling in the light. Her next step was to rush over to the open locker and pull on her suit. She activated her comms.

"Duncan? Duncan!" she hissed into the mic, but only static answered. "Shit."

Fumbling through her pockets, through the pockets of the other two suits, Thorne couldn't find the lazguns. She tried the desk, but the drawers were locked. It didn't matter. All she needed was her screwdriver.

All three lazguns were in the second from the top drawer on the left, plus a key card. Thorne pocketed it all. She retrieved the other two suits next and approached the door. All she could hope was that the hall was empty.

VII

Pharo paced. The cell was small and it only took him five steps from one side to the other, then five more steps to get back again.

"You need to calm down," Bando said.

Pharo glanced up at her. *I don't think she fully grasps the situation. Our captain was shot. We are in deep shit.*

"How long do you think it'll take?" he said. "How long for Thorne to get to the brig room and back?"

The Medical Officer shrugged and looked out the cell door. "We have to trust in her. She'll get us out."

Soft footsteps came down the hall and Pharo froze, watching the door. Bando backed away from the door, her hands clenched into fists. Distantly, something wailed, a long lingering bass note that made Pharo's hair stand on end.

"It's coming!" the prisoner yelled. "It's coming!"

Pharo swallowed, felt his throat click. *I wish I'd never asked Müller to let me lead today. I should have just stayed on the* Piasa.

The footsteps echoed, loud as the drums of death. *I should have been a Company netcast writer instead!* Pharo thought as he wondered if he would vomit, then Thorne appeared.

She didn't say anything, but Pharo could tell she was upset. Instead she swiped a card and the locking mechanism beeped, the door opened.

"I'm so glad you're okay, Thorne," Bando said, immediately going to hug the Second Engineering Officer. Pharo watched both women, feeling very much like an outsider.

"We should go," he said and noted the glare Thorne gave him.

"I couldn't reach Duncan through comms," the Second Engineering Officer said, her voice toneless.

"And Suzuki?" Pharo asked and immediately could tell that Thorne hadn't even tried to reach the *Piasa*'s Navigational Officer.

The Executive Officer bit back a reprimand. She was just a junior officer after all, he couldn't expect her to know what to do in all situations.

"Let's suit up," he said instead.

Thorne stood by the open door with her lazgun, waiting as Bando and Pharo pulled on their suits and armed their own weapons. Once ready, Pharo opened the private *Piasa* crew comms. "Officer Suzuki, are you there?"

"I'm here, Officer Pharo." The Navigational Officer's quick response startled all three of them. "What do you need?"

Pharo noted how calm she sounded. *Suzuki doesn't know. She hasn't noticed anything!*

"Suzuki, we have an emergency." Pharo knew his voice was trembling, that his fear was obvious. *Dad would be so disappointed in me right now.* "The Captain is dead. And Z'lomm. The Commander shot them both."

He heard the sharp inhale over comms as Suzuki processed what he'd just said.

"Bando, Thorne, and I are in the brig but we've gotten out," he added, then wondered if he should have said "Thorne got us out."

"Shit, Müller's dead?" Suzuki's voice was faint, weak.

"Suzuki, you need to secure the *Piasa*. Don't let anyone in until we get there." Pharo's head was burning up. An oncoming panic attack. The same feeling he got before every exam and interview. With every conversation he had with his father. "Alert the Company immediately."

"Yes, of course, sir!" Suzuki said.

"Suzuki, have you seen Duncan?" Thorne interrupted.

"Now's not the time, Thorne!" Pharo couldn't imagine what was going on in the Second Engineering Officer's head. What mattered was securing the ship. Not what her superior officer was doing.

"Duncan? He was in the Mech Room last I saw him, working on the program." The Navigational Officer sounded as confused at Thorne's panic as Pharo felt.

"Suzuki, you need to stop—" Thorne began, but Pharo cut her off.

"Second Engineering Officer Thorne. Now is not the time. The *Piasa* needs to be secured." he snapped. "Suzuki. Lock the ship up tight, then send a distress call to the Company. We'll make our way down to the docking bay."

"Yessir," Suzuki replied and signed off.

Pharo cleared his throat. *I sounded just like Dad then, and I don't really know how I feel about that.* He glanced at Thorne. She was furious.

"Duncan could be in danger!" she said, her hands in tight fists by her sides.

"*We* are in danger, Thorne!" he snapped back—*angry, always angry, like Dad. Am I just like him?*

"If that program is behind the erratic behaviour of the *Goremades* Officers," Thorne pressed on, squaring off physically. "Then Duncan could be at risk! We need to warn him but he's not answering comms!"

Bando stepped between Pharo and Thorne, hands up, palms out. "Thorne, I understand your concern. But Pharo is right. Our priority is to get back to the docking bay. We can't even know for sure that the program did anything at all."

Thorne shook her head but stepped back.

"Everyone, put your helmets on." Bando followed her own instructions, tugging her helmet over her head and locking it shut. "If there is something in the air causing this, we don't want to be exposed to it any more than we have been. We should have enough stored air to last us till we get back to the *Piasa*."

Pharo shivered. Bando was right. There could be some kind of a contagion onboard, though Pharo would bet money on it being a widespread case of space sickness. Still, he pulled on his helmet and secured it.

Thorne stepped out of the cell and went to the one next door. Pharo followed. He was curious too.

The prisoner was sitting against the far wall, dressed in a standard Company jumpsuit. She was an older woman, her hair pure silver, in greasy tangles around her face. Her thin face hung with exhaustion, marked by the deep, dark rings under her eyes. Thorne swiped the security card and the cell door opened, but the woman didn't move.

"Ma'am, you should come with us," Pharo said, forcing himself to step into the cell, holding out his hands just as Bando had done earlier.

The woman shook her head. "Nowhere is safe."

"We can take you back to Company HQ, or at least, the nearest station or planet we encounter first." He looked over his shoulder at the two women behind them, hoping they would do something, anything.

"I'll stay here," the woman said, her voice cold and oddly calm. "But you should hurry. They let you come. They wanted you here."

Pharo became hyper-aware of how dry his mouth was, how sour it tasted.

"What do you mean?" He rasped.

"They need your FTL drive," she replied, with absolutely no emotion on her face. "That's the only reason they let you dock, you know."

"Shit," Bando muttered.

The Executive Officer spun on his boot heel. "We need to get back to the *Piasa* right now."

Thorne and Bando nodded and he exited the cell. They left the door open.

"Everyone, have your lazguns at the ready," Bando said. "There's no telling who we'll encounter."

Pharo took lead. Not because he wanted to, but because he felt it was expected of him as the Executive Officer. His hands shook as he held his lazgun up. Through the hall and into the brig control room, which was still empty. Pharo's heart bashed against his ribs, echoing along with their own footsteps. He turned his wrist towards his face, activated its mini holo-display, pulling up the same schematic they'd reviewed on the *Piasa* during their briefing.

"We're twenty-seven levels up from the docking bay in this Block," he said, scanning the bright green display.

"That's a long way," Bando said.

"Duncan?" Thorne's voice crackled over comms. "Duncan, please respond!"

"Thorne!" Pharo snapped. "Keep the line clear for Suzuki!"

How long? How long will it take us? Will we be able to get on the elevator? His mind whirled, buzzed. He tried to take deep breaths. *Does it matter? I'm going to screw this up. I'm going to die!*

"Pharo?" The Medical Officer's voice pulled him out of the spiral. Pulled him back to the present.

"Let's go, no time to waste," he said, his voice husky.

He opened the brig control room door, pausing on the threshold, looking down one way then the other to find it empty.

Beyond that, from the map, he knew the *Goremades* to be a warren of corridors, rooms, and narrow spaces. The main elevator could take them straight down, but Pharo knew that it wouldn't be possible to use it without being seen, and they didn't have a chance in hell to overpower an entire space station.

There were smaller lifts located across the *Goremades*, but they only operated between four or five floors. Alternatively, there were service ladders. These were only used in catastrophic emergencies, so this was Pharo's goal.

"Keep to the side of the hall and create as small a profile as you can," he said, not knowing if it made any sense at all.

But they listened to him, keeping to one side, behind him, guns raised. *What would Dad do? What would he do?* The same thoughts ran round and round. He felt outside his own body, numb, but every nerve electric. Up ahead was the first junction of halls. Pharo desperately wanted to take off his helmet, to wipe the sweat that was collecting in his eyebrows, threatening like hot stormclouds to douse his eyes and blind him.

Instead, he looked down at his wrist, at the map. Left, left, right, straight, straight, and right to the first—Pharo was so distracted that, when he bumped into someone, his first reaction was to apologize.

A moment.

A shiver.

Pharo looked up from his wrist.

The man in front of him was dressed only in ripped, stained underwear and had his back to Pharo. He was slightly bald, his skin speckled with large dark spots, and loose skin hung from his sides, his arms. The stranger didn't turn around, didn't acknowledge the three behind him at all. Instead, he swayed back and forth, mumbling under his breath.

Pharo took a step back, kept his eyes on the swaying man, and opened comms.

"Uh…" His mind faltered, trying to think of a command. *What would Müller do? What would Dad do?* "There's a guy here."

Pathetic. He bit his left inner cheek hard.

"He seems…unwell," Bando replied.

"That's an understatement," Thorne replied and didn't wait for a command, for Pharo's order. She stepped around the Executive Officer and grabbed the man by his shoulder, spinning him to face them. "Oy, sir, do you know where you are?"

Pharo's heart dropped straight through his rectum and he reeled back from the two in front of him. The man turned slowly, hunched over his clasped hands. He didn't look up at them. He didn't seem to see that they weren't part of the space station crew.

"Why bother? Why bother?" the man muttered. "It all ends anyway. Why bother? Why bother with anything?"

"Yeah, he's out of it," Thorne said, walking past him. "Let's go."

Finally Pharo's fear was overruled—by anger. *Thorne had no right to lead. She was only a Second Officer! Not even a First!* He chased her, shouldering past, and took back the lead.

Left, left, right, straight, straight, and right.

They encountered more people, all seemingly lost in their own thoughts and in various forms of disarray.

A woman clutching her crying child, shushing the little girl, and promising that the end was soon and that all things served the end found in the moth's eye.

A man and a woman, slumped against a wall, holding hands, weeping, several bottles of pills empty next to them. Enough to kill them, Bando had said, checking their pulses. *Too late.*

A man in a Company jumpsuit, stood facing a corner, mute and nonreactive as they passed.

A woman raced up to them, nearly giving Pharo a heart attack as she gripped the front of his suit, shaking him. She screamed, "And the silence creeps as the winged messiah does, eyes as red as the crimson dawn, whose thirst will never be slaked!" Her words made no sense. Pharo pried her hands away. But her words haunted him as they left her behind.

Dozens of weeping people. Dozens of those stricken with madness. Oblivious to their presence. By the time they got to the first service ladder, Pharo's eyes were stinging with sweat, his mouth as dry as the desert planet Dunate that he'd interned on.

"Here we are." Pharo's voice cracked. "This should take us to level twenty."

"The elevator would've been faster," Thorne snapped. "Every second we waste could mean danger to Duncan and Suzuki."

"Officer Thorne, control yourself!" Pharo could hear his father's voice in his own and flinched from it.

"Shove it, Pharo." The venom in Thorne's voice was enough to shock him to silence.

"Thorne…" Bando stepped to the Second Engineering Officer, laying a hand on her shoulder.

"Duncan *never* ignores my comms," Thorne said. "I've even tried on the private engineering line, but nothing. There's something wrong. He was trying to rebuild the coding we got. If it was this program that made everyone here go—go *crazy*—"

The panic in Thorne's voice was obvious and Pharo was at a loss. She was actually worried about the Engineering Officer Duncan. She cared more about him then she did them, the three locked in the space station surrounded by hostiles.

"Thorne, if what that person said had any truth…we can't," Bando said. Thorne shook her head.

"Trust in him, Thorne," Bando continued. "He's a space veteran!"

"We need to keep going," Pharo said, feeling out of place again. "We have to keep moving towards the docking bay."

The service ladder was locked behind a wall panel, but Thorne's stolen key card allowed them access.

The narrow access ladder was dimly lit by pale blue strip lighting, the ladder rungs were thin, dotted with rubber beads for grip. Looking down at the access shaft, Pharo ran a bone-dry tongue over his cracked lips. *Smarten up, boy. Are you an officer or a coward?*

Pharo flinched away and reached out, grabbing the rung directly across from him. Then he descended. Running from the gore he witnessed in the Command Center, running from Thorne's obvious disdain, running from the voice of his father.

VIII

Thorne was halfway down the second access ladder when her comms buzzed with the telltale sound of the line opening.

"Lass." She nearly slipped off the ladder in shock at the sound of Duncan's voice. *He's okay!*

"Duncan!" she said. "Are you okay?"

But Thorne knew he wasn't. Knew it from the lifeless sound in his voice.

"Duncan....stop!" And distantly, nearly lost in the comms auto-background sound filterer, was Suzuki.

"Officer Duncan," Pharo snapped over comms, it was a party now. "What's going on?"

Thorne's line clicked. Duncan had switched to the secure engineering line, where Pharo and Bando couldn't hear.

"The *Hera*," Duncan said, in Thorne's ear. He sounded tired—so, so tired.

Thorne's heart was pounding, racing away beneath her ribs. Something bad was coming. Her thigh had never ached this bad, not since the accident. Below her, Pharo had stopped descending and she knocked her boot against the side of his helmet to urge him on. She could only assume he was still shouting into the general comms channel.

"You're a hero, Duncan," she said. "That's why I wouldn't let you refuse my application. You're the only one I'd ever mentor under."

He sighed, his breath like the heavy crush of space, echoing and empty. "I shoulda let it crash, lass."

"Duncan!" Suzuki's voice was louder—closer—and more desperate. "Don't do this, please!"

Thorne's feet kept bumping into Pharo's helmet as he slowed, faltering on the ladder.

"Did you run the program, Duncan?" Thorne wished she could just kick the Executive Officer down and leave them all behind. "Please tell me you didn't run it!"

The pause that followed told Thorne all she needed to know. Whatever had happened to all the maddened Citizens of the SS *Goremades* had happened to Duncan.

"I—I can fix this," she said—half to herself, half to Duncan. "Just wait, okay? I'll be back at the *Piasa* in no time!"

"Stay away, lass," he said. "There's no point in ya returning."

"Duncan, please!"

"I should have let her crash, ye ken?" he continued as if she hadn't spoken at all. "But I didnae know."

"You mean the *Hera*?" *If I can keep him talking, I can buy time.* "You're a hero, Duncan. You saved thousands of lives!"

"They stripped me of everything," he said. "But I dug, ye ken. I kept digging."

The ladder was endless. The three of them—Thorne, Bando, and Pharo— would starve before they ever reached the bottom. Before they could ever escape the SS *Goremades*.

"Do you know what I found, lass?" His voice was a whisper made hoarse from years of haunting regret.

"Duncan, please," Thorne begged. "Just wait, okay? I'm almost there!"

"The *Hera* was carrying biomatter for testing." Below her, Thorne saw Pharo land, open the access ladder door. But there was still so far to go. "Biomatter, hah. It was *people*, lass. People taken from non-Company colonies. Kidnapped."

It took a moment for it to sink in. Thorne's hands shook on the rungs and she had to stop. There had always been rumours. Dark gossip spread about the source of the Company's speedy turnaround on cutting edge pharmaceuticals and biotherm technology. *But they were just rumours, right? They wouldn't go so far as to kidnap people for testing, right?* But Thorne could believe it. *Company protocols condemned my father to death rather than risk anything to save him, after all. Human life was a mere statistic.*

"It woulda been faster for them to die in the crash. Less pain." Duncan's voice cracked and Thorne's heart cracked with it, at the sound of his barely held back tears. "I condemned them. To the torture, the testing, the agonies."

"Duncan, no." But what could Thorne say to make anything better? "Please, please, promise you'll wait for me?"

"I have an old war buddy, someone who went through the Tx'el Rebellion with me." Duncan wasn't listening. "I asked him, nay, begged him ta tell me. To *show* me."

"Duncan, please stop!" More than not wanting to hear it herself, Thorne didn't want him reliving it all again. Trapped in the hungry grip of bad memories.

Thorne's helmet jerked as Bando gave her a brisk nudge with the side of her boot. *That's right. I have to go. We have to hurry. I can still fix this! I will save him!*

"What I saw of them. These people. Innocents," he continued. "Carved up, skinned, full of poisons and tubes. Treated like they were less than human. I did that. I shoulda let us all burn."

Her boots touched the floor and she shot out the access door, avoiding Pharo's reaching hands. Everything teetered on a knife's edge. If she could just get to Duncan in time, she could prevent everything from shattering. From breaking.

"Joel Duncan, you listen to me!" she shouted. "Whatever happened to those people was not your fault. It was the Company's fault, not yours! So you sit down and you *wait* for me, Duncan!"

She dashed down the hall, dodging a weeping man, his fingers digging furrows into his face.

"You're right, lass." And for a terrible, hopeful, moment, Thorne thought she'd reached him. Then he continued. "The Company is at fault. That's why I must do this, ye ken? So stay away, lass. Let me do wha' I needta do."

His terrible calm, his finality, reminded Thorne of the last time she'd ever spoken with her father—an engineer on their home space station—who had used his last moments to reach her over comms. To say goodbye. She had listened to him calmly tell her he loved her, tell her how proud he was of her getting the elusive Nova Oculus Scholarship to the Academy for engineering, all the while choking to death on the leaking core fumes as he died trapped in a secondary core room in an auxiliary factory block on a routine check. Learning at the Academy bore a terrible repercussion. Thorne had followed in her father's footsteps, but also learned that he could have been saved. There would have been time, except…except for Company Protocol, which valued "the bigger picture." So her father's colleagues—cowards—had sealed him in.

"Duncan—" But she was speaking to a closed line.

Thorne made to turn a corner when a hand gripped her elbow and whirled her around so forcibly that she slammed against the wall.

"Officer Thorne!" Pharo glared at her, still gripping her elbow tight. Bando was just behind him, panting as she caught up.

"Duncan—he's going to do something bad! We have to get back!" Thorne realized she was on the verge of tears.

She straightened up, bit the inside of her left cheek hard, until she tasted the bright tang of blood. *Get your shit together!*

"We know! He's locked Suzuki in the cargo bay and is pulling out the *Piasa*'s FTL drive," Pharo snapped. "I've ordered her to take whatever measure is necessary to stop him."

Thorne's whole body went cold. She could picture Duncan, tainted by whatever poison that program put in his head, digging into the *Piasa*'s engine. Suzuki behind him, lazgun raised. A killing shot.

"Duncan is not our enemy!" she hissed.

I can save him. I won't let him die, not like my father. I can save him.

"Isn't he? He's trying to steal our FTL drive! We'd be stranded here!"

"He is NOT our enemy!" *Why is he doing this? Why is Pharo turning on Duncan?* "We can talk him down! Not attack him!"

A hard grip caught Thorne's arm. She was jerked around and found herself facing a towering man dressed in a standard Company jumpsuit, whose insignia indicated he was some kind of teams supervisor—likely for a mining shift. His gray hair was shaved close to his head, his lips stained black and the front of his jumpsuit crusted with rusty stains, his hands painted crimson with fresh blood. Facing him, Thorne's arm was twisted cruelly, but she couldn't get out of his grip.

"Interlopers," the man said, his voice hoarse and scratchy. "Your coming was foreseen."

Footsteps from behind Thorne. She glanced over her shoulder. Four more Citizens blocked off that direction and, when she looked back, there were three more behind him.

They all held wrenches, drills, plasma-cutters. Thorne felt something hard press into the side of her neck: a bolt-cutter, just like the ones Commander Wayt and his men had had.

"Put down your weapons, outsiders," the man said.

"You can't legally detain us!" Pharo shouted through his helmet. "We are representatives of—"

One of the Citizens behind the Executive Officer stepped up, wrench raised. The sound of its heavy impact against the back of Pharo's helmet echoed down the hall. Pharo collapsed to the floor with a faint moan.

Bando looked up at her, then at the man directly behind her, she held up her hands, slowly sinking to her knees and surrendering her lazgun on the floor.

"Take them," the man said.

IX

Pharo's head was pounding. The pain drew him out of unconsciousness like the beating of a drum, a siren's call pulling him, unwillingly, back into the present. The first thing he noticed was the taste of blood, thick and sour. His tongue probed out, recoiled at the gaping hole in his bottom lip. *That bastard hit me.*

Next came the struggle to open his eyes, fighting against the blinding light. He brought a hand up, touched the bump at the back of his head with tender fingertips. Then he was struck with a nauseating rush of panic, realizing the only way he'd be able to feel the bump was if his helmet was gone, which meant he was at risk if there was something in the air.

He tried to sit up and the room gained orbit, spinning, spinning, spinning.

"Lay back, Pharo, take it easy." Bando's voice came to him, though he couldn't focus his eyes, couldn't see clearly, only in throbbing pulses. Her hands pressed him back.

"Is he okay, Bando?" Thorne's voice, quieter.

"Pharo, open your eyes for me," the Medical Officer said.

Pharo hadn't even realized he had closed them. He opened them and flinched again at the bright light.

"I need you to keep them open, okay?" A light went left, right, left, disappeared. "No concussion as far as I can tell."

"My helmet," Pharo forced out past a gummed-up tongue.

"I had to remove it to check your injuries, Pharo," Bando replied. "You got hit pretty hard, but it looks like you're no worse for wear."

"My head." He didn't know what he wanted to say. *My head hurts, I feel like puking, I wanna go home.* But his father's voice was loudest. *Get over it, boy. You think your pain means anything? Smarten up!*

Weren't those his words when he'd fallen down the stairs of their home? He'd broken a wrist. He'd cried and his father had yelled. He'd only been eight.

"I'm about to administer some pain relief, okay? You'll feel a sting."

He didn't feel anything at all. Until the cool numbness rushed over him. He sighed. *I didn't have to ask for it. I'm not weak.*

His head went still. Finally. The pain faded. His vision sharpened. He sighed again.

Pharo sat up, slowly, with Bando's hand on his back supporting him.

They were in a small room, the floor covered by a faded red rug, the walls adorned with old-fashioned, Pre-Calamity styled religious tapestries. Several plexicarb pews had been pushed against a wall, and there was a single desk against the back wall, covered in electronic tablets and religious icons.

There was only a single door. Thorne had her ear pressed against it.

"Where are we?" he asked.

"They took us to the religious centre of this Block," Bando replied. "We're in the office."

It was then he noticed the sound. The chanting. Beyond the door, into what he could only assume was the general hall of worship, people were chanting.

Pharo stood, Bando still at his side, holding his elbow. The medicine she gave him had been powerful stuff—as he stood, his skull didn't so much as throb.

"Why did they take us here?" he said.

"I … I'm not completely sure." Bando looked over to Thorne.

The Second Engineering Officer finally turned around. She avoided looking at him. *This is her fault. If she hadn't run off like some kid…*

"They were saying something about seeing all this before it happened," she said. "The religion hall was all messed up. Black stuff all over the walls and floor. There's about three dozen of them in there, all with black lips and weapons."

"Does it have something to do with that program they've been talking about?" he asked.

Thorne shrugged.

The door hissed as it opened. Standing at the threshold was the same looming man that had caught them in the halls. Beyond him, Pharo could see the religion hall, full of pews and various motivational sayings, even some towering stained glass themed holo-displays on the walls.

"Outsiders," the man intoned.

A bit overly dramatic, Pharo couldn't help thinking and snapped, "What is your name, Citizen?"

"I am General Manager of Cybernetics, Harold Juniper," the man replied with a black-lipped smile.

Juniper gestured grandly, ushering the three out into the religious center.

Pharo meant to be the first one out, but Thorne took the lead. This time, he didn't hold it against her. He was still shaken from the previous attack, his hands were trembling.

Still, he checked his belt. The lazgun was gone. From the gauze covering the large, hard bump at the back of his head, he could only guess that the Citizens had left Bando her med kit. *No idea if Thorne still has her handy secret tool kit though.*

Out in the center, Pharo was assaulted by the thick reek of incense—spicy and heady—and coughed, choking on it. Dozens of Citizens were sat on the crooked pews spread through the hall, heads bowed with tears or prayer.

The black sludge Thorne had mentioned streaked the walls, slimed the floor. In the nearest corner, three children knelt near a mound of the stuff. They scooped gelatinous chunks into their mouths, slurping it down and giggling.

Pharo pulled his eyes away. Juniper led them and other Citizens fell in behind them, hands clasped, and lips stained black. Surrounded and closed in, Pharo let himself be led to the centerpiece of the hall: a massive altar, beneath the row of stained glass holos. It was a dais, in front of a choir area. Along the right wall were various tools for worship.

A woman stood behind the altar, topless, her chest smeared with the same black gunk that stained the walls and floor. Her white-blond hair was slicked back with the same substance, away from her face, so that Pharo could clearly see the oozing holes where her eyes had been.

Juniper went and stood by her side, looking down at Pharo, Bando, and Thorne. He knelt at the woman's side and pressed his forehead to the back of her hand. She tilted her head towards him in acknowledgment, revealing the burned, scarred tissue where her ear should have been.

The woman turned her eyeless face to the three *Piasa* Crew Officers.

"All lines converge in the eye of the moth," she said in a musical voice, its soothing sound in discordance with her horrific injuries. "And so the outsiders are here in the hall of moth, to be enlightened."

Pharo looked over to Bando. Her orange eyes were wide, glittering in the neon-coloured holos.

"We don't want any trouble," the Medical Officer said.

Pharo cleared his throat. "Who are you?"

The woman was disturbing to look at. There were black rivers of dried blood on her cheeks, leaking from her eyes. Yet she was calm, poised. She spread out her open hands, looking like one of the many saints the people of Earth had once held sacred in the old religions.

"I am become nameless," she said. "To act as a vessel for the saviour, the one who sees all, whose red eyes pierce the very veils of time and have brought us visions of the future to come."

"Wow, okay. Helpful," Thorne snapped. "But we're leaving, even if I have to blind the rest of you!"

"Thorne!" Bando hissed.

The crowd behind them murmured, clothes rustling, the tension as thick as the incense. Pharo licked his lips, gripping his helmet tightly in his hands. *I need to manage this carefully or this could become a mob situation.*

"Ma'am, we are representatives of the Company and are here on official Company orders," he started, but she held a hand up.

"The Company is the enemy of truth," she said. "You need enlightenment. You will not be harmed. But you will see."

The crowd cheered, their voices an aural assault again Pharo's brain, reawakening the throbbing in the back of his head. He could feel the energy rising, creeping towards a violent threshold. It was a sensation he was used to, from the fights his parents would have behind closed doors. Beneath the jubilant shouts of the *Goremades* Citizens, Pharo could swear he heard his mother's muted cries of pain.

He shivered. *This has all gone sideways. I just want to go home. I should've been a Logistics Clerk like mom.* But it didn't matter. He was the *Piasa*'s Executive Officer and, with the captain dead, he was in charge. He had to protect the remaining crew.

"When we found the ship, lost among the rocks," the woman intoned, "We were blessed with the holy software to give us sight into the future. We have seen the corruption, the betrayal, the loss of humanity. We also discovered the location of the saviour. We brought him back."

"What are you talking about?" Bando asked.

The woman, the twisted prophet of this damned congregation, gestured at Juniper. He stood, turned, and went to the altar that had been pushed back against the wall.

"Let us go," Pharo said, trying to sound like his father. "Or you'll make it worse for yourselves when the Company hears of this!"

Thorne glanced at him. "Yeah, you got them shaking now."

Juniper pulled an old, yellowing VR headset from the storage space in the altar, returning to stand next to the eyeless woman. The Company usually outfitted its religion centers with outdated VR sets that could be loaded with various religious videos and programs, used by Citizens during their off-shift hours. Pharo was well familiar. His mother had spent a lot of time in the religious center of the CSC *Miska*, searching, yearning, never satisfied with her own place in space and needing to find something that could give her life meaning. It was the same reason she'd had a kid, though in motherhood she'd found only disappointment.

Juniper raised the VR set up high. Behind Pharo, the Citizens erupted in cheers. "Enlightenment! Enlightenment!"

Slowly, every inch of his body quivering with religious fervour, Juniper lowered the set and held it out to the prophetess. The eyeless woman took it from him without fumbling, as though she could sense exactly where it was. She brought the set up and kissed it softly, smiled. Pharo couldn't stop staring at her crooked right canine tooth. The crowd hushed immediately, eerily.

"Things will be better for you when you know the truth," she said, the overhead lights sparking on that crooked tooth. "Ignorance is not bliss. Not anymore."

Juniper nodded. Pharo felt, more than saw, the crowd converging on him. On the others. Two men grabbed his arms, pulling them back so hard they nearly wrenched them from their sockets.

"Let go of me, assholes!" Thorne screamed, thrashing.

Pharo wanted to shout too, to struggle, but his whole body was alive with buzzing, numbing wires. Everything slowed down and he felt frozen, a viewer rather than a player in this mess. Two men and a woman picked Bando up bodily off the floor, carrying her up the two steps to where the eyeless woman stood. The Medical Officer kicked and squirmed, but they dropped her to the floor, falling to their knees on her arms and waist, pinning her.

"Enlightenment is our only hope," the woman whispered. Tears, stained with blood and pus, slipped down her cheeks. "And our curse."

Juniper knelt, gripping Bando's jaw in one large hand, as the eyeless woman thumbed the power button on the side of the headset and slipped it over Bando's head.

"Bando!" Thorne shouted, twisting and trying to bite the hand of the person holding her right arm.

The Medical Officer turned her head left and right, as if searching for a way out. Something grabbed her attention in the set—her head drew forward, her limbs quivered—then she seized up, thrashing against the three that kept her pinned. "Please! No! Please!" she cried and then went still, quiet. The three holding her down stepped away, melting back into the crowd.

"Bando?" Pharo whispered.

The Medical Officer's hands trembled against the faded carpet, her lips moving in a rapid, silent mantra.

Dad would rip free. He'd throw punches. He'd fight. Tentatively, Pharo strained against the hands gripping his upper arms, only to feel them tighten. *At this rate, I'll end up with two dislocated shoulders.* Pharo's heart went into FTL gear. He felt as he did as a child, when his father had found something to get fired up about—Pharo's grades, his attitude, his lack of interest in sports—and Pharo's father would grab him. If Pharo was lucky, he'd just get shaken. If not, then he'd get swung into a wall, a table, a counter. Worse yet, if his mother were home. She'd try and stop Pharo's father, step in, make him madder, make it worse.

She never fought back for herself. Instead she would just go…limp.

Pharo sucked in a hissing breath through his clenched teeth and just let his knees go. The men holding his arms stumbled forward, pain exploding in his shoulders like supernovae, but he slipped out of their grip and fell to his knees to the floor.

One thing his father had gifted him—a higher pain tolerance.

Before the blinding pain in his shoulders had even begun to fade away, Pharo sprung to his feet, throwing himself against the nearest Citizen, sending them flying into the people holding onto Thorne. The group of them went down into a pile. Thorne didn't stay down though—in a moment, she'd squirmed out from underneath the pile, her nose dripping from a new cut across its bridge, and was scrambling towards Bando.

Juniper pushed the eyeless woman behind him, reaching for his boltgun. Pharo had never felt so numb. So cold.

A man groaned at Pharo's feet, trying to pull himself from under the muddle of Citizens, a lazgun in his outstretched hand. In a controlled swoop, Pharo stomped on the man's hand, the delicate bones snapping under his boot, and Pharo snatched up the lazgun. The man howled. Pharo raised, levelled, aimed—just as Juniper, himself, aimed back.

Pharo was faster. The bright blue blaze from his lazgun caught Juniper right in the throat. The towering man bowled over, falling to the floor with a thump as he clutched his throat.

Thorne was at Bando's side, yanking the VR set off her face. The eyeless woman stumbled over Juniper's prone body, her hands out, the fingers curled into claws. Bando lay still yet, stunned, blinking slowly as she stared at the ceiling.

"How dare you!" the eyeless woman shrieked. "How *dare* you!"

Pharo's next shot took her in the right shoulder, spinning her in a wild circle. Behind him, as one, the crowd of crazed Citizens wailed. Thorne hooked her hands under Bando's armpits, pulling the Medical Officer to her feet. Pharo spun, caught a Citizen raising a crowbar, fired, down they went.

Three more shots. Three more people down. The numbness was gone. The cold, gone. Pharo almost felt like he was dancing, the buzzing of his lazgun punctuating a strange tempo of the mad crowd around him. Every shot was perfect. Every move precise.

"This way, Thorne!" he shouted and felt every part an Executive Officer as she immediately obeyed.

Pharo forced the crowd apart with stun shots, dropping anyone who refused to move. Back on the raised dais, the eyeless woman wailed and snarled. Pharo could see the double doors leading out of the space station's sanctuary. They were almost there. But he could also see the battery gauge on the side of his lazgun blinking yellow. Almost depleted.

Scattering the last five Citizens in front of the doors, Pharo threw himself forward. The pneumatic gears hissed and the doors slid open, allowing him to reach the hall beyond.

There were more Citizens out there, but they were less cognizant, and just sat along the walls of the corridor, staring blankly in one direction or another.

Left or right? Pharo hadn't memorized the *Goremades* blueprint and had no idea where the docking bay was in relation to the religion center.

"This way!" Thorne pushed past him, dragging Bando along to the right.

Back in the religion center came a howl of rage. "Get them! Bring them to me!"

And like the poor quality video of the Biblical Flood his mother had made him watch every day after school for a month, they came pouring through the doors. In the multitude of eyes Pharo saw only madness, a void, nothingness—like the leagues of space beyond.

Juniper appeared at the front of the pack, his lips pulled back in a snarl, shoving people out of his way. Pharo caught the flash of overhead light on the barrel of Juniper's boltgun and ducked.

He heard, rather than saw, the bolt puncture the ceiling, hitting a pipe and releasing a hiss of steam into the corridor. Pharo rushed through it, easily catching up to Thorne, who was being slowed down by the dazed Bando.

"We gotta hurry up!" he said and Thorne shot him a glare.

"Oh, I thought we were just taking a cozy stroll, Pharo," she snapped. "Bando's fucking out of it, I can't get her to snap out of it!"

Behind them, thundering footsteps closed in and ahead, Pharo saw movement.

"Shit." He shoved Thorne and Bando down a corridor on their right.

"This isn't—" Thorne started.

"There's more people up that way," he hissed. "Is there another route?"

Pharo's heart dropped when Thorne bit her lip and shook her head. Then she stopped.

"Watch her." The Second Engineering Officer dropped Bando's arm, then sank to a knee near the wall.

She pulled her toolkit out of her boot and that's when Pharo spotted the maintenance hatch. Echoes of shouts and screaming bounced around the corner, closer and closer.

"Can you hurry?" Pharo said, checking his lazgun levels for the hundredth time, as though it would somehow recharge itself on his anxiety.

"Can you shut up?" Thorne slipped her screwdriver between the wall and hatch. "If I damage the outside, they'll know where we went."

Pharo tried to swallow but his throat was bone-dry, his tongue was a dead piece of meat in his mouth. Staring so intently at the corridor junction, he flinched when the panel popped off.

"Alright, you first," Thorne said. "Then Bando."

Pharo shook his head. "I'm the Executive—"

"Pharo, I can't reattach the panel from the inside without a magkey," she said, staring up at him. He could see that her hands were shaking. "I'll hold it up from the inside until they pass."

He still hesitated. Torn by duty and common sense.

"Go Pharo!" Thorne stood up, gripped his upper arms, spun him, and shoved him towards the access hatch.

So he went, dropping down and slipping his legs into the darkness. He had expected a tunnel but instead, his feet dropped off into a void. Pharo found the first rung, the next. Jamming the lazgun into a pocket, he began his descent.

"Come on, Bando." Thorne's voice from above. "Get your ass down there."

The light of the hall was blocked briefly as the Medical Officer followed Thorne's instructions and began to descend the ladder. The inside of the maintenance tunnel was pitch black, overly warm, and the air was sour. *How do Engineering Officers stand these tunnels? Day in and day out, like rats.*

His heart got louder and louder, a violent crescendo that surrounded him as he groped blindly with one foot and then the other to find the rungs of the ladder.

Then it was too much—Pharo couldn't descend any further. His mouth was gaping as he panted, trying to suck in air, trying to center himself as his palms went slick and his knees shook. Pharo looked up and watched the light disappear as Thorne pulled the hatch over the access panel.

The shouts and cries of the insane Citizens grew louder, bounding against the closed-in walls of the maintenance tunnels and drowning out Pharo's heart. His left hand seized in sudden pain as a boot came crunching down on it—Bando.

Pharo yanked his hand out from under her boot, skinning his knuckles, and nearly biting through his split lip trying to keep from crying out. He continued down, eyes so wide they were aching, until his boots hit floor instead of rungs. Still swathed in the absolute darkness, Pharo fumbled until he found a tunnel and ducked inside of it, just to get out of the way of Bando. Crouched there, as in a mechanical coffin, Pharo covered his face with his hands and just listened. He counted Bando's boots tapping against the rungs until they stopped.

"Pharo." Not a question, just a hushed statement.

"I'm right here, Bando," he replied, not moving.

Maybe it would be better to stay here. To hide until the Company comes.

He sensed more than heard the Medical Officer kneel in front of him. Her warm hands sought out his shoulders, his head. She rested two fingers on his neck.

"Your pulse is accelerated," she said.

Pharo looked up and saw the bright orange of Bando's augmented eyes, round circles flicking this way and that in the midnight depths of the tunnels.

Above them, boots thundered and voices screamed by in a banshee flurry before fading. Pharo licked his dry lips, panting, his breath out of control, short and shallow, short and shallow, his head becoming light. Bando took his hands in hers. He couldn't look away from those vivid rings of orange.

"Five counts in through the nose. Seven counts out through the mouth." She squeezed his hands in beats, counting out five, pause, five more. "Five in, Pharo. Seven out. There's no need to panic."

He forced himself to follow her words. *In, three, four, five. Out, five, six, seven.* His heart slowed. His breaths deepened. He could think again.

"No need to panic, Pharo," she whispered warmly. "It's pointless. Pointless to panic now. With what's to come. With what *will* come."

X

In the veins of the leviathan known as Space Station *Goremades*, Thorne crouched near an unopened panel and swept the tips of her fingers over the sides of the tunnel closest to it. She halted when she found the engraved plaque and slowly read the word on it with her fingers.

"Where are we, Thorne?" Pharo hissed, further back in the tunnel. "How much longer?"

Thorne ignored him. It was obvious he was on the verge of panicking and she had run out of patience. Plucking the screwdriver from her toolkit, she felt until she found the seam of the panel, then leaned in, pressing her ear to the polycarb and listened.

Silence besides the hum of machinery. Thorne felt along the edge again until she found the latch and flipped it off. As quietly as she could, Thorne pushed the cover off the hatch, catching it before it could fall to the floor. A flood of light swamped the tunnel and Thorne blinked a few times, waiting for her vision to adjust.

Thorne peered into the room.

True to the plaque, the room beyond was the *Goremades'* cybernetics laboratory. Currently it was empty, long workbenches scattered with materials and prototypes, tools hanging from swinging ceiling hooks alongside spiralling power cables. Large storage lockers were bolted along one wall, parallel with the door leading to the hall. An archway led to another space— likely a building workshop or testing area. The plexicarb floor was streaked with thick black-green iridescent stains. A half-built mining droid slumped in the corner, like a dead giant.

"Looks clear," Thorne whispered and crawled through the hatch.

Bando followed, then Pharo. The Executive Officer groaned as he stretched, pressing his hands to the small of his back.

"How do you stand it?" he asked.

Thorne tiptoed over to the lab doors and pressed her ear to it. The muffled sound of weeping. "Stand what?"

"Being stuck in those all the time?" He pressed the heel of his hand on his chin and cracked his neck.

Thorne turned away from the door and, for the third time since leaving the sanctuary, she tried to raise Duncan on the comms. And for the third time, received nothing but static.

"I didn't know they had a cybernetics lab here." Pharo picked up a circuit board, then put it down just as quickly.

"The file Captain Müller sent us made it seem that there was a small team of researchers here trying to improve on AI-powered mining machines." Thorne left the door and walked past the workbenches, glancing down at the items strewn across them. Most were half finished repairs of survey drones and auto-drills.

But there were other things. Strange things.

Thorne picked up a collection of pistons, wires, and titanium rods that had been cobbled together into a rough mechanical arm. The shiny metal was stained with the same ooze as the floor. Thorne brought the half-made arm close to her face. Sniffed.

Right away, she picked up on the scent of oil, metal, but there was something else. Something *organic*. Coppery tones—*blood?*—a musty reek like a wet animal, rotting meat. Hot, sour smells.

Putting the arm back down, Thorne went to the test room in the back. Pharo had abandoned his exploration of the circuit boards and moved to Bando's side.

The Medical Officer stood in front of the broke-down droid, running her fingers around and around its single optical lens. Pharo reached for Bando's shoulder but, at his touch, the Medical Officer flinched away.

As soon as we get to the Piasa, *I will talk some sense into Duncan. Everything…everything is going to be fine. All Bando needs is a little stay at a Company Mental Recovery Station and… and everything will be fine.*

Thorne took a deep breath. She would fix this.

The testing room was large, twelve foot high ceiling, reinforced walls, marked with burns and gashes from previous experiments. Midway up, bright lights were installed, flooding the room with illumination and chasing away every shadow. A diagnostic panel, opposite the archway through which Thorne entered, was blank.

Black ichor caked the floor and the walls, to about seven feet high. So much of it, in fact, that it had saturated the air with its reek. A standard-issued Company medbay bed had been moved to the middle of the room.

Why did they bring a bed into the lab? Thorne tiptoed across the floor, hearing and feeling the thick substance crackling beneath her boots.

The bed's mattress was soggy with the black goo, old ripped straps hung from the four points of its metal frame—which was bent out of shape, near broken in some places.

"What the hell?" Thorne breathed.

"Thorne?" Pharo called from the lab.

The Second Engineering Officer was more than happy to leave the eerie testing room behind and return to the lab. Pharo grabbed Thorne's arm and pulled her in close.

"There is something seriously wrong with Bando." He glanced over his shoulder where Bando still stood by the droid, stroking its "face."

The harsh overhead lights caught the tears in Bando's eyes, prismatic motes like gemstones that slipped down her cheeks.

"She's just had a scare," Thorne said.

"They showed her the program, didn't they?" He wouldn't let go of her arm.

Thorne stared at Bando, noticing how still the woman held herself, as though injured, how she let the tears run freely down her cheeks, making no effort to wipe them away.

Thorne nodded. She could feel her hands shaking, so she clutched them together tightly to mask the movement.

"And if what they say is true," Pharo said. "Then she's going to end up like the rest of them. Like Duncan—"

"Stop it, Pharo!" Thorne lowered her voice after realizing she was shouting. "She'll be fine. Duncan will be fine. As long as we get to the *Piasa*!"

"Thorne." She had never seen Pharo looking so stern. "She's not okay, Thorne. She's—she's…"

He closed his eyes and sucked in a shuddery breath before continuing. "She's acting like my mother did. Right before… right before she killed herself."

Thorne's breath caught in her chest as a chill ran over her body. She shook her head. Pulled away from Pharo. "No."

She pushed back from him, went to Bando's side. *This can't happen. I can fix this. I can fix all of it.* She took hope in the fact that Bando didn't flinch away from her touch.

"Bando?" Thorne's voice dropped to a whisper. "Are you okay?"

"Humans are such complex things, aren't they?" Bando said. "We create."

The Medical Officer touched the droid again, brushing her fingers through its exposed wiring. "We create. We destroy. Destroy more than we create."

"What happened when you watched the program?" Thorne asked. "What did you see?"

"Our wombs are not as prolific as the hands we use to kill." Bando's lip trembled and the tears fell faster as she closed her brilliantly orange eyes.

Thorne reached out and gripped the Medical Officer's hands, squeezing them tight. *There couldn't have been a worse time for Bando to lose it than now.* A bitter, shameful thought.

"Bando." She squeezed the woman's delicate hands tighter. "Please be strong…for me, okay?"

Bando opened her eyes and met Thorne's gaze, then nodded. Behind her, the lab door hissed open.

Thorne spun, shoving Bando behind her. A man and a woman walked in, backwards, pulling a big bag along with them. Thorne glanced at Pharo, who had taken out his lazgun and levelled it on the two. Thorne caught his eye and then held up her hand, shaking her head.

The two were dressed in stained lab coats and looked worse for the wear, but not as wild as some of the Citizens had been. Wholly occupied with dragging their bag into the lab, the two didn't notice their guests. Thorne waited until the two were inside and the lab door had closed once more.

"We have a lazgun aimed at your backs, Citizens," she said as forcefully as she could. "Put your hands up and turn around slowly. Unless you want to hit the ground seizing."

The two stopped, dropping their grips on the bag, and turned slowly. As the bag fell to the floor, several containers of freeze dried rations spilled out, along with some bottles of water. The man sported a thick, unkempt beard, his eyes sunken, his skin sallow. The woman's face was strained, her bottom lip was split, a wound that had to be days old based on the look of the scab. Both their eyes were wide and terrified.

"Please, please don't hurt us," she said.

"We won't," Thorne snapped. "Unless you give us a reason."

"Who are you?" Pharo asked, keeping the lazgun aimed at the man.

The man and the woman exchanged glances, the woman gave a slight shrug.

"I'm Heidi Loom, Cybernetics Engineer," the woman said, her voice hoarse.

"Nro'ren Dem, same as her." The man kept his eyes on the floor, his hands shaking in the air.

"You're the crew of the *Piasa*, aren't you?" Heidi asked and, shooting Pharo a stern look, knelt and began to herd the escaped food back into the bag.

"Yeah, and your Commander gave us a hell of a welcome," Thorne said.

Nro'ren held his hands out. "I'm sorry. We heard about… what happened. The Commander is not well. Many people here are…unwell."

"From the program?" Thorne felt Bando tense behind her.

Nodding, Nro'ren rubbed his face with his hands, exhausted. Thorne gestured at Pharo and he lowered his gun.

"We never should have gone to that place," Heidi said, her shoulders slumping. "We never should have brought it back."

"Stop wasting our time and just explain what the hell is going on!" Thorne took a step forward, her hands clenched into tight fists.

Heidi flinched, cowering over the bag of supplies, and Thorne was overcome with a feeling of shame.

"Please," she tried again. "We just want to get back to our ship, and for that, we need to know what's going on."

"And what caused it," Pharo chimed in.

Behind her, Thorne could feel Bando trembling. Heidi nodded then stood again, wringing her hands.

"The Pre-Calamity satellite started all this," she said.

Nro'ren nodded. "Automated survey drone captured images. We retrieved it. Pulled the data."

"Its records dated it back to when Earth was still populated," Heidi said. "It held coordinates to an off-world laboratory that held some classified technology."

She exchanged a look with her companion, took a deep breath, and pushed onward. "It was an order from Earth-side Company Command, to shut down experimentation on a program they called the Eye of the Moth.

"The Commander was intrigued. He thought the Company might reward us somehow. He sent a ship to the coordinates, it was by one of the moons of Jupiter. A research station, Pre-Calamity of course, rather primitive. Unpowered.

"The crew lasered through the airlock and investigated."

She stopped, breathless. Nro'ren took over. "Decades of raw data. But in the days prior to an emergency evac, they found the files for the program. And the monster."

"Monster?" Pharo asked.

"A monster, dead and not," Nro'ren said.

"The data from the derelict station was precise," Heidi said. "Humans back on Earth believed in a strange creature that appeared to predict disasters. And—based on the dates—it seems apparent that the sightings grew more frequent as the Calamity approached, but they wouldn't have known that of course."

"Get on with it, Heidi," Thorne snapped. *This is insane, a doom fore-telling creature?*

Heidi clutched her elbows, hunching over her crossed arms. "The Company, as it was back then, created a task force. They captured the thing and held it in a lab. They wanted to unlock how it was allegedly predicting the disasters. I've seen the videos, the reports. They tortured it and cut it open. Did all sorts of tests. Burrowed into its brain. And they did it. Or maybe they did. Based on its synaptic and transorbital scans, they managed to mock up a program that mimicked its brain activity."

"The Eye of the Moth," Nro'ren added.

"And the monster?" Thorne asked, wondering if a smack upside the head would help Heidi hurry up.

"Still on an operating table. Humanoid, but covered in a delicate dark fur, and with ten foot long wings—or wing, as one had been cut off. As was an arm.

"The team decided to bring it back with them, along with the program. It was left in a storage room for a while, then the Commander and his team watched the program. The beginning of the end."

"But you didn't watch it," Thorne said.

"No," Heidi replied. "Some of us didn't."

"We saw what happened to the ones who did." Nro'ren shook his head, staring off into the distance, past the walls, into some distant memory. "Some went completely mad, weeping, drowning in sorrow. Others... others were consumed with what they saw and were obsessed with it. They thought the monster was some kind of a messiah. You couldn't predict how a person would turn after seeing whatever it is the program shows. Probably something to do with their biology, their psychological profile maybe."

"A plague of despair," Heidi said.

"Then the Commander wanted us to repair the monster, with the technology we had here." Nro'ren gestured at the lab around them. "The Commander sent out a station-wide broadcast. He said the Company had doomed us all. That humanity's hubris was the event horizon of our future. That's when the Security Officers came for us, Heidi, me, the six other cybernetic scientists. He locked us in here with that thing and we weren't allowed to leave."

Heidi nodded. "He said that creature, the Mothman, was our only hope for salvation. Madness. How were we supposed to bring it back?"

Heidi broke off, covering her face, masking her tears.

"But it wasn't dead. Not in the truest sense," Nro'ren said. "Its brain was resting, a kind of dormancy. When we combined it with what we had here: robotic limbs, wires, an inner power core. It woke up. The thing woke up angry. Insane. As mad as the Commander."

"It did all this." Heidi pointed at the black ichor, the damaged walls. "It ripped this place apart. It was the saviour the Commander thought it would be and now it haunts our halls. Its red eyes are harbingers of the fall of *Goremades* and its people."

Thorne looked over at Pharo. He seemed as baffled as she felt.

"You don't believe me," Heidi said and shrugged. "But you have to help us. Get the Company here."

"Then come with us," Pharo said. "Come with us to the *Piasa* and you can escape!"

Thorne glared at him. *We have no idea if these people are a threat, what is he thinking?* It didn't matter though, the two scientists shook their heads.

"That's your funeral," Heidi said. "We'll stay here until the Company comes with more than a bunch of children."

"Come on, Pharo," Thorne spat. "Leave these cowards to hide and wait."

She reached back and grabbed Bando's hand, finding it cold and clammy, with a slight tremor. Striding to the lab door, Thorne slammed her fist against the door release. The door hissed as it opened, revealing an ichor-streaked corridor that was—thankfully—empty.

Pharo wavered a bit before following after, slipping ahead of Thorne to take the lead with his lazgun at the ready. Thorne gave Bando's hand a squeeze, catching her eye and forcing a smile. The Medical Officer didn't return the smile, just looked blankly at Thorne with no expression at all. *It's somehow worse than when she was crying. Like she's already dead. A walking corpse.* Thorne shivered but kept the smile, bared teeth, a false show of confidence.

"We may be cowards," Heidi called through the open lab door. "But at least we'll be alive at the end of the day."

Thorne stopped, turned. The cybernetics scientist was standing by her bag of stolen food, arms crossed, a smirk on her face. Never had Thorne felt more rage in her life, not since her father had died. She dropped Bando's hand, knelt, and pulled her toolkit from her boot, then marched back to the lab door, which had begun to close. Heidi's smirk died on her face and she stepped back, raising her hands in front of her, as if afraid Thorne was going to attack her.

"Thorne? Thorne!" Pharo yelled.

The thing about scientists, Thorne thought, as she stabbed her screwdriver into the door's panel. *They think they're hot shit, but they always come running to the engineers when something is broken.*

Heidi cried out as she saw the sparks. The door stopped, only a quarter of the way closed, its internal gears whining, then going quiet. The scientist covered her mouth, staring at the dead door.

"Good luck hiding now, coward." Thorne smiled and turned away, returning to Bando's side and taking her hand again.

Pharo waited until the two caught up, keeping an eye on the corridor ahead. He didn't say anything as Thorne and Bando approached. No one did.

The three of them just kept going. It was all they could do.

Thorne's boots crunched over the dried ichor, dragging Bando with her. The Medical Officer was sluggish, trembling, head down, and shoulders slouched. Thorne could hear Bando muttering something, her free hand jammed into her suit pocket. Thorne was struck by the stench of shit and piss. *It's like whatever they saw made them give up their humanity,* Thorne thought as they passed a woman using a wrench to pull out her teeth, one by one.

Left, right, left, following Thorne's instructions as she displayed the station's blueprints on her wrist holo-display. They passed Citizens, most huddled against the walls or pacing the corridors, muttering, praying, crying. None were threats, but all served as a warning. Of what the program—one that Heidi claimed could show people the future—did to people.

Finally the three were in front of the elevator that would take them to the same level as the docking bay. Thorne clutched Bando's hand, counting the seconds as they waited for the lift to arrive, biting her lip, tasting copper-bright blood.

Pharo faced the hall, his back to the lift, as he kept watch. But there was no one except one man weeping, prone on the floor, whispering to himself in a frenzy.

The lift dinged and the three stepped back, watching the doors slide open. Thorne held her breath. *I'm so tired of the danger. I just want to get back to the ship. I just want to make sure Duncan is okay.*

The elevator was empty save a smear of black goo. Thorne dragged Bando into the lift and Pharo followed, his lazgun still raised. Thorne slammed her palm against the button for level three, then held her thumb against the close door button.

Over her head, tinny generic music played from tiny speakers in the ceiling between the flickering lights. Thorne gritted her teeth. *Ridiculous.*

She lurched as Bando fell to her knees, yanking her hand out of Thorne's as she did. The Medical Officer curled over herself, rocking slightly on the floor. Thorne knelt next to her, and put a hand on Bando's back.

"Bando?" she said. "What did you see?"

The Medical Officer said nothing.

Thorne tried again. "Tell me what you saw!"

Finally the Medical Officer looked up and in her eyes Thorne saw a void, a lack of humanity. Thorne shivered.

"I saw the end," Bando breathed.

Thorne glanced up at Pharo. He shook his head. What that meant, Thorne didn't know.

"What end, Bando?" she asked.

The Medical Officer looked up at her. "I saw it. How it ends. Sooner than ever imagined. The heat death, event horizon, the reckoning that claims us all."

"Bando." Over Thorne's head, the lift ticked down the levels in overly cheerful dings. "That program...it's not real. It's just some flawed...flawed code. No one can predict the future. It's not real."

"Thorne." Bando reached up and cupped Thorne's face with her hand. The Medical Officer's orange eyes were painfully bright. "Have you ever had a dream so real that for a moment, when you wake, you wonder if it was a memory?"

Thorne didn't know how to respond. Of course she had those dreams. Usually about working on an engine, turning gears, searching for tools. Mundane. Generic. Bando didn't wait for a response.

"But you always can tell in the end," she said. "Reality versus dreams. So I know. I *know*. The end. It's coming. We're a part of it. All humans are. The Company is the source, the point of no return, the dark spot in the light of a star. The doom. The despair. What can we do, Thorne? What can we *do*?"

"Bando, I—" Thorne started.

"When did we become so comfortable with corruption?" Bando interrupted. "With pain? When I think about my life—I put everything into learning medicine, learning how to save people, but—but humans don't want to be saved. We don't want to be saved, do we?"

Thorne looked up at Pharo, he just stood there, mute. *Useless bastard.*

The elevator dinged again, reaching the floor they needed. The mechanics hissed, the doors slid open, revealing a dark hall, the lights above either broken or short-circuited.

"What was the point, Thorne?" Bando dropped her hands, slouching further to the floor. "I dedicated my life to saving a species intent on extinction. I saw it all. Such certainty. There's no escaping it. Like a ship caught in the pull of a black hole, we are drawn to oblivion."

Thorne shook her head. "Whatever you think you saw, Bando. It wasn't real. That program is Pre-Calamity for one thing. Humans back then could barely wipe their own ass, let alone code software—not to mention they *caused* the Calamity!"

The Second Engineering Officer hooked a hand under Bando's arm and pulled her to her feet.

"Come on, Bando," Thorne said, trying to sound gentle and not as frustrated as she felt. "We're almost back to the docking bay. Just a bit more, okay?"

Pharo stepped out into the dim corridor, peering down the left side, the right, then straight. "Looks clear so far."

Thorne pulled Bando out of the elevator, nearly slipping on a streak of black ooze that reeked of mechanical grease, blood, and something else— something *other*.

"What the hell happened to the lights?" Pharo muttered.

Thorne opened her mouth to snap at him to keep his eyes on the halls, but went mute as she looked up and saw what he meant. The ceiling had been gouged in violent furrows, splattered with more of the ichor, which had dried in delicate obsidian stalactites. The overhead plasma lights had been shattered—quite the feat, considering they were designed to withstand a lot of wear and tear.

"You don't think that woman was telling the truth?" Pharo's voice was a hoarse whisper as he backed up against the wall.

Thorne's skin prickled with goosebumps and she looked down one hall, then the other. "That what? They used cybernetics to bring a dead monster from Pre-Calamity Earth back to life?"

She tried to laugh, but it got trapped in her throat. Off in the distance, deeper in the station, something wailed. Thorne looked over at Pharo, whose eyes were wide orbs in the darkness. Her entire body was covered in a cold sweat. *It was just one of the Citizens, crazed and screaming.* She looked down one hall, then the other, then the third.

"Uh?" Pharo took a step along the wall, then stopped and looked at Thorne.

It wasn't a monster. There's no such thing. It's just some crazy person— The wail rose again, a screeching, ululating cry as mournful as it was wholly inhuman.

"Let's go, the docking bay is that way," Thorne whispered, pointing down the leftmost corridor.

Pharo nodded and sucked in a deep breath, turning and taking lead. Thorne had to give him credit for his bravery at least. She had just started to follow when she realized Bando wasn't right behind her. She turned and saw the Medical Officer, looking down the right hand corridor, breathing shallowly, almost panting.

Returning to Bando's side, Thorne tried to take her hand, but the Medical Officer pulled away.

"Bando!" Thorne hissed, her frustration getting the better of her. "Now is not the fucking time, okay? Have your breakdown on the *Piasa*, okay?"

"Thorne?" Pharo called quietly from down the hall.

She reached for Bando's hand again, determined to drag the Medical Officer all the way back to the ship if need be. At Thorne's touch, Bando pulled back her hand and slapped Thorne right across the face, sending her stumbling into the wall, her right ear ringing and head buzzing.

Stunned, Thorne pressed her hand to her burning cheek, as she stared at Bando. Her body went hot, cold, hot, a battlefield of confusion, hurt, and rage. Bando looked down at her hand and tears trickled down her cheeks. *What is she crying for?* Thorne thought bitterly. *She wasn't the one who just got slapped.*

Another wail, echoing Thorne's hurt, bounced down the corridors everywhere at once and seemingly coming from nowhere. Her heart picked up, racing in her chest. The cry was closer, that much Thorne was sure.

"I trained most of my life to help people," Bando said, unmoved by the screams of whatever it was that was coming their way. "I wanted to heal people. I wanted to save people. But none of it matters. None of it ever mattered."

Thorne gritted her teeth and dropped her hand from her cheek to her side, clenching it to a fist. Unbidden images—fantasies—of punching Bando square in the face raced through Thorne's mind and she wanted to draw blood. She wanted to see the shock and hurt in Bando's orange eyes, to see her own pain mirrored. Most of all, she wanted to shock the Medical Officer back to her senses.

Another wavering scream, close enough to make Thorne's ears ring and throb with pain. Bando reached into a pocket and pulled out a small screwdriver, the type used for circuitry. *She must have taken that from the cybernetics lab,* Thorne thought dumbly, opening her mouth to say something, anything.

The moment shifted forward in jumps, broken fragments of time that seemed false, seemed like a fabrication, a sick VR program gone wrong.

Bando gripped the screwdriver with both hands, holding it so that its head pointed straight up. Thorne was deafened. The not-so-distant screams, her racing heartbeat in her ears, the rasp of her breath as it roared down her throat, and she stepped forward. She reached out.

Bando rammed the screwdriver into her left eye, spraying a small pop of clear viscous liquid into the air. Still crying, half her tears now thick and bloody, Bando yanked the screwdriver out without even a whimper.

Somewhere far, far away, Thorne heard Pharo calling, screaming. His voice mixing with that of the other screams. Hers, maybe. Or whatever the thing in the halls was. Certainly not Bando. Silent, weeping Bando. Still gripping the screwdriver with both hands, the Medical Officer finally seemed to remember she wasn't alone. Bando looked at Thorne with her remaining orange eye and a bloodied socket brimming with gore and jelly.

"Don't cry," Bando said. "None of this matters."

Then the Medical Officer stabbed the screwdriver into the side of her neck, yanking it right back out after, letting loose a crimson spray. Thorne flinched back, stumbled against the wall, covering her eyes and sank to the floor, trembling.

"No." Her mouth moved around the word, but Thorne heard nothing over the screaming. "No."

Bando knelt slowly, in one graceful motion like a falling star. Her arms were limp at her side, letting her heart pump out her life from the wound in her neck. *She would know exactly where to stab. To make sure it was quick and permanent. She would know. She would know exactly where. Where to cut. Where to puncture.*

On her knees, Bando fell to the side—Thorne felt the thump of the Medical Officer's head hitting the floor—and a scarlet pool grew beneath it.

Thorne couldn't look away, couldn't pull her gaze from Bando's remaining eye. A vivid orange well of sorrow. Of complete despair.

A hand appeared in her line of sight—Pharo—he grabbed her collar and yanked her to her feet.

None of this matters, Bando's tortured voice bounced through Thorne's brain, relentless. *None of it ever mattered.*

The hall shuddered and Thorne fell back into the moment, into herself. She pulled away from Pharo, towards Bando. "We have to help her! We have to stop the bleeding!"

"Thorne. Get a grip," Pharo hissed. "There's *something* down there."

The tone of the Executive Officer's voice stopped Thorne in her tracks. In that moment of pause, she felt the rumbling in the floor, and Thorne looked past Bando and down the hall. There, in the darkness, at ceiling level, two round, crimson lights hovered.

No, not lights. Thorne took a step back. *Eyes.*

Two blazing blood-red irises, unblinking, filled with an intense alien intelligence and — and pain.

Thorne took another step back, looked down at her friend. Bando was still, her marred face reflected in the pool of her cooling blood. The thing in the dark chittered, its eyes tilting left then right, assessing them. Assessing the body on the floor. Thorne bumped into Pharo, right behind her, and she reached back, not knowing what she sought. He took her hand, his palm was cool and dry, unlike her sweaty one.

"What is that?" he asked.

The lurking thing screamed in response, lunging forward, its lumbering footsteps shaking the hall. Thorne spared one last glance for Bando—it was all she could give her friend—and then she fled. Down the hall, into the darkness opposite that which hid the creature with the scarlet novae for eyes.

With every step Thorne took, sprinting blindly down the hall, she felt an answering one behind her as the thing in the shadows gave chase. Pharo quickly gained distance, dropping her hand, passing her. Ahead of them, a junction in the halls where the lights were undamaged and still shone, masked slightly by smears of ichor.

"Left!" Thorne cried, hoping her memory of the station's layout was accurate.

Heart pistoning against her ribs, the hair on the back of Thorne's neck prickled. She imagined she could feel hot breath on her back, the heat of the beast closing in. The turn came and Thorne's left boot landed firmly on a fresh glob of stinking ooze. It acted as the catalyst, her momentum the fuel, and Thorne's foot slipped out from under her, throwing her along the hall to go sliding past the turn. *This is it. This is how I go.* Crying out, she twisted, trying to catch herself and, instead, landed hard on her hip and elbow, sending bright sparks of pain through her joints.

Up close, the reek of the ooze burned her nostrils, coating her suit and making her skin tingle. She looked up, just as the creature stepped into the light.

It was humanoid—towering so high that its head dragged along the ceiling—yet it was anything but human. Shiny black fur, caked in ichor, covered its body. Its left leg was spindly, ending in a taloned foot more like an insect than any mammal Thorne recognized. Its right leg was gone, replaced by the sleek titanium limb of a survey drone.

Its missing arm had been replaced by a less sophisticated, mechanical joint that had been shattered at some point, so that it ended in a sharp point, exposed tubes, and sparking wires. This tortured limb leaked the thick, iridescent gore that coated the walls and floor, the creature's blood mixed with mechanical lubricant and rot. Its remaining arm was wounded, exposing bone and muscle, leaking a rancid yellow pus. A great ragged wing dragged on the floor behind it, limp and useless. Topped with furry antenna, its angular head was broad, furred, dominated by furious crimson eyes, glowing with tortured intelligence.

Clawing at the titanium plate bolted to the back of its head, the thing shrieked, its call warbling off at the end. Then it looked straight at Thorne. She shrunk back, fear making her go cold and numb. Thorne had no idea what to do. Her head buzzed like a live wire, meaningless white noise, and she froze as the monster slunk towards her—its taloned foot silent, the other clanking with every step.

None of it mattered. None of it ever mattered. Bando's voice whispered in her head, utterly useless and insane. The creature lashed out with its ruined metal arm, gouging a deep furrow into the wall and sending ribbons of polycarb through the air. *It'll dig that into my back, slash over my face, I won't be able to fix that—I won't be able—*

Pharo leapt out from the other hall, spread his feet in the muck, and fired his lazgun. The bright bolt struck the creature's left shoulder, fizzling out, filling the air with the stench of burnt fur and meat. The creature paused, turning to look at its burnt flesh. It screamed and Thorne clutched at her ears, trying to block out the sound drilling into her eardrums.

Pharo fired once more, then a second time, a third, then the creature—its fur sizzling, its new wounds leaking chunky black rot—lunged, reaching forward and grabbing Pharo's throat with its bio-claw.

His shout was cut off as the creature tightened its grip. Dropping the lazgun, Pharo clawed at the creature's arm, kicking as it lifted him from the floor, drawing him closer.

The monster's eyes sparked, blazed a deeper red, and Pharo went limp, his arms and legs dropping away as he stared deep into the creature's crimson eyes.

No. Thorne scrambled to her feet, thinking of the crazed Citizens, thinking of Duncan, thinking of poor dead Bando. Thinking about the eye of the moth program. She grabbed the lazgun. Its charge bar was flashing red—whether that meant it still had shots left or was already empty, Thorne had no idea. She knew the bolts had little effect on the monster. Perhaps having been dead for centuries had made it comfortable to pain. Made pain a way of life.

Pharo whined, a low, tinny sound, deep in his throat. Desperate, Thorne spun around, then spotted a small fire extinguisher—Company standard—and yanked it from its cradle. She could feel time ticking away.

Pulling the fire extinguisher back, Thorne swung it forward, throwing it up into the air towards the monster and Pharo. Stance wide, as she'd learned to do in the Academy, Thorne held her breath. She'd always been shit at aiming. She fired.

The lazbolt hit the extinguisher square center as it passed the creature's head and the bright yellow canister erupted in a cloud of opaque powder, clogging the air, obscuring everything. The monster screeched.

Lunging forward, Thorne dove into the cloud, finding Pharo slumped on the floor. She grabbed his arm and pulled him up, leading him forward—towards the corridor they needed—hoping she wouldn't run into the beast as she did so.

The powder-choked air coated Thorne's lips and throat, stinging her eyes and making tears run down her cheeks. Ahead, she could see a hulking shape within the cloud. She didn't wait. Clutching Pharo's hand in a death grip, she pulled them down the corridor, towards the docking bay.

XI

Pharo knew he was on the Space Station *Goremades*. He could feel the plexicarb floor beneath his boots, Thorne's hand gripping his hand enough to hurt, the burn of air rasping down his throat. But it all felt far away. Felt false.

In the eye of the moth, things had felt more…real. Concrete.

You have to be good, Pharo, his mother whispered in the back of his mind. *Be good, you have to be good. That's the only way you can go to Heaven, if there is one, baby.*

He shook his head, trying to shake the memory-faint echoes. Instead, he saw stars. The far ones, distant ones—not in distance, but in time, the stars in the eyes of that *thing*—stars that were bright and brilliant. It made him feel sick and small.

And the Leviathan waits to consume all. He felt his mother's breath on his ear, felt phantom hands tucking him into his childhood bed, the dampness of tears on his cheeks—his or hers, he couldn't know. *Our sins, Pharo. Our sins define us. But humans are born of sin. Can we ever stop? Does any of it matter?*

"Please stop," he said, his voice hoarse through his damaged throat.

He tried to focus on the back of Thorne's head, caked with white powder, on her sweaty palm in his, the sound of their boots. But his mind spun, reeling him back. His vision grew fuzzy and he fell back into a crimson-tinged despair again.

Nothing we do matters, Pharo. Mother wept, her hands covering her face, her bruises. *I try so hard, so, so hard. And they tell me to find a hobby. To create my own meaning.* She looked up, lip split, eye blackened. *I can't be the only one. The only one with darkness in my heart. Am I really that bad, Pharo? Do I deserve this?*

The scarlet future, tainted with the choking taste of blood and burning flesh. He saw them, all of them—us, everyone—dead. A broken vision of stations haunted, ships adrift, and it went onwards, stretching forward and always and forever, trapped in a—yes—trapped in an event horizon of absolute certainty. An inescapable future. *She was right. Mom was right. We are all full of darkness, sin, we aren't even trying to save ourselves.*

Never had Pharo felt so tired. So heavy. *When will I start to look at sharp objects with desire?* His thoughts detached themselves. He viewed himself like a specimen, to be examined without attachment.

He tried to focus again. The thud of his boots on the floor, his own heartbeat thumping a tempo in his chest, Thorne's hand in his. But it was too much effort, he was too tired, and his mind drifted back. Back four years, to when he found his mother.

He'd gotten his first assignment and rushed home to share the news. He knew his dad wouldn't care, as it was a minor posting standard for recent graduates, but he'd expected his mom to celebrate.

Instead he'd found her in bed, the blankets a mess, four empty pill bottles on the floor.

Sleeping pills. She'd saved them up. Planned her permanent escape from the darkness she felt every day.

Now, being pulled down one hall, then another, past blank-faced Citizens who cried or screamed or stared silently at him, Pharo wondered if she had felt relief in her last moments.

She hadn't left a note. Nothing to show that she'd thought of him in her last moments, if she'd cared what it would do to him to find her there.

"Pharo!"

His father had gotten home late from his mistress's home that night. Company medical officers had already taken his mother away to be processed. He hadn't even reacted when Pharo had told him the news.

"Pharo!"

She was weak, Pharo. That's what happens to weak people. They break.

He'd spent weeks hating her for leaving him to bear his father's fists alone. Then Pharo was deployed. Distance from his father. Distance from the hurt.

Everything was crimson. Everything was red. Everything was ending and the people were dead.

"Pharo! Please get up!"

She wasn't weak. Pharo pictured her. Her tears, her bruised face, but also her laughter, her smiles that she saved just for him when it was just the two of them. *The universe isn't black and white like Dad wants.* He remembered how she would stand between him and his father when his father was in a rage—for a bad grade, for a bad day, for anything at all. She would shelter him from the rain of abuse. She would take it all.

She held out as long as she could, didn't she? Because she would have gotten a notification from the Company about his deployment. She would have known that he would be free from his father and maybe—maybe that's why she chose that day. To escape the pain, to leave nothing for him to come back to.

Because Pharo would have gone back. He would have gone back for her.

But with his mother gone, there was nothing.

And I am not my father. Not wholly. I am her too. I am her, and him, and strong, and weak and...

The red faded to gray to black. Pharo's cheek stung and he looked up—he hadn't even realized he'd fallen to his knees. His head ached and he could taste blood from where he'd bitten his cheek but he was there, he was present.

Lightheaded and nauseous, Pharo stood, one hand sliding up the wall for support. To his right, six people dressed in tattered, ichor-stained jumpsuits knelt in a triangular formation. They held their right hands out and pressed the index and middle fingers of their left to their foreheads. As one, they hummed a noteless tone.

An enraged cry drew his attention.

The monster—named Mothman by the scientists—dominated the hall, towering over Thorne, who looked like a toy in front of it. Its eyes blazed like scarlet spotlights and, remembering the trap they represented, still haunted by the after-images of a crimson stained future, Pharo looked away. Thorne's uniform was stained black and crimson—her blood and the monster's? Pharo stumbled to the side, nearly collapsing.

The Mothman slammed its head against the wall and let out a screech that ended in a warbling whine. Thorne answered it with her own scream, a wrench in one hand, a screwdriver in the other—two things that looked useless next to the creature's shattered metal spear of an arm and bulk.

She didn't leave me. Even with no chance to win against it, she didn't leave me to die.

The creature swung. Thorne didn't react in time and Mothman caught her on her shoulder, throwing her against the wall. By some miracle—*Mom would have said that some god intervened*—the jagged end of the creature's arm only ripped her suit, rather than her skin.

The Second Engineering Officer cried out in pain, dropping her tools as she clutched her left arm. When she stood, Pharo saw her eyes were closed. Protecting herself from the monster's influence, but also making her absolutely useless in a fight.

Yet still she fumbled, found the screwdriver, and gripped it tight in her good hand, left arm hanging limp at her side. Thorne stood fast, between Pharo and the beast. Stood fast as it screamed again, eyes sparking like the fires of hell. *We don't need to go to hell, Pharo.* His mother's memory wept in the back of his head. *We're already there. Every day.*

"Messiah!" A chorus of voices that made Pharo flinch—the Citizens behind him had stopped humming. Now they were praying. "Messiah of the Future Eyes! We are not worthy! Please save us! Save us!"

"Shut up, you assholes!" Thorne screamed in return, swinging her tool back and forth in front of her.

"Thorne!" Pharo finally found his voice, though it cracked with use.

"Fucking finally, Pharo—"

"Duck!" he shouted.

She dropped, narrowly avoiding Mothman's swipe. Thorne spun on her knees and scrambled away, towards Pharo.

"This way!" Pharo called. "Keep going!"

"Yeah, like I was planning to stop," Thorne said.

The creature slumped, its bio and metal hands touching the floor, its exposed muscle and tissue dripping globs of black ooze to the floor. It let out a forlorn cry, its furry antenna dropping. Pharo felt an unexpected wave of pity wash over him at the sound. *It almost sounds...sad...*

He reached down, caught Thorne's reaching hand, and pulled her to her feet. Only then, bleeding, panting, and pale, did she open her eyes.

"Messiah! Messiah! Save us!" the Citizens continued to chant.

Mothman flinched, cradling its head in its arms, as it wailed. *It's acting just like an animal that's suffering.* The mammoth monster thrashed back and forth, into one wall then the opposite, still clutching its head and crying out as fountains of ichor spurted from its wounds. Pharo tore his eyes away from the creature, and together they ran.

Around the first corner, a roar followed, then all-too-human screams of the Citizens who'd been begging for salvation.

"How far?" Pharo asked.

Thorne was dragging behind him, panting, her other arm still limp at her side. "Stop, Pharo. I have to stop."

Pharo slowed to a stop, looking behind them. The corridor was empty. Thorne pulled her hand away and slumped to her knees.

"Let me see." Pharo kneeled next to her.

"I think my arm is dislocated." Thorne's eyes were far away, glazed.

Shock. Pharo spotted a door close by and pulled Thorne to her feet. "Come on, we can't be out in the open."

The floor trembled under his boots and down the hall, the Mothman screamed. Caution aside, Pharo slammed his palm against the door release and—as soon as it was wide enough—pushed Thorne through, closing the door behind them.

The room was a large conference space, its table scattered with asteroid surveys and logistical reports. Someone had been using it also as a toilet, considering the mess in the far left corner. Pharo wrinkled his nose against the smell, then turned to Thorne, who had sunk to her knees again.

Blood dripped from a cut across her left eyebrow, painting her cheek red, and freckling the scuffed plexicarb floor. Kneeling next to her, Pharo took stock.

That cut on her forehead will need stitches. The right side of her uniform, just below her armpit and down to her waist, hung open, revealing another gash along her ribs. *So much blood.* Pharo looked up into Thorne's eyes again, they were still distant, blank.

Pharo had failed the mandatory first aid training that Company Officers had to take, but his father had used his connections to ensure his graduation anyway. Still, Pharo had had extensive experience dealing with the wounds his father had inflicted on his mother—a dislocated shoulder was something he was sadly familiar with. He gripped her forearm in one hand and braced his other against her collarbone.

"This'll hurt," he told her and didn't wait for her response.

Her shoulder jolted back into place and, with it, Thorne. Her eyes sparked to life and she cried out, reeling back from him. She fell onto her back, clutching her arm, and he fell on her, covering her mouth with a hand.

"Sh!" he hissed.

Tears streaming down her powder-caked face, Thorne bit the meat of his palm. Pharo hissed again, pulling his hand away, and stumbled away from her. "Goddammit, Thorne!"

"You asshole!" she whispered back.

They both went quiet, listening. Beyond the door, the behemoth stomped past, whining a low hum. They waited until the whine faded.

Thorne sighed, slowly, painfully, pushing herself up to lean against the wall. She reached to her side, touched the edge of the wound tenderly and winced.

"Fuck." She let her head fall back against the wall and she closed her eyes.

Pharo sat too, dropping his elbows to his knees and cradling his head. A headache beat a furious tempo at the back of his eyes. *The adrenaline wearing off. Exhaustion will come next.* He sucked in a deep breath and stood, afraid that if he sat too long, he'd never get enough energy to stand back up.

"Thorne." He looked at the blood seeping through her fingers. *She's dying, isn't she? She's dying because she stayed behind to protect me.* "I just want to say—"

"What did you see?" she said, her eyes still closed, her breathing laboured.

Pharo took a step back. "What?"

"When you looked in the eyes of the moth. What did you see?" She finally opened her eyes and looked at him. The tears were gone. The only thing left was a cold resolve. "What did it show you?"

A flash of crimson—eyes. Smell of rot. A feeling of absolute vertigo, falling into the heart of the universe where chaos reigned.

Pharo pressed his hand against his mouth, swallowing back vomit. Swallowed back the visions. He thought about lying to her for a brief moment, thought about telling her that he'd seen just nonsense, muddled images. He thought about protecting her from it.

"I saw the end," he said.

"The end?" Thorne tried to shift, then winced, falling back over her injured side. "What do you mean? The end of what?"

"Of everything." The images threatened to overwhelm him again—*a star growing, growing, red and infinite, swallowing everything. But not a star. A hunger. Planets drained dry. People drained dry. Endless white halls of corpses in Company uniforms. An incomprehensible sorrow. Grief spanning galaxies. Ennui ruling the remains*—Pharo tasted copper, came back to himself with blood in his mouth, a bleeding tongue. "It's hard to explain. It was a feeling as much as images. But I think…I think the Company destroys everything."

Thorne shook her head. "So that's what Bando saw? What these assholes saw through the program? Some holo-flick about the end of the universe?"

Pharo sucked in a shuddery breath. Madness lay at the edge of his mind, a scarlet haze begging to be let in. "If it was…fake…then it felt really real. It felt like I was there. I saw it all. I knew it to be true. I *know* it to be true."

The Second Engineering Officer met his eyes and whatever she saw made her nod. "Are…are you okay though?"

Pharo shrugged. "It's there. The thing's influence. It's like it's just being held at bay, like a fever. But I think I have it under control."

"Good." Thorne reached into her bloodstained boot and pulled out her toolkit. "Because I need a favour."

The star pierced by a darkness blacker than space itself. A sea of golden horror. The event horizon. The end of—Pharo knelt, forced back the thoughts, the visions, the feelings of pain and crippling hopelessness. "Sure, anything."

"There's a mini sealant pen in there," she said, holding the toolkit out to him.

Opening it, Pharo found most of the tools missing—lost in their desperate flight through the Space Station *Goremades*—all that remained was a mini phillips head screwdriver, a few zip ties, a couple slim shiny metal rods, and the sealant pen.

"What am I supposed to do with it?" He pulled it from the case and looked it over.

It looked like a slim stylus, except one end was tipped by a small, faceted crystal. A dial on the side showed the word OFF.

"Do you know what the pen does?" Thorne turned, raising her arm with difficulty, revealing the tear in her side.

Now Pharo could see the extent of it. The creature had managed to cut her in a way that a flap of her skin lay on her side like a piece of fabric, exposing the glistening tissue underneath. Pharo looked away, swallowing rapidly to keep his gorge down.

"Pharo, please." Thorne's voice snapped him back and he looked at her, trying to seem calm, confident.

"No," he choked out. "I—I don't know what it is."

Thorne grimaced, shivering against a wave of pain. "It's used to seal hull damages or repair minor damage to wires, circuitry…usually it is used in conjunction with those solder sticks, but—" She shuddered again, her arm dropping a bit before she recovered. "But what's important is that, to work, it emits immense heat. I think…I think at the lowest setting you could cauterize my wound."

"Thorne." Pharo's body went ice cold, numb, then hot, too hot. "I—I can't. That's…"

"Pharo, you have to," she said. "I can't make it like this. If you don't, I'll—I won't make it."

She nearly died for you and you're here whimpering about a wound? Pharo's father's voice was like a slap across the face. But he wasn't wrong. *This isn't the time to be faint of heart.* Pharo gripped the pen tight and nodded. "You should lie on your side."

Thorne collapsed to the floor, her arm draped over her head. Her breathing was laboured and her skin flushed, glistening with sweat. Pharo looked down at his hands, stained with blood and ichor. *I'm as likely to kill her with an infection as save her by touching her.* He pushed the pen's dial with a thumb, clicking it over from OFF to LOW. The crystal at the end of the pen began to glow with a fierce white light, staining Pharo's vision with a prick of shadow. He clicked the dial back to OFF and set it on the floor.

"I can't promise that I can be careful enough not to hurt you," he said.

Thorne barked out a harsh laugh. "I know it's going to hurt, Pharo. Do you have something I can bite down on?"

Pharo froze, then patted his side. His left pocket. Reaching in, he pulled out the small digipad he always carried—the one he'd been asking her to fix for months.

"Here," he said, feeling tired, feeling scared, but most of all, feeling sad.

Thorne opened her eyes long enough to see what he was offering and took it, shoving it between her small, white teeth, biting down hard. She then returned her arm over her face and Pharo could see her physically brace herself against what was to come.

This is just a job. Like cleaning your crew quarters. Pharo reached out, gritting his teeth. *Just making the bed, tucking in the sheets, the usual.*

He slipped his index and middle fingertips beneath the flap of Thorne's flesh. The skin was cold, compared to her warm body. *Sheets. Tucking in the sheets.* He tried to imagine the stiff sheets on his cot. Then, gently, oh so gently, he flipped the flap of skin back on top of the crimson swath of flesh.

Thorne hissed around the digipad. Pharo picked up the sealant pen and clicked the dial to LOW, looking away from the crystal as he did.

"Ready?" he asked.

Thorne didn't respond, just clenched her teeth harder, the screen cracking with the pressure. Pharo gently pressed down on the flap of skin, moving it so its edge aligned with the raw edge of Thorne's side, ignoring her hisses of pain. With his other hand, he brought the pen in, biting his lip.

"Here we go," he said, as much to himself as to Thorne. Then he touched the tip of the crystal to one edge of her wound. Her skin sizzled under the heat.

Instantly he could smell the aroma of cooking meat and, horribly, his mouth watered. He hadn't eaten in hours, it felt like days even. He swallowed back his saliva and began to burn Thorne back together.

He watched her skin stitch together with curls of smoke, reddening—blackening when he wasn't fast enough with the pen. The whole time, Thorne was still, the pad screen cracked and bits of screen fell to the floor as she bit down, but she didn't flinch, she didn't shy away.

He followed the curve of the brutal slash, right, sloping upwards, then left over Thorne's ribs, finally up and up and up, right to her armpit. She wept, whimpering low in the back of her throat, her eyes screwed shut, tears streaming down her face.

Up, up, up—*like that time I had to glue a cut above mom's eyebrows shut, like colour inside the lines, Pharo*—to the very end. As soon as he could, Pharo pulled the pen away, clicking it OFF.

"Are you okay?" he asked, setting the pen aside.

Thorne groaned, holding a hand to her side as she shoved herself back up into a sitting position. She opened her mouth. Pharo expected her to say something, but instead she turned to the side and puked down the white plexicarb wall. The vomit was thin, yellow, dribbling down the wall in narrow drips.

"Do I look okay to you?" she asked hoarsely, once she had stopped retching, wiping her mouth with the back of her free hand.

"Yeah, you know what?" Pharo gave her a wry smile. "I think I should switch to being a Medical Officer. I did an amazing job. You look great."

Thorne snorted out an abbreviated chuckle before wincing. "Yeah, great bedside manner."

"Do you think you can walk?" Pharo stood and offered out his hand. "We need to get back to the *Piasa* and off this station."

Thorne nodded and grabbed his hand. Cognizant of her wounds, he pulled her slowly to her feet. She wavered, stumbled against him. Pharo wrapped his arms around her shoulders, holding Thorne against him. Feeling her in his arms gave him a sense of calm, of warmth. Then she pushed away from him.

"I'm fine, let's go," she said.

Gripping the sealant pen in one fist, Pharo peeked around the corner. Three men in stained robes had surrounded a Citizen in a standard Company jumpsuit, who was crouched against the wall, covering his head with his hands.

"Do you see?" one of the robed men asked. "Do you see?"

"Please don't hurt me! Please!" the man begged. "I have a family!"

"Do. You. See?" chanted the robed men.

Pharo backed away from the corner and glanced over at Thorne, who was scoping out the other direction. "Is it clear?"

She shook her head and crept over to him. "There's six people down there. I recognize a couple from the religion center. I think they are part of the cult. Black gunk all over their mouths."

"Dammit. There are three down this way."

Thorne sighed and sunk to the floor, head dropping. "Alright. Well. Three isn't bad, right?"

"Are…" Pharo stared at the top of her head. "Are you being serious?"

Just the thought of confronting those three men made his stomach curdle and a cold sweat broke out on his forehead. Coward. His father's voice was a cruel echo. *Just like your mother. Just like your good for nothing m—*

"There's an electrical panel right there." Thorne interrupted his thoughts and pointed at a near invisible panel set in the wall across the hall.

"It's in sight of both groups," Pharo whispered.

The two *Piasa* officers were crouched in a T junction. The left corridor had the three men, the right had the group. Both would be able to spot the officers should they attempt to access the panel.

"I can do it," Thorne said. "It would only take a few seconds and, I don't know about the people you saw, but mine were examining a bunch of bodies on the floor. They wouldn't notice me."

"Thorne—"

She shook her head. "We don't really have an option, Pharo. I can kill the lights in this area and we can sneak past them in the darkness. We have to do it. This is the fastest way to the docking bay."

She stood, screwdriver in hand. Their last resort weapons, all pulled from Thorne's toolkit. Pharo wanted so badly to beg her to reconsider. That they should turn around and find another way, a safer way. *Coward,* his father's voice hissed. *Be brave,* his mother said. *That's it, I'm officially nuts,* Pharo thought.

"Be careful, okay?" he said, instead. "We'll run if they see us."

She nodded, turned, and tiptoed out into the corridor. Pharo slid along the wall and peeked around the corner.

The three robed men were still standing around the weeping man. Hands held together, heads lowered, as though they were praying.

Down the other side, he could barely make out a crowd of people, though not what they were doing. Thorne reached the panel, slipped her screwdriver in the panel's seam, and popped it open. It swung on tiny hinges, revealing a complicated nest of wires. Pharo flinched against the sound, despite how soft it was.

She reached in, intent on her task, not hesitating, not looking right or left. A strange pang reverberated through his chest.

Jealousy.

Even injured, even scared, she was fighting. She never gave up.

I'm supposed to be an Executive Officer. I'm supposed to be a leader, but I haven't done anything. Despair. And two rings of deep red. *No, no, no, not now, not*—screaming, running, and blood in waves on the floor, behind the scream of a dying thing yet undead and dead and not dead at all and—Pharo pulled himself back, slowly, as though through a vat of oil. He felt his knee on the floor, the ache in his lower back, the pain in his jaw from clenching. And almost with a jolt, Pharo was back to the present. Slightly nauseous, he looked to the right. The crowd seemed the same. To the left, the three men dropped their hands. They exchanged looks, then the one in the middle gestured, and the other two pulled wrenches from their belts.

"Please! I have children! I have—" the crouching man cried.

The two robed men fell on him. The man on the floor let out a cry that was quickly cut short as the wrenches rained down. The robed men operated in silence, their arms pistoning up, then swinging down, up, then down. Arcs of blood filled the air and painted the ceiling and walls. Pharo wanted to take his eyes away. He wanted to hide away. But he was trapped. Trapped in the horror and the gore. Watching the victim go from man to mound to mush under the blows.

A click.

The lights flickered once, then went out, dousing Pharo in merciful darkness.

Down each hall, people cried out against the sudden loss of light. Pharo strained to hear every sound, to identify every noise, trying to track every-one's movement. He was concentrating so hard that he nearly screamed when a hand landed on his chest.

"It's me." Thorne's voice from the darkness. "Time to go. Let's stick to the opposite wall. Most people freeze in place when the lights go out."

Her hand crept down, found his hand, and together they slipped through the darkness. For a heart-stopping moment, Pharo felt lost—lost in space and time, the only anchor Thorne's sweaty hand in his. Then they found the wall and Pharo pressed his shoulder against it.

"Slowly now," he whispered, to himself or to her, he didn't know. "Slowly now so they don't hear us."

One shuffling step at a time, Pharo slid along the wall, positively aching with the act of listening for any sound, for all the sounds.

"Do you see?" a man shouted ahead of him.

"I see, I see!" another replied.

Pharo shivered. *They can't see us. They are just nuts, spouting nonsense. They can't see us… can they?*

"Who turned off the bloody lights?" echoed a voice from behind.

Thorne's grip on his hand tightened slightly.

Another step, then another, another. Painfully slow. The three men were there, somewhere in the unknown dark. Pharo could hear them breathing, harsh, ragged sounds. *It's as if they are waiting for us. Watching us slink towards them, with their wrenches raised.* Pharo tried to lick his lips, but his tongue was dry and raspy. *They can probably hear my heart, pounding away like a drum.*

A chorus of screams raced down the hall from behind him. Pharo caught his own scream in his throat, clutching Thorne's hand as tight as he could. He turned, peering in the darkness and saw distant scarlet sparks. *Eyes, red eyes.*

"I see! I see! Do you see?" The voice was right next to him. Pharo pressed himself hard against the wall, freezing in place.

"Saviour! Messenger of Truth!" cried another.

An eruption of movement, someone stomped on Pharo's foot. The sounds faded off into the direction of the eyes, the screaming. A lonesome cry dominated the cacophony, bouncing off the walls and floor, filling the darkness.

Thorne squeezed his hand, snatched the pen from his other hand, then pulled. Pharo didn't resist. Risking a collision, they ran.

The Mothman gave chase.

A tiny light flared to life—the sealant pen—faintly illuminating the corridor. They passed people, struck to stasis by the darkness and then the sudden light, while behind them the screams rose and rose and rose. The floor shook, it felt like the whole station was trembling.

Pharo risked a glance behind him. The rings of fiery crimson were closer, piercing the absolute black with a fury. He could recognize the difference in the Mothman's steps: one silent and lighter, the other a screech of metal on floor along with a terrific thud. Step, thud, step, thud. It screamed again, calling for them, calling for them all.

Pharo wished they could slip down one of the branching corridors, but Thorne had already laid out their route. The docking bay was straight down this corridor, no deviations, no turns. Which meant no escape from the thing barrelling down behind them.

Further ahead, Pharo picked out a distant light. *That must be the next section—what did Thorne call it? An electrical block?*

Another screech and a red haze invaded Pharo's vision—his limbs grew heavy, and he slowed. It felt like his mind was falling—no, being pulled, left, down, down, down—a crowd, reaching, pulling Thorne from him. The pen drops from her hand. A fist to his stomach, he falls too. A hand grips his hair, shoving his face to the floor, a knee to his back. The faceless woman chokes Thorne, the life flees the Second Engineering Officer's eyes, leaving nothing, leaving death—another scream throws him right back, though he's trembling, his knees want to give out.

The light grew, gave definition to the walls, the floor, the ceiling. The corridor ended in one last T junction. And within sight—the docking bay doors, salvation.

Then *she* stepped out. The eyeless woman. Followed by a crowd of her insane followers.

Pharo thought of the scarlet toned vision. He thought of Thorne's eyes going blank.

He tried to stop, but his momentum carried him right into the crowd.

"Take them!" the eyeless woman cried, her lips pulled back in a cruel snarl.

Thorne yelped in pain as three men yanked her away from Pharo. *I know what's coming next.* Moments caught in time like snapshots, broken schematics, waiting for the next slide. He dodged left and the punch aimed at his stomach missed. Lunging forward, Pharo scooped up the sealant pen.

Thorne was pinned to the floor, clawing at the eyeless woman's hands, which were wrapped around her throat. Flicking the pen to max heat, Pharo slipped through the hands reaching for him, and stabbed the faceless woman in the throat.

The stench of burnt flesh saturated the air and the woman howled, reeling back and away from Thorne, her hands now around her own neck, where the skin was blackened and peeling. Pharo crouched over Thorne, who had rolled into a fetal position, coughing dryly. Holding the pen out, he swiped at anyone who came near. Most had surrounded the eyeless woman, trying to help her, mobbing her with concern.

"Thorne, get up." Pharo slashed out as a robed man lunged at him, then flinched back from the intense heat of the pen.

The floor shook—thump, metallic scream, thump.

"Kill them! Kill them both!" the eyeless woman screamed and her followers turned as one, raising their boltguns, their clubs, their sharpened bits of metal.

Pharo reached down with his free hand, blindly seeking Thorne, and finding a shoulder. A towering woman with a shaved head squared off at Pharo, raising her boltgun. Pharo's heart dropped. He stood, straddling Thorne between his feet as if he could protect her.

Thump, screech, thump, screech. The Mothman barrelled into the woman before she could take her shot, shoving its savage metal spear-arm straight through her rib cage. The crunch of bone was audible, blood arced through the air as the Mothman lifted her above its furred head. With a scream, the monster flung her into three others, sending them all to the floor.

"Saviour!" the eyeless woman croaked from where she knelt on the floor. "Guide us, Bringer of Truth!"

She reached out in the Mothman's direction. Her neck was blotched black and red from burns, blood leaked down her collarbone. The creature screamed back in response, its fur prickling up, and its antenna jabbing forward. Thorne stood, wobbling on her feet, clutching at Pharo's sleeve to steady herself.

"Get the outsiders! The Saviour wants their blood!" the eyeless woman cried.

"We have to get to the docking bay!" Thorne said.

"Okay," Pharo hissed back. "Well, if you can figure out how to get past all those people, we will!"

Six cultists had lined up between them and the docking bay doors, weapons raised.

A blonde man with a hammer and a brunette woman with a crowbar lunged towards Pharo. He stumbled back, pinning Thorne against the wall behind him, the pen raised as a futile defense against the oncoming attack.

Faster than what its bulk should allow, the Mothman shot between Pharo and the cultists, grabbing the man around the throat with its bio-arm and slashing the woman with its spear. Her chest opened up in a crimson valley, showing ribs and glistening organs, she fell to the floor with a wail.

"No!" the eyeless woman cried hoarsely. "Saviour!"

The creature snapped the man's neck with no effort, tossing him to the side like trash, and stepped on the prone woman's head. It shifted its whole weight onto its bio-foot and her skull popped, splattering gray brain matter, blood, and skull fragments across the floor.

Pharo reached back, found Thorne's hand, and took it. The Mothman shook its head, flinging black ichor across the walls and the people around it. Globs of it smacked against Pharo's face, filling his nose with the reek of rot.

"What have we done?" The eyeless woman stood, clutching her throat, slipping backward, using her followers as shields. "How have we angered you? We seek the truth! We seek *your* truth."

The creature spread its wing, as much as it could in the corridor, crushing them against a wall, the ceiling, and shedding dozens of rotting scales as it did. It turned and caught Pharo in its fiery red gaze.

Pharo fell.

The present became nothing. The future, forever.

But Pharo knew this journey well now and he pulled himself back, out of the eye of the moth. Instead of the barren crimson death of the universe, he saw a being in pain. The Mothman turned away and set upon the cultists. It swung its arm, throwing two against the wall, their shrieks silenced. Slashing and spearing, it decimated the Citizens, who were too blinded by their own obsessive fate to even fight back against the monster they had created.

In return for their obedience, the Mothman painted the walls, the ceiling, the floor with their bones, blood, and bodies. The air was filled with a chorus of screams, of breaking bones, and the Mothman's howls.

"Come on." Thorne's breath in his ear. "Now's our chance!"

The way to the docking bay doors was clear. *As long as you don't count all the dead bodies.* Pharo followed Thorne's lead, running along the wall, towards the doors. He slipped a bit on the blood, running thick over the plexicarb. He tried to pretend he didn't know what his boot crunched was an exposed femur bone, half a skull. He tried to ignore the pop of a blue eyeball beneath his heel.

Thorne slammed her hand onto the door release pad, her other hand pressed against her side. Pharo turned around. He didn't want to look, but at the same time, he couldn't help himself. There were only two cultists left. A man and the eyeless woman were in the sea of carnage. The woman was on her knees, her hands clasped in front of her face as she prayed.

The creature towered over them all, its wing shoved against the ceiling, crushing the lights and sending sparks down around it. The man raised his wrench, but his hands shook and tears ran down his cheeks as he stared into the eyes of the beast, lost in whatever scarlet hell he saw. The Mothman pulled back its bio-arm, claws spread, and thrust them through the man's chest. The man let out a single groan as blood bubbled up and over his lips, down his chin, to dribble to the sea of blood at his feet.

Dropping him, the Mothman turned towards the eyeless woman.

"In the eye of the moth, I find salvation," she prayed. "In the crimson future, I find truth."

Behind him, Pharo felt the whoosh of air as the doors opened. The creature ran its claws down the side of the eyeless woman's face almost tenderly, then wrapped its long fingers around her face. She didn't resist. *Maybe she still believes her faith will save her.*

"We don't have time for this, Pharo!" Thorne said.

And yet he still couldn't move. The creature tightened its claws and the woman prayed all the faster. It took seconds, minutes, an eternity, and no time at all. The Mothman crushed the woman's skull with its hand. Her brains oozed out between its fingers, blood poured down her chest, and her words were finally silenced.

"Pharo!" Thorne yelled, grabbing the back of his jumpsuit and trying to pull him into the docking bay pressurization room.

Releasing the woman's pulverized skull, the Mothman turned. Its eyes blazed, red rings that no longer seemed so deadly to Pharo. He looked over his shoulder at Thorne.

"I'll be right there," he said and pulled away.

Dropping down, he pulled a boltgun from the grip of a disembodied hand.

"What are you doing?" Thorne called. "That thing is dangerous!"

The Mothman tried to fold its wing behind it, but it was too broken, too injured, so it draped to the floor instead. Pharo kept its gaze, letting its scarlet haze fill his. *Warm. It feels warm now, not dangerous. But I can see its pain. It never wanted this.* The Mothman bowed its head slightly, its antenna dropping. Pharo raised the boltgun and placed its large barrel against the Mothman's furred skull, right between its large crimson eyes.

"I'm sorry we did this to you," he told the creature.

Pharo had no idea if the Mothman's alien intelligence could understand, but as the creature's antenna gently brushed against the back of his hand, he wanted to believe it did.

Pharo pulled the trigger. The recoil whipped his hand back, his arm buzzing with the shot. The bolt shattered the Mothman's skull, sent up a spray of ichor. The creature's head fell, its antenna drooped, its eyes dimmed. It fell backward onto its wing, crushing the bones in it in a crackle of pops. Pharo stepped around its outflung bio-arm and knelt by its head. *It doesn't seem so big now.*

Its eyes faded from red to brown to white, changing into blind milky orbs, capable of seeing nothing—no futures, no present, finally at rest. But Pharo wanted to make sure—he owed the creature that—so he placed the boltgun's barrel to the Mothman's temple and fired again. And again. Reducing the creature's skull to a pool of flesh and circuitry, bone and wires. Releasing the Mothman from its cybernetic prison.

"Rest now," Pharo whispered and stood.

Thorne was waiting, her hand on the door release, her face screwed up in frustration and pain.

"Come on!" she shouted. "We need to save Duncan!"

He jogged through the gore and into the small room that acted as a pressurization room between the *Goremades* and the docking bay.

As the doors to the space station closed, Pharo's mind screamed in shades of red.

There is the First Engineering Officer, his hand on a flashing red button, overhead yellow lights flashing. Thorne running towards Duncan, the docking bay external doors open, the air sucks out, suffocation.

Pharo gasped as he fell back into the present and out of the scarlet-tinged future. *Another one. Another one just like before. Are these just echoes of the Mothman's power?*

Or something permanent?

The doors to the docking bay slid open, revealing the cavernous bay that housed the station's fleet of mining ships, survey drones, and the CRS *Piasa*.

A panel was missing from the side of the *Piasa*, exposing machinery and wide tubing. A body lay near one of the *Piasa*'s airlock doors.

"Suzuki!" Pharo darted across the uncomfortably open space between the ships, holding the heavy boltgun at the ready.

His heart dropped when he saw the rusty pool that haloed around Suzuki's head. Kneeling next to her, Pharo placed a hand on her shoulder. The front of Suzuki's uniform was stained, stiff with dried blood. Her face was turned away from him. *I don't want to see, I don't want to*—Pharo used two fingers to bring her head towards him, revealing a puncture wound just below the woman's cheekbone and another one above the opposite eyebrow. Blood lay in a cracked starmap across her face, stained her eyes pink, had dried in clumps on her eyelashes, and painted a false lipstick on her mouth.

"Oh, Suzuki." Pharo couldn't pretend he had ever liked the Navigational Officer or thought she'd liked him. Her personality had reminded him too much of his father. But she'd been good at her job and that was something he could, at least, respect.

"Duncan!" Thorne's voice caused Pharo to jump to his feet, whirling with boltgun raised.

Thorne stood facing away from Pharo, towards a raised, plexiglass walled room—the docking bay's control room. The glass on one side had been broken, bent inward, a hole big enough for a man.

Duncan, the CRS *Piasa*'s First Engineering Officer, stood in that room. He pressed a button and, overhead, the docking bay's comms speakers buzzed.

"You shouldna have come, lass."

XII

"Duncan!" Thorne called, then realized he couldn't hear her and pressed her suit comms button. "Duncan, come down here. Please."

Beside her, a scouting ship hummed. It was geared up and, from the look of its patchwork side, it had been worked on recently. Thorne's stomach dropped to the floor. The panel that gave external access to the *Piasa*'s FTL drive was open, but its FTL was gone. Thorne could only guess where it was now, but as to why, she was at a loss.

"Go back inside, Thorne. Where it's safe." Duncan's voice was resigned, dead.

Pharo appeared at her side. "We need to get out of here!"

She shook her head. "Duncan. I know what you saw in that program. I know how it must have made you feel, but we can fix this!"

"I shouldna be here. I should've died on the *Hera*, lass." Duncan hit the button on the panel in front of him.

"Depressurization of docking bay initialized. Personnel, please relocate to safe zone areas." blared the overhead automated voice as a yellow light flashed.

"Duncan, you're better than this!" Thorne screamed into her mic. "Stop it!"

Please, please let me get through to him! A thought similar to one she had years ago, when her father had commed her, as he lay dying. *Please, please let him be saved!*

"A cargo hold full of children. It woulda been a mercy to let them die." Duncan's voice cracked, broken by regret. "The Company may not have been responsible for them, but they collected taxes on them, looked the other way. It's time I atoned. The future is red and full of horror, Lynn. It would be better for all of us if we were dead."

"Duncan!" she snapped. "Don't do this!"

"Depressurization sequence begun."

"Thorne! We can't stay here!" Pharo grabbed her arm, pulling her away. She tried to fight, but her side screamed in pain as the burnt flesh pulled against itself.

"I can get through to him, Pharo." She stomped on his foot, causing him to let go.

"I loaded all the explosives I could on that ship, Thorne." Duncan said. "It's set to Company's HQ on Huresa. It's their reckoning. And mine. Go now, lass. Go."

"Docking bay doors sealed. Exterior doors opening in thirty seconds."

"Joel, please." Thorne was crying, though she did not know when she'd started. "I can't lose you too."

"Goodbye, lass." he replied, his voice finally cracking with his own tears. "You were the one light after the Hera. You were the daughter I ne'er had."

The overhead comms crackled as the line shut off. Thorne lunged forward. *I have time, if I can get inside the control room, I can—*

Pharo's fist struck her side and she cried out, doubling over. The Executive Officer flung her over his shoulder, her side throbbed in agony as she bounced, he ran, straight to the *Piasa*'s open airlock.

As soon as they were inside, Pharo dropped Thorne without ceremony. The impact sent a bright shockwave of pain through her body and Thorne's vision freckled with black spots. He punched his fist against the door button and the airlock door hissed shut, its locks thunking closed. Thorne struggled to her feet, slammed an open hand against Pharo's back.

"I could have stopped the sequence, Pharo!" She hated the sound of her voice cracking, the feel of hot tears down her face. "I could have saved him!"

"No." He turned to her and she froze at his grave expression, the barest flash of red in his eyes that made her shiver. "I saw it. You would have died."

He's insane. Whatever that monster did to him, he didn't actually recover. Thorne stumbled back from him, hugging her injured side as she keyed back into comms.

"Duncan? Duncan, are you there?"

The only answer through the comms was the howling rush of air being sucked into the unforgiving void of space. Thorne rushed past Pharo, ignoring her pain, her fear of him, and stared out the porthole.

The outer doors opened, a gaping maw revealing a gullet of endless space and brilliant stars. The control room was empty, the broken glass sucked out, as well as Joel Duncan, First Engineering Officer of the CRS *Piasa*, hero of the *Hera*. Thorne screwed her eyes shut and sucked in one shuddery breath after the other.

I didn't even get to say goodbye. To tell him how much he helped me. How much I needed him.

"I'm sorry, Thorne," Pharo said.

She hated him more than anything at that moment.

For stopping her, for pulling her away, for not letting her try to save Duncan.

"We have to get out of here," he continued.

"Without an FTL drive, it will take us decades to get anywhere," she whispered, feeling numb, feeling tired.

"What—what do you mean?"

Thorne turned to him and saw the shock on his face. "Duncan took the *Piasa*'s FTL and installed it into that scouting ship that just took off. He programmed it to go to the Company's planetary headquarters."

She could almost laugh at Pharo's gaping mouth and wide eyes.

"That's why they wanted the *Piasa*," she said. "Not for help. For our FTL drive in their stupid crusade against the Company. Based on the equipment lying around, I think he turned the scouting ship into a bomb."

"We have to stop it!" Pharo turned, slamming his fist on the interior door lock button.

"Do we?" Thorne turned and looked back out the window, still searching for any sign of Duncan. The docking bay was still, empty, the only movement the still flashing yellow lights.

"Thousands of people could die if it reaches HQ," Pharo said. "Don't you care?"

"It's what Duncan wanted." She rested her forehead against the glass.

He didn't deserve to die with regrets. He was a hero.

"Was it?" Pharo gripped her shoulder, spinning her around. "Look at me and tell me that the Duncan you knew would have wanted to kill hundreds of people."

She didn't want to look at him, didn't want to see a hint of red in his eyes, so she stared at his neck, at the pulse in its side. *The Hero of* Hera. *Joel Duncan.* Sadness washed over her heart, waves as heavy as a black hole, dragging her down, all she wanted was to sleep. Her shoulders slumped, her knees wanted to buckle, and she let her head fall against Pharo's shoulder.

He wrapped his arms around her and she listened to his racing heart. A comforting tempo, deep. The sound of living.

What would Duncan want? What would he really want?

She wanted to sleep, to just forget about the *Goremades*, forget about the horror and the death and the pain. *I grew up always asking myself, what would Dad want? What would he think is best? She bit her lip. And then when I started working with Duncan, I began to ask what would he want? What would he expect?*

But what about me? What do I think is best? I think Duncan's guilt got the better of him. But he wasn't a killer. He saved the Hera. *He wouldn't want his last act to be one of mass murder.*

"We have to get to the ship." She pulled away. Tired, but resolved. She knew what she wanted now. "We have to get to it before the FTL drive revs to full power."

"How long do we have?" He followed her into the *Piasa* proper, as she led the way, through the empty ship, to the bridge.

"Forty-five minutes, give or take."

"And you think we can board the ship and stop it?" He was hopeful.

"No. We don't have the tools for boarding," she said.

"So what? What are we supposed to do? Ram it?"

She stopped at a junction. One hall would take them to the bridge, the other to the engineering room. "With the tools I have, I can open the external panel and access the FTL drive. There's no way to stop it once the jump has been initiated, but I can reroute the grounding wire so that it feeds back into itself, which should cause the drive to overload and explode."

Pharo stood in front of her and looked her over. *I know what he sees, my pale, sweaty face, the way I'm hunched over my injured side. He doesn't think I'm strong enough.*

"Thorne—"

"There's no other way, Pharo. I can't drive the ship. You can't rewire the drive. This is the only way." *And I want to be the one to save Duncan's reputation, his memory. It's the least I can do.*

A pause. Then Pharo nodded. "Alright. Let's go. Time's running out."

She turned and started down the corridor that would lead her to the engineering room. Pharo called out after her. "Thorne? Be careful, okay? I don't want to lose you too."

She didn't turn back. Didn't want him to see her face. Who knew what his new red eyes would see. *Maybe he'd see straight into my mind. See that I think this is a suicide mission.*

Back in the portside airlock, Thorne painfully pulled on a suit, wincing at every bend and shift. Her wound had opened up again. At least this time, she was able to grab gel patches from the med bay and paste them across her side. The numbing gel did wonders on the pain, but it couldn't get rid of it completely. Thorne couldn't risk painkillers dulling her mind though.

She sealed the suit, checked her oxygen levels for the third time, then strapped on the heavy toolbelt. Thorne had attached every single tool she thought would be needed. The hiss of comms startled her.

"Pulling up now, Thorne," Pharo's voice came through. "Are you ready?"

"As I'll ever be. In airlock three, opening exterior door now."

The door opened, the sound swallowed by the void of space. She stepped onto the threshold, her toes hanging out into the emptiness. She hooked her belt tether to the external hook by the door. If she did manage to do the job properly, she'd want a fast escape.

Directly in front of her, a full hundred meters away, was the *Goremades* scouting ship. The writing on its hull identified it as the *Istka III*. It had stopped, its thrusters glowing a brilliant blue as the FTL drive warmed up. Thorne could feel the warm thunder of its distant power. If sound existed in the hostile environment of space, she'd be able to hear it purring, a purr that would grow to a growl, to a roar.

Time was running out. *One small step...* She jumped outwards and blasted her suit's thrusters, shooting through space, hurtling towards the *Istka. I have to do this right. Too little thrust, and it will take too long for me to get there—too much and I'll bounce off the hull.*

Her breathing picked up as her heart raced. Her visor fogged and she felt warm—too warm. Her waist vibrated with the unreeling cord, still attached to the *Piasa*. She hadn't thought to make sure she had enough. Hadn't checked.

She flew, a shooting star of delicate flesh and breakable bone, a thundering heart and the tiniest hope.

The scouting ship grew and the distance shrank. *Closer...closer... closer...NOW!*

Thorne hit the reverse thruster, slowing her approach just enough. She slammed against the ship's hull and her side screamed through the bumping pads, but she caught hold of a handlebar and held tight.

"Thorne?" Pharo's voice was distant and it crackled over the comms.

"I'm on the ship," she gasped.

Still holding onto the bar for dear life, Thorne looked down the hull and spotted the panel. It was obvious. Duncan hadn't been careful when bolting it back on and he'd missed a corner, which jutted up from the hull.

She held her breath, lunged for the next handhold, and caught it. In this way, she hopped along the length of the hull.

"Tell me what's happening." Pharo's voice was like a bug in her ear. Usually when she and Duncan worked, they were quiet, unless something necessary needed to be said.

She'd reached the panel now, clipped herself to a nearby bar, and slid out in front of the panel. She removed each of the knuckle sized bolts, tucking each one into a pocket out of habit. Once free, she removed the panel and stuck it to the side of the hull with magnetic gum. With the panel removed, she could see the *Piasa*'s FTL drive, deep within the scout ship, glowing blue with building energy. *I don't have much time.*

"Thorne?!"

"I'm here, Pharo. I need to concentrate."

She reached in and pulled out a bundle of wires, tied together in Duncan's signature neat style. It had been a long time since she'd had to deal with an FTL drive and she struggled against the pain in her side to remember the meanings of the wire colours.

"I'm sorry, I—I just want to know you're okay," he said.

Blue is usually grounding, isn't it? But it looks so thin. Her heart was racing. One wrong move and she could cause the FTL to explode instantly.

Thorne reached for her wire cutters, her hands were shaking, shaking so hard they almost slipped out of her grip.

"I'm okay," she lied. "Almost done."

Please be blue, please be blue.

Unbidden, a memory of trying to study in an Academy dorm room. Her notes displayed across several screens and in all colours of text. One stood out and she heard her own voice say, "cut the blue, and you're through". An old rhyme to remember. A silly thing for an exam.

"Cut the blue and you're through," she said, pulling the wire cutters away from the blue wire, her skin cold with the knowledge she'd almost killed herself.

"What was that?" Pharo asked.

"Cut the blue and you're through. Yellow is the grounding fellow." And she snipped the thick yellow wire, shutting her eyes.

Seconds ticked by, with no blast.

"I was jealous of you, you know." Pharo's voice again.

She opened her eyes again, panting. The FTL drive was brighter now. It would be ready to jump soon. "What?"

"In the Academy," he replied.

She stripped the grounding wire a bit, then located the mini energy cube that powered the drive.

"That's why…that's why I acted the way I did, back then," he continued. "You had everything I didn't. A father who loved you, talents, the grades. You were going somewhere. I was just…I was nothing compared to you."

Thorne paused, holding the wire and the cube. "My dad died, Pharo. He wasn't around then."

Why does it matter now? Why are we doing this now? Why am I still so bitter?

"At least you knew he loved you. Everyone likes you, Thorne."

"Pharo…"

The hull was vibrating, shaking Thorne's very bones as the FTL drive neared readiness.

"You don't have much time left," he said. "I won't forgive you if you die, you know."

She inserted the grounding wire into an open port. With that in place, the power would be caught in a loop. An explosion was guaranteed. Already the cube was heating up and the FTL's light wavered in violent throbbing pulses.

"It's done, Pharo!" she said. "I'm coming back, be ready to get out of here!"

She hit the retract button. On her belt and the mechanism whirred, but instead of being pulled back towards the *Piasa*, Thorne was yanked left and smashed against the hull. Her injured side flared, knocking her senseless. She spiralled off towards the stars. *Idiot! You're hooked to the scouting ship!* Thorne reached down and gripped the rope, her belly roiling at the rapid spins. She pulled herself along the rope, back to the scouting ship, which was now shaking out of control. *Not much time now.* Reaching the anchor, she fumbled at it.

"Thorne? Where are you?"

She managed to unclip herself, then hit the retract button again. Nothing. "Fuck, fuck, fuck."

"Thorne!"

She kicked off. She'd used all her thrusters getting to the scout ship. The suits didn't have much to begin with as they were mainly meant for minor external repairs, not leaps across the void. So she reached for her trailing cord and pulled, hand over hand, desperately. She could feel the vibrations of the overheating FTL drive in space itself.

Hand over hand, hand over hand, she told herself and yet at the same time, her mind yelled back, *I won't make it. I was never going to make it.*

But she didn't stop. She refused to stop. Hurtling towards the *Piasa*, she jerked the rope at the last minute, spinning herself at an angle, straight through the airlock door. Thorne slammed into the interior door.

"Go, Pharo! Go!" She reached out and slammed her hand against the airlock button. The exterior door hushed shut, closing off her view of the scout ship.

Pharo didn't respond, but she felt the *Piasa* rumble. She knew the ship's every vibration, every sound. Its engines were a familiar purr and she closed her eyes.

Moments later, she felt the explosion. It vibrated through her bones, through the ship's bones, making the *Piasa* grumble. But they were out and away, into the endless void, into the unknown, and the uncertain. *Enough moping on the floor.* Thorne sat up, leaning against the airlock door, and pulled off her suit. Blood seeped from beneath the gel patches on her side and the pain was nearly unbearable. But she was alive. *I did it Duncan. For you. But I won't forget what you said.* She stood on shaky legs. *I won't forget about the Hera.* She hit the door release button and stepped out into the hall.

"Thorne!" Pharo raced around the corner.

She turned to face him and was shocked when he embraced her, crushing her against his chest and burying his face into her neck.

"Get—get off me!" she gasped, her side flaring up.

"I'm sorry!" He stepped back, his hands stayed on her shoulders.

He looked older now, his face drawn and tired, his eyes a strange amber colour, when they used to be blue.

"I think I might need stitches," she said, trying to hide the fear she felt.

Pharo barked out a short laugh. "Come on, let me take you to med bay."

Thorne stood in the middle of the bridge, leaning slightly to favour her injured side. She stared at the external holo-display of stars and swirling galaxies. *Never before has this view seemed so lonely.*

Pharo stepped up to her side. "I set up the distress signal. Hopefully a Company ship picks it up soon."

Thorne thought of Duncan's last moments, his despair and his hatred of the Company. She thought of Pharo's own words. *The Company is the cause of the end. So it was seen, so it must be so.*

"It won't be long," Pharo said, slipping his hand into hers. She let him, didn't look at him, avoiding his new strange amber gaze. "They'll find us. We'll be okay."

Is that something he sees? Or just reassurance?

The holo-display flickered, readjusted to account for distance travelled. *The Company will come. And what will I do then?*

I'll find the truth. I won't stop. I will dig and dig and bury them if I have to.

Pharo squeezed her hand and she pulled away.

"I should rest," she said and turned to leave.

Days, weeks, or months. She would find her way back. She would find her way back to the Company and then she would find Duncan's truth.

"Thorne."

It was Pharo's tone that made her turn, that made her finally meet his strange eyes.

"I'll help. When we get back. I promise you, on my mother's life, I will help you find the truth."

And for the first time that day, Thorne smiled.

Once Upon a Time in Turu

Directed by Ryan Marie Ketterer

Once Upon a Time in Turu

Ryan Marie Ketterer

Malse

The mothmen need to die.

Malse repeated this over and over in his head, reminding himself of what he was doing here. He shoved aside a few drunk chupacabras, their stench overwhelming even in the trash-strewn streets.

Rusted metal signs hung from crumbling brick facades, each offering booze or merwomen, oftentimes both. Malse was interested in none of that though. He was on the hunt.

As if on command, a spindly alien rounded the corner, bumping into Malse. The low-life fell to the ground, his long, green fingers getting stuck in the mud. Malse pounced, his Jersey devil speed too quick for the other-worldly being beneath him.

"You aliens are trash, ya know that?" Malse glared into its big eyes.

"I paid up," the alien said, attempting to squirm from Malse's strong devil grip. "You know I'm all paid up!"

"I'm looking for Elrong. I seen you two drinking down at that bar, the one with the merwhores, Pashimi's?"

Elrong is the city's most ruthless mothman. And the mafia's number one enemy.

"I ain't seen 'im since last week," the alien replied. "Ya know he owes me money, too!"

It was unlikely this little fink knew anything. Malse grumbled and pushed himself up.

"I'm tired of lookin' at ya face, get outta here!"

The alien slipped in the mud as he scrambled away.

Malse stood at the mouth of a dark alley, mist in the air sparkling with the reflections of flickering neon lights from the bars surrounding him. Pashimi's wasn't far.

He lit his pipe and started walking. The hashish inside lit quickly, and he put it into his long mouth, taking a drag. His wings twitched as the drug worked its way into his system, and he primed himself for another night prowling the streets of Turu.

Pashimi's place held a raucous crowd. In the corner, a lizardman band smacked on drums and screamed at the crowd. Chupacabras and aliens danced—or maybe fought?—in the middle of the dance floor.

Why was this place filled with a bunch of stinkin' deadbeats? Malse shoved his way through the drunk monsters.

Pashimi smirked at him from behind the bar. She floated in a tank, her normally shimmering fins dulled by the murky water.

"My very favorite customer," she said, the sarcasm evident. "The usual?"

Malse grunted and rolled his eyes. She always judged him, as if she was so much better, selling her body for cash.

She slammed a tin mug in front of him, foam spilling over the edges. "What trouble are you in today?"

Malse watched a chupacabra empty an ashtray into the pool Pashimi swam in, the black flecks of dust dancing across the oily surface of the water. The miasma of rot that hung in the air around the bar almost drove Malse to leave, but he needed information.

"I'm looking for the leader of that mothmen gang. Elrong, his name is."

"Well," Pashimi said, her deep eyes glittering with the reflection of the murky water. "Maybe I can help. Tell me about this ... *Elrong?*"

"Got into a bad fight, last I heard. Only has one eye."

"A mothman with only one eye, how unusual." Pashimi grabbed at her chest and hardened her gaze. Her hand covered a lumpy scar that ran across half of her chest, where one of her breasts once was.

"What's that? Did Elrong do that to you?"

"No, silly." Pashimi giggled and winked at him. "This is an old wound, maybe older than you. The mothmen have always been too rough, though."

Malse flushed, his anger renewed. They should be eradicated from Turu!

"Tell me, Pashimi." He was trying not to beg. "Tell me what you know!"

"The bar cleared out for a bit earlier, apparently there was a fight over by the abandoned factory. I heard something about mothmen, but who knows how accurate that is."

Turu was a decaying city of monsters. The buildings were in ruins, the roads and houses unkempt.

But that factory was haunted.

The factory rose before Malse: several stories of disintegrating brick, a couple useless smokestacks, and a whole lot of nothing around it. Distant metal creaks sounded in the distance, through shattered glass window panes. There were no monsters in sight now.

His Jersey devil night vision kicked in and he scanned the street for any sign of a disturbance. If there was a fight here tonight, Elrong may not be far.

Malse noticed a set of footprints as he got closer to the building. He knelt next to the disturbance in the dirt, hoping he might recognize the multi-pronged claws of a mothman, but the prints were too frantic in appearance to be made any sense of. A damp, musty scent made its way to him, and wrinkled his nose.

He followed the markings around the side of the factory and into an alley, holding his breath to avoid the sour air. Malse kept his wings raised, ready for flight, as he entered the narrow walkway.

A sudden clang of metal echoed into the damp, night air, and Malse spun. But it was only a rat, scurrying from behind a dumpster.

See? Ghosts aren't real.

At the end of the alley were piles of trash. What's the point of the dumpster? His lips curled in disgust.

Malse was about to turn around and call it a night when he spotted something sticking out from the refuse. Was that a paw?

What in the name of Nessie?

He moved closer and immediately recognized the body of a jackalope. The head was smashed in, and sticky blood pooled in the dirt around the body. Crimson art painted the deteriorating brick.

The beady, black eyes of the dead monster stared back at Malse.

Flashbacks flooded his mind.

His poor childhood in Turu.

Chasing those big antlers everywhere they went.

Laughing with her when he caught up.

Rayna Ares was his best friend back then, but they hadn't spoken in years, not since she married into wealth and moved to the other side of the city.

Even though he never met him, Malse knew. The dead jackalope in front of him was Kevan Ares, Rayna's son.

Orli

Orli had managed to scavenge a pair of Turu street rats on her way home—a delicacy on this side of town—and couldn't wait to sink her teeth into that meat.

She was Turu's only policefoot—the only bigfoot for that matter, too—and her days had gotten longer and longer lately, what with the gang violence and the growing divide between the rich and poor. But now? Now she was going to slurp up some delicious vermin blood and turn her mind off for a bit.

Just as she sunk into her dirt-ridden cushions, there was a furious pounding at her door, accompanied by muffled shouts.

Apparently one night off was just too much to ask for.

When she swung the door open, she was shocked to see Malse. He was panting, as if he'd flown a marathon to get here.

Malse and Orli went way back. Them, plus Rayna Ares, were the tightest of friends, and the biggest of troublemakers, back in the day.

"Kevan," he said, gasping between each word. "Kevan... Ares... at... factory."

Kevan was Rayna's son. Her and Malse hadn't seen their friend in so long, not since she moved over to Royal Kire. This was not good.

"Slow down, bud." Orli opened her door all the way and let the Jersey devil stumble in. "What's going on?"

Malse collected himself and recounted what he saw.

Orli brought Malse to the station, sat him down with some shroom tea, and told him not to move. She ordered her owlmen on the night shift to report to the factory—it was all hands on deck tonight. To get to the crime scene, she navigated the poorest neighborhood of this forsaken city with ease—this was her home after all.

Dead bodies were not all that uncommon in Turu, but someone like Kevan Ares? The son of not just one of the richest families in this Nessie-forsaken place, but also the son of her childhood best friend. Rayna would not take this well.

Orli had a deep sense of regret for never getting to know Kevan, but her close relationship with Rayna dissolved after the jackalope started running in the rich circles. Maybe Orli should have tried to reach out once in a while.

After setting up lights in the alleyway, Orli and her team began collecting evidence. Most of the footprints were distorted and would be impossible to match, or even to narrow down to a single species, but they collected imprints of what they could.

She photographed the body, the blood. There was so much, splattered across the crumbling bricks like abstract art—a canvas of violence.

Kevan's head was crushed to pieces, chunks of bone and bloody fur strewn about and covered in dirt. She was unsure what might cause this sort of damage to a monster's skull, but nothing present at the scene stood out to her. She had her owlmen bag and tag everything regardless.

There was a dull shimmer on the jackalope's body, like a worn out disco ball. She wondered if Kevan doused himself in some sort of shiny perfume. Maybe it was something the bougies did?

She made note of the abnormality.

It was time to head back to the station and start piecing this together.

Orli looked across the table at the lizardman medical examiner. Between them lay the cobbled body of Kevan Ares. The many pieces of his skull were arranged haphazardly on a sheet of wax paper next to his twisted form. Dried blood matted the fur all over his body. Orli stifled a gag and didn't take her eyes from the gruesome sight.

"His head was caved in, probably from something large. A rock, or maybe a brick," the examiner said. "There are some claw marks here, too, along his back and side. Something very sharp made these. The spacing is odd, they're almost too far apart to have been made by a single paw, or…"

"Interesting." Orli snapped a photo of the wounds. "We have a source that speculates the involvement of a mothman."

"Mothmen have sharp claws, but they're far too thick to have caused these wounds you see here," the lizardman said, unfurling his long tongue and sucking it back in. A nervous tic. "That odd spacing would make more sense with a mothman, though."

Orli thought about how many monsters in Turu had claws or nails. It was going to be hard to narrow down all the possibilities, but she knew this clue might be the key to solving the murder. The medical examiner seemed to have read her mind because he said, "Maybe start by looking at the big cats? They could've created the odd pattern intentionally, to throw you off."

"Yeah, thanks. Let me know if you find anything else."

Orli grabbed a mug of stale shroom tea and a pair of pus-filled donuts on her way to see Malse, who she had left alone in her office.

"Orli," he said as she stepped in. "Finally. Where have you been?"

He was frantic. Nervous.

"Well," she said, taking a bite of one of the donuts, some of the pus getting stuck in the brown fur around her mouth. "I had this crime scene..."

"Yeah, yeah, yeah. But what happened?"

"I should be asking you that. What were you doing over there Malse?"

"Don't worry 'bout that," he said, waving his hands at her. "But I have it on good authority that Elrong was out there looking to pick fights that night, right out there where Kevan was."

Orli took a swig of her tea and almost gagged when she realized the liquid was cold.

"Stupid mothmen..." Malse muttered.

Orli's eyes shot up and she wiped pus from her face. "What's that now? You have some beef with the mothmen?"

Malse sighed and threw his head back in frustration. "Yes, Orli. You know the trouble those light-chasers been causing all over Turu."

Orli returned his smart-ass response with a raised eyebrow. "Trouble they're causing *you*, as in the mafia."

Malse was getting upset with Orli's line of questioning so she toned it down.

"Okay, okay, we don't need to talk about your extracurriculars," she said.

"I was looking for Elrong, askin' around," Malse continued. "Everyone down at Pashimi's says he was out there, by the factory, pickin' fights, ok? Trust me, Li. Can't you just trust me on this one?"

Orli cringed at the use of her childhood nickname. It'd been over a decade since she last heard that.

"Sure, sure," she finally said, choking down her tea. "But only until I can corroborate."

They continued to sit there in silence, the thick, somber air unmoving.

"What about Rayna?" Malse finally said.

Orli shook her head. "What about her?" Seeing her again would be hard.

Pashimi's was desolate during daylight hours and the lack of a monster crowd revealed its true state.

The floor was cracked and splintering wood, stained with dirt and monster shit. Piles of trash and bile were scattered throughout the main room. Orli wondered why anyone would set foot in such a place, but the grinning merwomen floating in various pools throughout the place reminded her.

"Don't worry, we clean up before we open again." The voice came from an older merwoman floating in a tank behind the bar. "Then you can have any of these women you want."

Orli walked over to Pashimi and pulled a small recording device from her utility belt.

"I'm not here for that. I'm investigating a crime." She clicked on the recorder and asked, "Did you serve any mothmen recently?"

"Recently?" Pashimi laughed. "The mothmen hate Pashimi's. They rarely set foot in here."

Pashimi spun her fin under the water, leaned forward, and winked at Orli.

"Then why have I heard from others about a mothman fight here?"

"A fight at Pashimi's? Oh, guppy, there were no fights here."

Orli was getting frustrated with the swim-around. "Why don't you share what you do know about the mothmen then?"

"Certainly," she spun her tail once more. "This bar cleared out, monsters shouting about mothmen. But did I see any? No."

Pashimi floated away and started stacking tin mugs.

"You're no fun, you know that," the merwoman said. "Always business. I don't know anything about the fights these monsters busy themselves with. But, we did have a werewolf in here last night too, maybe that caused a stir. Been a while since they came 'round.'"

A werewolf in Turu? It'd be a long time since she'd last heard about one of those. As the one and only bigfoot in Turu, Orli always felt a kinship towards werewolves, being so scarce and all.

With their human-appearing bodies, werewolves were not known to last very long in Turu. But when they did transform, they had some pretty sharp claws.

Malse flew over the rocky path that zig-zagged up the side of a steep cliff outside the walls of Turu, sucking the thin air deep into his lungs. The flowers were in full bloom, surrounding him with the colorful scents of spring.

The Devil's Syndicate preferred a secluded base of operations, away from the prying eyes of the overbearing and far too observant Orli. He hoped his long absence wouldn't raise any red flags. At the top, a bustling crowd of Jersey devils ran to and fro, some directing traffic, while others moved wooden boxes from one small hut to another.

For once, he had no idea what was in those boxes; just another illicit item getting trafficked in and out of Turu, no doubt. This whole mothman rivalry was starting to affect him and his interactions with the mafia. The boss couldn't find out the mothmen were encroaching on their territory. Malse just had to figure out a way to stop them, or at the very least, slow them down.

He thought about what he saw last night, what he heard at the bar. If Elrong was involved in Kevan's death, then maybe Malse didn't need to kill him. Maybe all he needed to do was put Orli on his tail.

Malse walked across the cliff ledge towards the hut he called home, one he shared with several other devils. The plateau was filled with these rickety structures, some for storing the Syndicate's latest product, others to house the creatures that made this operation run. They barely stood up straight, made of thin sheet metal if they were lucky, or rotting particle board if they weren't.

Malse could hear a conversation drifting from within his abode.

"Boss 'as me goin' down to infiltrate that stupid 'unting club today," someone said. "Down at the church. Wants to make sure we control all the bets getting placed. Control the bets, control the money, amirite?"

Malse paused outside the hut so he could listen in. He recognized the voice as Sigrun, a Jersey devil favored by the boss, and also his roommate and rival.

"What a load of shit!" Malse didn't immediately recognize the voice that replied. Maybe it was Ronic? "Why does he trust you with the fun projects anyways? I'm stuck talking with that stupid human."

"Because I get results, ya understand." Sigrun laughed. "Unlike Malse, that devil's a fool."

The two monsters continued to laugh as they bickered about who was a better mafia grunt.

Malse backed away, a cave opening inside his chest. The only monsters that he ever seemed to click with were Orli and Rayna. But one left to be rich, the other a narc.

He'd prove everyone wrong. He'd solve this mothman problem and show them. They were so clueless, they didn't even know there was a war going on right outside their door! Malse was the hero the Syndicate needed.

A hunting club? Malse wondered what Sigrun had meant by a hunting club. And something about bets, too. There was a lot more going on in Turu than even Malse knew about, but maybe it was important. Maybe if he could find out about all of these secrets, he could find Elrong and end this. Or, worst case, point Orli in the right direction. She had to trust him at some point, right?

Orli

After organizing her thoughts and her paperwork on the murder case, Orli was finally ready to inform Kevan's family of last night's discovery. She cringed at the thought of having to walk over to that side of Turu, to see Rayna again. She no longer knew anything about her old friend. She was basically a stranger.

Orli loaded up her belt: camera, check! Swabs, check! Fingerprint reader, check!

She had to be ready for anything.

As Orli jogged through the streets of Turu, she thought back to her childhood.

Her, Malse, and Rayna originally met when they skipped out on classes about their deity Nessie. They spent days on the playground pretending to be rich and famous and nights hunting the fabled piasa.

The three of them hadn't grown up with much, but she was thankful for those memories.

Rayna didn't seem to agree though, because she escaped that life—one where she grew up among the slumbags—as soon as she could, marrying Banut Ares at a young age. Orli hadn't seen the jackalope since those early days, before Rayna ran away, and she didn't look forward to seeing how much she changed.

Orli finally reached the sprawling Royal Kire neighborhood. While the rest of the city had dark towering walls looking down on them, Royal Kire was located in the corner of Turu where the walls had long since crumbled. The rich families that lived in this neighborhood took advantage of the collapsed wall, building a new, thriving monster community that looked out over a collection of crisp blue lakes just outside of Turu.

Bright, green grass radiated on the small lawns in front of each house, all tended to immaculately. Each home was painted a different color so the new, thriving locale shined like a rainbow.

Out in the lakes, mermen and merwomen lounged in the water, laughing. Long tentacles occasionally broke the surface, some holding baby creatures, others engaged in a synchronous, rhythmic motion. Kraken yoga?

Orli finally came to the largest house in Royal Kire: the Ares mansion. The stark white structure stood out amongst the colorful houses and towered several stories high. It had large, wide windows and doors, built specifically to accommodate the antlers of the jackalope family. A kaleidoscope of flowers lined all sides of the property, and Orli wondered how something so beautiful managed to grow in a place like Turu. In a place that routinely smelled of rotting carcasses. It didn't look like the Turu that she knew, that she grew up in.

She stepped up to the wide door and knocked as loud as she could. Her heart thumped frantically against her chest, rattling with each beat. She rubbed her arm, her fur shedding more than normal on the swept clean landing. Maybe Rayna won't be home.

Orli fiddled with her belt, double checking that everything was in its place for no reason at all, when the large door slid open.

And there she was. Rayna Ares.

Her tall jackalope antlers were adorned with a sparkling gold lace that Orli couldn't even fathom the cost of, and a deep blue shawl was draped over the long body of her childhood friend.

"Orli," she said, holding a tight smile in place as her eyes bounced around, trying to find meaning in her old friend appearing after so long. "What are you doing here?"

"Hi Rayna." Despite her attempts at sounding professional, Orli stuttered. "May... May I come in?"

Rayna's smile remained, now very clearly forced, as she opened the door further and welcomed Orli inside. The jackalope scowled as she watched Orli's mud-soaked feet step inside her home.

The bigfoot suddenly recalled a time when she and Rayna threw owlmen droppings on a random house's lawn right here in Royal Kire, perhaps her brain's defense mechanism against the conversation that was coming. Orli stifled her inappropriate laugh at the poorly timed memory and tried to remain calm.

"Banut," Rayna said, yelling up the stairs to her husband. "The policefoot—"

Rayna turned back to Orli, her beady eyes confused and concerned, before continuing. "Orli is here."

As they got situated, taking seats in the living area, Banut hopped into the room.

"Orli," Banut said. "What's going on?"

"Rayna, Banut. I'm so sorry to be the one to tell you." Orli paused, unsure of how to continue. Tears welled in her eyes. "We found Kevan's body—"

"Kevan? No, you must be mistaken. He was just here yesterday..." Rayna's voice drifted off and her body started to vibrate. Banut wrapped his paws over her shoulder.

"What happened, Orli?" Banut asked.

"His body was found last night by the abandoned factory. We've begun a formal investigation–"

"Kevan wouldn't be over there. At that factory? No. The one over by all the merwhore-houses right? Kevan wouldn't be over there." Banut sputtered his words, his face a mask of disbelief.

"I know how hard this must be. Please, come down to the station sometime today. You'll be able to confirm it's Kevan. I am so, so sorry for your loss."

"My son! My son is not some piece of trash that goes over there!" Rayna said, her words cutting deep, like she knew they would. She had been sitting silent, but now breathed heavy, her anger taking over as her thick fur coat stood on end.

Orli tried not to let it in, but that accusation was a knife in her gut. An accusation that the other side of town was filled with low-lives and unworthy creatures. That was her home. She looked down, doing all she could to avert her gaze from Rayna's glare. Orli's fur shed an unnatural amount on the chair she sat in.

"Once again, I'm so sorry for your loss." Orli struggled to remain calm. "Please, come see us today if you can."

Rayna sobbed and clutched a cushion on the ostentatious couch while Banut still stood, his brow furrowed and mouth turned down.

The policefoot turned and left the living area, walking down the long length of the entrance way towards the front door. As she approached, Orli noticed a dark smudge behind the door handle. She was out of view of the family, so she knelt down to get a better look.

As soon as she got close, she could smell it: that iron-rich stench of blood.

Kevan

The morning of the murder

"Kevan! Honey!" His mom's grating voice rattled Kevan's tired and hungover mind. "Kevan, wake up! Breakfast is ready!"

Kevan pawed at his crusty eyes, rubbing them until he could see. Harsh sun poured through the large windows in his room, and he shielded himself from the sudden brightness. He rose from the bed, eyes still squinting, and felt around for his short bristle brush.

When he managed to find it on the floor, hidden under debris from last night, he walked to his mirror and brought it to his body. The bristles rubbed against his brown fur while he stared at the bedraggled state of himself.

Last night's activities had clearly taken a toll on him: rough fur, bags under his eyes, and… was that glitter on his antlers? He thought of her and smiled. He thought of her warm embrace. And that glitter! So. Much. Glitter.

He finished brushing and started to wipe down his antlers with a special lotion, smearing it until all traces of the glitter were gone. If anyone noticed it… Best to not let that happen.

He wrapped a lush blanket around his body, peeked one last time in the mirror, and hopped downstairs in search of food.

"Honey! You slept so late today, I was getting worried!" Rayna bustled around the kitchen, placing silverware on the table and turning plates to they were just right.

"Mother, you know how important my beauty rest is! I looked an absolute fright this morning." Kevan chose a spot at the table and pulled his improvised cloak tighter around his body.

"Oh honey," she said. "I'm so sorry for waking you!" She rubbed her chin on the top of his head. He relaxed a bit, satisfied, and smiled.

Platters of carrots, spinach, and other green nonsense were set on the elaborate table and Kevan groaned when he saw the options.

"Ugh, Mother!" Kevan pouted as he dropped his fork carelessly. "Why are we having plants for breakfast again? They have no taste!"

"Oh, Kevan, honey. They'll give you good bones. Eat up. And tell me how your night was."

"Just hung out, nothing special." A little white lie never hurt anyone.

"Sounds lovely, dear. Were you with your friends, Jahat and those boys?"

"Yes, Mother." Kevan was becoming annoyed at the incessant questions. "Same people as always."

His night certainly started with Jahat and Draak, but it ended somewhere else. A place where his heart could soar. He shoveled more of the flavorless green mush into his mouth before storming from the room, and shouting as he left.

"Going out again, bye!"

Kevan walked past the colorful row of houses and towards the lakes, on his way to meet his friends at the edge of the forest. His long paws sunk into the freshly cut green grass as he hopped past the largest of the lakes.

"Hi Kevan," a voice shouted from the water.

He looked in that direction and a merwoman giggled and waved, whispering something to her friends. One of the kraken rose up from the water, commanding her attention instead, its long tentacles splashing the merwomen. Kevan kept hopping past, never slowing down.

He arrived at the small clearing last, Draak and Jahat laughing, no doubt reveling in their memories of the exploits from last night.

Draak purred when he saw Kevan approaching, and Jahat fluttered his wings, rising from his rock perch and into the air. Draak was a mngwa, one of many that lived in the Royal Kire neighborhood, the black stripes along his long cat-like body accentuated in the morning light.

Jahat was an ahool from a storied genetic line with roots all the way back to the beginning of monster exile in Turu. The ahools were not the only monsters in Turu with broad wings that let them sail across the city in minutes; it was their strong, bursting chests and long limbs that made others fear them, that let them tower over others, even when firmly on the ground. Doesn't mean they couldn't be friendly, though.

Jahat smiled at Kevan, his sharp white teeth clicking in excitement, as he lowered himself back on the rock, his large claws clicking as he relaxed.

"Kevan! Tonight's the night, friend," said Jahat with a grin across his face.

"I know, I know. Do we know exactly what time the moon rises today?"

Draak purred again, stepping forward, and said, "Not sure exactly, I think sometime after nine."

"Good. With Jessica, we should finally be able to stand up to those mothmen." Kevan sounded calm, despite the hard look on his face.

"Do either of you know where she stays between moons?" Jahat asked, batting his wings in anticipation. "I know she tries to stay inside, not show her face, blah, blah. It'd be nice to pay her a visit before things get too crazy."

Jahat looked like he was going to keep babbling on about nothing, when a loud crack echoed from the forest. The three friends spun, looking towards the noise. Despite the morning sun casting long shadows around them, the forest was dark. Darker than it should be. A chill ran through Kevan.

Another loud crack, this time closer, followed by another, rang out. Jahat fluttered his wings, once again rising above the rock he was perched on, while Draak moved into a defensive position in front of his friends.

"Perhaps it's time to get out of here," Draak said.

Jahat laughed at Draak. "What are you afraid of? The scary piasa?"

"It could be anything!" Draak was growling now.

"You guys are both dumb, the piasa isn't real. It's just a stupid story," Kevan said. "I gotta go anyway. What's the plan for later?"

"Ya know, my uncle knows creatures who hunt the piasa," said Draak. "There's a whole group of 'em that believe–"

"All nonsense," said Jahat with a short laugh. "That's all nonsense."

"Focus!" Frustration coated Kevan's words. "We need a plan for tonight. Find Jessica and then what?"

"Let's just go to Pashimi's again. The mothmen don't typically show themselves there," Draak said.

They all agreed and made their way back to Royal Kire.

Malse

Malse needed to figure out how he was going to prove the mothmen murdered Kevan, but the information Sigrun had just revealed was a good start.

He waited at the Devil's Syndicate base for his comrades to finish their gossiping so that he could follow Sigrun back into Turu. It wasn't hard. His rival was awkward and not at all sure-footed, an embarrassment to all Jersey devils. He also appeared a bit worse for the wear, his face swollen and bruised.

He was hoping that Sigrun would head straight to whatever hunting club he referred to back at basecamp, at a church he recalled. But of course, Sigrun couldn't keep himself away from the merwomen.

Malse waited outside as Sigrun burst into Pashimi's, the bar having just opened. If Malse walked in, Sigrun would notice him in the thin crowds. Instead, he slunk around the side of the bar, hoping to find a window to peer into the place.

As expected, there was almost no one inside except for a couple of aliens, already drunk from the hair of the demon. Malse could barely make out the conversation, catching only a few words here and there.

"...later if you...another..." Pashimi giggled after winking at the aliens.

Sigrun made his way to the other end of the bar, the side closer to the window, and Malse ducked lower, hoping not to be spotted through the grimey glass.

"What can I do for you, Sigrun?"

Sigrun leaned over the bar, a hungry look in his eyes, as he said, "You ladies still offering the mermosa special?"

Pashimi scoffed and swam back to the aliens, shouting her reply across the bar. "No, everyone pays for their drinks and their merwomen. No special treatment, especially not for you!"

Everyone at the bar gazed at Sigrun with untrusting eyes. Malse never liked his roommate, but this was a new low. Trying to get out of paying for sex? Pathetic.

"C'mon, I had a rough night. Can't you tell?" Sigrun asked, not giving up. His face had changed then, no longer determined, as his eyes dropped and a note of desperation entered his voice. "Why not help out a devil in need?"

Pashimi returned to Sigrun's side of the bar and dropped a tin mug in front of him. "What, not enough monsters to beat up?"

Sigrun's jaw dropped open in mock offense. "What, me? I would never."

The haggling continued for several more minutes, and Malse was about to abandon the window, when he thought he heard one of the aliens say something about mothmen.

"...fight last... factory..."

"Oh that fight? Those guys are fuckin' losers," Sigrun said, laughing. "Chased me down but I got the best of 'em! I'm too strong, ask anyone, they never had a chance."

Sigrun was there last night. This revelation shocked Malse. Maybe he saw something; hell, maybe he was even involved! No, that can't be true. The mothmen must have done this. Malse hated everything Sigrun stood for, but there's no way a devil killed Kevan Ares.

Right?

Orli

Orli stepped away from the Ares household, gazing at the massive structure with a sense of distrust and sadness. There was something they weren't telling her. Something happened there, something that no one wanted to talk about.

It was the blood that truly concerned her. Smeared on the inside of the Ares' front door, it had long since dried and darkened. Maybe it belonged to their son? Or perhaps something more sinister was afoot.

Even though they'd grown apart, she could never envision Rayna lying to a policefoot, especially one she once considered a friend. Maybe it was Banut that knew more than he was letting on? How could they not have noticed that blood? It was right there on the front door.

If the blood belonged to someone that lived inside that house, it might not break the case open, but it could shed additional light on what was going on. Hopefully her team back at the station would be able to provide more information.

A low growl broke her from her reverie and she spun. A young mngwa stepped towards her slowly, its sharp, dark eyes never wavering from her. The big cat had its teeth bared, a sign that it didn't trust Orli. After a long pause, the creature finally spoke.

"Are you the one that's gonna find who killed Kevan?"

"Who's asking?"

"Draak. Kevan was my best friend." The mngwa paused, dropping his head. "We were together last night, but we got split up. If I had stayed with him…"

The monster looked downcast. His gray fur was accentuated by shiny black stripes, common of mngwas, and his paws splayed wide on the ground. Maybe too wide?

"It would be a big help to this investigation if you could tell me what happened," Orli said. "From the beginning."

Draak nodded.

"It was stupid. These mothmen had been following us the past few nights, beating up on us," Draak said. "We tried avoiding them, ya know, but they seemed to always know where we were."

"How many?" Orli asked.

"Three or four. We ran into them a couple times. Elrong was the ring-leader. He was always there."

Orli made a mental note. This was the second time the name Elrong came up in her investigation. The first time was from Malse, who thought the mothmen gang presented a threat to the Devil's Syndicate.

"Okay," she continued. "Last night, where were you?"

"Well, first we all met up at Pashimi's–"

"Who's we all? More than you and Kevan?"

"Yeah, us, plus Jahat and Jessica."

Orli recalled Jahat, the son of the rich ahool family living in Royal Kire. Turu founder's blood, if she recalled. The name Jessica was unfamiliar, maybe foreign?

"Who's Jessica?"

"She's… she likes to stay hidden. No one in Turu likes her."

Orli recalled her conversation from earlier that morning with Pashimi. "Is Jessica a werewolf?"

"Yes, ma'am. Last night was the full moon, we thought with Jessica turned…" Draak shook his head. "Them mothmen still managed to beat up on us good. Probably would've killed us if they didn't run off."

"They ran off? Why?"

"Sorry, ma'am, I don't know. They were fighting us full force, then they were just gone. Like maybe they were chasing someone else."

Orli's eyes lingered on the cat in front of her, watched his thick paws tap the uneven ground they stood on. Something about his demeanor gave her an odd feeling.

"And what about after the fight? What happened?"

Draak turned his head in shame.

"We scattered. I just ran as fast as I could, I thought everyone was with me. When I stopped, no one was there. None of them could keep up, I guess. I never saw Kevan again."

"Draak, would you mind if I looked at your claws?"

The request surprised the mngwa, and he raised a paw, examining it himself. Was he checking if there was something incriminating?

"Don't see why not."

Orli pulled out a picture of the scratch wounds from Kevan's body and knelt down in front of Draak. Holding the photo up next to his paw, Orli could tell immediately that it didn't match. The medical examiner's note about the spacing was correct. There was no way a single paw could've made those marks.

She rose. "One last question, Draak. Do you know where I can find Jessica?"

"Sorry, no, she likes to move around. Prefers to stay inside, away from everyone, unless it's a full moon. She doesn't feel safe here in Turu," Draak said. "Last night, Jahat found her and brought her to Pashimi's, but he didn't say where she was."

Orli thanked Draak, and decided she needed to visit the ahools.

Orli walked through Royal Kire towards the lush treetop homes of the ahools. It had been a while since she set foot there, and as it came into view, she was in awe.

Large structures sat nestled in the crooks of tall, thick trees and the ground was overgrown with jungle plants. She stepped into the area and the oppressive humidity of the rainforest climate immediately pressed down, her heavy brown fur only making things worse. The smell of rich vegetation overcame her.

Since this scattered jungle home did not have any semblance of a front doorbell, she just decided to shout.

"Jahat? Policefoot Orli here. I'm hoping to talk to you about last night."

A rustling came from one of the treetop structures and a groggy ahool stepped into view.

"Yeah, I... Just give me a second."

Orli waited several minutes before Jahat finally lowered himself from the tree, beating his wings to slow his descent.

"Sorry, long night."

"Yeah, that's why I'm here. Can you tell me what happened?"

"Yeah, sure, but why? Went out with a few friends, got in a few fights. Definitely had too much to drink, ha, but nothing illegal I promise. Why you askin'?"

Orli's face fell. "I assumed you knew…"

"Knew what?" Jahat laughed nervously. "I'll tell you now, I definitely hurt a mothman last night but that's the craziest my night got."

"Jahat, I'm so sorry. We found Kevan's body early this morning. Your friend's been murdered."

Jahat's mouth opened so far, Orli was able to see his spiky teeth all the way in the back. "What? No, there's no way. We fought the mothmen, but we all got away. We all ran away."

"Yes, I've heard some about that fight. Where did you go after?"

"Me? I came home. Everyone went home, I assumed. We just kinda ran away fast, trying to get away from them."

"So you came straight back here?"

"Um, well no. We scattered, yeah, but then eventually ended up together somewhere near all the bars," he said. "We were all pretty shaken up and just decided to leave, stop with the nonsense for the night."

A slightly different tale than she'd heard from Draak.

"You all? Who's that?"

"Oh, sorry, yeah, it was me and Kevan and Jessica and Draak. We all just decided to call it a night."

"Jessica, huh? Do you know where I might be able to find her?"

"She moves around a lot. Yesterday I think she was at one of those sketchy inns on the outskirts of the city, the ones no one really goes to. She might still be there…" Jahat raised his foot to his face, scratching the side of his head with long, thin claws.

Orli eyed him as he scratched, his fingers moving quickly up and down, and said, "This is just procedure, doing it with everyone, but can I take a look at those paws of yours?"

Jahat laughed nervously again. "Sure, course…"

A chill ran down her spine as she noticed the claws on the winged creature were much thinner than those she saw on the big cat earlier. The spacing between them, though. Still not quite right.

"I think that's it for now, okay Jahat? I might need to ask some more questions later, as we start to figure more out, if that's okay?"

The ahool nodded and flew back to his nest above.

Jessica

Jessica peeled open her crusty eyes, confused by her surroundings. As shadows began to form in the milky darkness around her, it all came back to her. The mothmen, the fight.

At some point today, she was going to need to get dressed and step outside this disgusting factory, but she was going to put that off as long as possible. She rose from the concrete floor as her eyes continued to adjust, the skeletons of heavy machinery surrounding her.

The creatures in Turu thought the abandoned factory was haunted, killing monsters without regard.

The noises, the clattering metal and crunching concrete? She convinced herself daily that none of it fazed her, just an old building and probably someone else claiming their space.

Jessica came to a window, the pale morning light leaking through the cracked panes and illuminating her ghostly white skin. Jessica looked over herself, confirming there was not a drop of blood in sight. She must have licked it off last night when she returned.

Her human skin contained not a mark on it. Her wolf body was stronger, more resilient. Minor scratches wouldn't transform when her body returned to its weaker state.

Jessica climbed onto the window's ledge and peered into the street. It was empty, just how she liked it. The creatures in Turu feared humans, so she did her best to stay away from the public eye. Sleeping in alleys, only coming out among the lowest of low-lives. That's how she met the devils. Devilish they were, alright, swindling the poorest monsters in the city for an extra buck.

But hey, she had to make her living somehow. For so long she'd found success as the eyes and ears of the Devil's Syndicate. No one could have a secret conversation around here without Jessica listening in. It was easy, especially in her nimble human body, to fit into small hideaways that were too cramped for the usual residents of Turu.

Things changed though, when she heard that little jackalope bragging to his friends about money. The Bougie Boys, she'd called them. They were cute. Young and stupid, too. When she mentioned the conversation to Ronic, one of her mafia contacts, he agreed it was an opportunity.

Next thing you know, Jessica was rolling with the richies. She was hoping the jackalope would fall in love with her. That's why she always stood up for him, getting mixed up in that shit with mothmen. Stupid. Stupid, stupid, stupid!

She thought back to the fight. Kevan trying to be a tough guy, using his antlers to shove at their opponents. She landed a few very good blows, at least. The mothmen would be hurting today. She still wasn't sure why their opponents all left though, almost like they got distracted. It at least gave her and Kevan a chance to run. They managed to get into the crowded streets without further issue.

What happened to his little rich friends though? Ah, what did she care? The silly creatures were going to get themselves killed, and it wasn't her problem one bit.

Jessica climbed down from the mantle and lowered herself to the ground, leaning against the aged brick wall. The shadows in the dark factory shifted, as if the ghosts of its past still lingered, watching and waiting.

The sudden sound of clattering metal bounced off the walls, echoing with a persistent rattle. The unexpected noise broke Jessica from her reverie and she tensed as she heard the commotion.

Not haunted, she reminded herself. The noises were completely normal.

Nonetheless, she slid behind a crumbling pile of boxes and pulled her knees close to her chest.

A quiet voice spoke through misty blackness.

"Jessica? Where are you? It's me."

Jessica rolled her eyes and considered staying hidden. Ronic, of course. The Syndicate always came calling. She didn't feel like talking to him right now, but she had to. She stood and stepped into view.

"What do you want now?" she asked, annoyance spilling between her words. "How did you even find me?"

"C'mon, you're never that hard to find. I can smell a human from anywhere," he explained. "I came to ask for an update on the Ares situation. This was your idea, your op. Not sure what changed, why you're trying to avoid me now. What's the status?"

"Kevan doesn't carry his riches around with him. He's dumb, but not that dumb. This is going to take time. He needs to trust me, love me."

"The boss is getting antsy." Ronic sighed. "The longer this goes, the higher the chance of failure. Of Kevan finding out your plan."

Jessica was avoiding eye contact. There was no update to give, but she needed to think of something. "I need him to invite me into his home. In Royal Kire. That's the first step. I'm working on it, Ronic."

Ronic nodded at that. "Well, be careful. There's tons of investigators roaming the streets out there. Must have been a busy night in this shithole. I had to fly in to get close enough to this damn factory."

Jessica nodded, folding in on herself. She definitely had to be careful.

Orli

Orli stood at the end of the alleyway, feet away from where Kevan Ares' gruesome murder took place. She came straight here after visiting Royal Kire, hoping that maybe she'd notice something she hadn't before. One of her chupacabra guards stood nearby to prevent meddling.

Along the right side of the alley was a green dumpster, dented and rusting. As she stepped past it, she glanced into it for any clues, but instead was met with the smell of rotting lizard shit and standing water.

She stopped there, in the middle of the alley, and took in the scene. Chunks of brick occasionally fell from the crumbling facade, and the air around her was still. Almost too still.

But no matter how long she examined this place, nothing stood out.

For decades, Turu had avoided major conflicts between the bougies and the slumbags, and she was always hopeful that maybe things were starting to get better. Sure, there was the occasional robbery, usually some rich socialite meddling in the ghetto with a creature that had nothing to lose. She'd seen a few break-ins over in Royal Kire as well, desperation bringing out the worst.

But this? A murder? Why would Kevan Ares seek out trouble over here? Why were the mothmen bothering him? Was he hiding something? There was something she was missing.

Orli continued forward, broken glass crunching underfoot.

Several broken bags of refuse lay strewn past the dumpster. Pools of blood from the murder were still there. Orli glanced around, and then raised her eyes. At the top of the building was a wide, shattered window. No real surprise there, most of the windows at this abandoned factory were destroyed, but what caught Orli's eye was the blood that tinged the edges of the glass.

She took a few steps back, hoping for a better angle, when she heard loud metal crashing echoing from within the building. She jumped, wondering at first if maybe someone had spotted her and tried to run. But there was no one there, no one in that window above, at least.

Orli rushed back into the street, looking for her chupacabra standing guard.

"You," she said to him, forgetting his name. "Did you just hear that?"

The lanky creature spun at her voice and cowered against the outside wall of the factory, before realizing who was calling for him. What a useless creature.

He regained his composure and shook his head in reply, and Orli said, "Okay, well, I'm going into the factory. Stay here. If I'm not back in twenty minutes, come find me."

Orli walked down the street to the nearest doorway. The rusted door was cracked, welcoming in any who dared enter the supposedly haunted building. It let out an ear-piercing creak as her large paw opened it further, and she ducked inside.

Darkness surrounded her. Without hesitation, Orli found her flashlight on her belt and flicked it on. A long hallway opened in front of her, shadows dancing as the yellow beam moved with her slow steps. The light was unable to penetrate the gloom so she continued forward carefully, not sure where the long passageway led. Skittering, muffled noises surrounded her. The place must be infested with vermin.

Eventually, an empty doorway stood in front of her, broken hinges on the left. At least she doesn't need to break in.

Her light bounced around, highlighting large machinery and vaulted ceilings. She searched for the broken window she saw outside. A metal stairway led to a catwalk running along the edge of the large room. There were several wide windows near the ceiling. Only one of those windows was shattered. She began to climb. When Orli got there, dried blood coated everything. The metal grates below her feet, the brick wall, the broken glass.

Her earlier assumption was wrong. The murder didn't happen down below, it happened up here. This is an entirely new crime scene.

She collected multiple samples of the blood, labeling each. *Window. Floor. Wall.* Then, she looked down onto the alley below. If the murder occurred up here, Kevan must have been thrown from the window.

Or did it occur up here? Was he alive when he was thrown out the window?

The sound of muffled conversation stilled her and Orli turned off her light, hoping to hide her presence. If someone was here, they may have witnessed something last night. The conversation sounded far off, possibly from the other side of the dark factory.

She tried to remain quiet as she made her way back to the lower level, but her lumbering body caused the metal stairs to creak. Orli needed to move quickly if she wanted to find out who was here.

On the ground floor, she moved towards the voices. Towering machinery lined her way, retired mechanical beasts that once performed some function unknown to her. Thick cobwebs dampened the little light that managed to leak in. There was a rather large hole in the ceiling above this part of the building, small pieces of crumbled cement occasionally falling nearby.

Eventually, she reached the other side of the building, which had far more natural light and was lined with windows. The sound of scuffling attracted her attention.

"Ronic, I thought you were leaving," a female voice called, as a head came into view behind piles of boxes.

Orli continued towards the unfamiliar creature. "Who's there?"

"Shit!" The voice sounded frantic, and the other monster ran from Orli, ducking back behind the boxes.

Orli pounced at the boxes, her massive body crushing through the rotting cardboard and bounding after whatever moved. It was a tiny thing she chased, and her seven foot tall body easily tackled it from behind. She rolled them over and eyed the unfamiliar face.

It was a human.

"Who are you?"

"I'd rather not answer that," the human answered back, an unfortunate smirk plastered across its face.

It seemed Orli had found Jessica.

Kevan

The afternoon of the murder

Kevan was in love. There was no other way to put it. His heart ached with longing as his group roamed on the edge of Turu, in the shadow of the towering cliffs.

"Why you so quiet, Kevan?" Draak said.

"Ah it's nothing." Kevan forced a smile. "Think I'm still just a little tired after last night."

Kevan continued to hop forward, wishing he could be wrapped in that tight embrace. He longed for her despite knowing it would never be possible, not long-term.

"She's late. Why is she always so damn late?" Jahat was frustrated as he fluttered his wings, hovering. They waited for Jessica so their day could begin.

"Is your entire family that impatient?" came a snarky reply from behind them.

Kevan spun as Jessica approached. The full moon would be rising tonight, but until then, Jessica remained human-appearing. She was thin and small compared to the monstrous trio, but once converted she was taller, faster, and more dangerous than all of them combined.

"Well I don't got all day, ya know?" Jahat rolled his eyes at her.

Jessica glanced at them all but when her blue eyes landed on Kevan they lingered. Her eyes were so hypnotizing, and he couldn't pull his gaze away.

"Kevan," she said with a smile. "It's been a while."

He chuckled and bounced away, saying "I brought some bootleg booze, if you guys wanna start early?"

"Is it that same shit you stole from your dad?" Draak asked as he followed. "That gives me the worst hangovers!"

"Do you want free booze or not, my dude?" Kevan said over his shoulder.

Jahat shoved his way past the others and wrapped a winged arm around Kevan, a single nail poking Kevan's shoulder, and grabbed the bottle with one of his clawed feet. He took a swig before giving the bottle back. With his wing still wrapped fondly around Kevan, Jahat looked at him and said, "I just want you to know how much I 'preciate this okay?"

The ahool's jagged teeth were bared in what some might consider a threatening manner, but Kevan knew Jahat better than that. Their friendship went back further than anyone else.

Jackalopes weren't exactly the most common monsters in Turu, especially not in Royal Kire. There were lots of water creatures, like kraken and merwomen, as well as the big cats, like Draak and his family of mngwas. The ahools were the kings, though. Their wingspans were intimidating and their jungle subdivision took up a large section of Royal Kire.

So when Kevan first went to school with the other monster kids, he stuck out like a sore thumb. But Jahat never batted an eye.

"Hey dude," the ahool had said, a friendly grin plastered across his face. Kevan found it hard to turn away from the smile ever since.

He looked back at his best friend, wrapped his own paw behind Jahat's wings, and leaned in. "I know you appreciate it, Jahat."

"Okay boys, stop being all lovey-dovey, you make me wanna puke," Jessica said.

Jahat released Kevan and stood taller. "Shut up, *human*."

Draak laughed. "Someone pass me that damn bottle."

It was passed, round and round again, as the group of friends slowly began to inhibit themselves for what they hoped would be the night they finally got the mothmen off their backs.

Malse was still reeling from Sigrun's revelation. The Jersey devil was there last night, he was involved in a fight with Kevan Ares, maybe even involved in the jackalope's death.

After knocking back several more mugs of ale and continuing to heckle Pashimi, his rival finally decided it was time to move on. Malse was thankful. His position outside the window was uncomfortable, and the stench of the nearby trash in the alley was starting to wear him down.

Sigrun led him on a winding path past more bars and merwhorehouses, towards the center of Turu. They passed through the neighborhood Malse grew up in, and the familiar building facades gave him a sense of nostalgia. He couldn't wait to escape this place and his broken family, but now? He missed it, longed for those warm summer nights playing make-believe with Orli and Rayna. The area had fared worse since he left, graffiti—*MOTH TRASH SUCK NESSIE'S DIK,* it screamed—marking the sides of not only abandoned shops, but also the homes of his former neighbors.

It saddened him that people lived here.

Eventually, they arrived at The Church of Our Deity Loch Ness. The one place all of Turu felt safe.

It was right on the line—yes, a literal line in the sand—that divided Royal Kire from the rest of Turu. The vandalism and violence was slowly starting to seep into Royal Kire, the emotions of the lower class finally starting to boil over, that line in the sand blurring more every day.

Sigrun stepped into the building where every monster went to worship. This must be where this hunting club is. Malse still didn't know what in the world they might be hunting.

He waited several minutes before following Sigrun in, hoping he wouldn't be spotted. There were several rooms along the long hallway in front of him, muffled voices drifting out of one at the end. Malse set up in the room next door, able to hear and see nearly everything through a small hole in the paper thin wall.

The room had several chairs set up, plus a few tables. There were what appeared to be pastries and the like arranged haphazardly. There was a decent group of monsters attending: chupacabras, aliens, owlmen, and lizardmen.

There was also an ahool, which surprised Malse. He'd assume this crowd was too lowly for a rich ahool.

"Seems like we got a newbie here, eh?" The ahool said, eating a hunk of dried skin with glittery frosting. It looked like some sort of mermaid scale cookie.

"That's right, Jahat," an alien replied and then turned towards Sigrun. "Why don't you introduce yourself? How'd you find us?"

"Yeah, I uh…" Sigrun cleared his throat. He was nervous. "I overheard some talk at Pashimi's. About hunting the piasa? Yeah, I was curious, figured I'd come check it out."

Malse held in a laugh, nearly choking as he did so. The piasa was a child's tale, a fabled monster he doesn't remember hearing about since he was young. He suddenly recalled a memory from his childhood, running around a fire somewhere in the slums of Turu with Orli and Rayna. They sang a song about the evil beast.

Once around the berry bush
Opening wide its hungry maw
Twice around the northern star
Comes the ferocious piasa.

He smiled at the thought.

"So, you're *not* a Syndicate grunt then?" Jahat asked, jarring Malse from his reverie.

"I swear to Nessie, absolutely not," Sigrun said. He was a good actor.

"Well," the alien continued. "Let me officially welcome you to the Piasa Hunter Acquisition Team. This group formed decades ago, with the sole purpose of finding the piasa."

"I always thought that was just for children…"

"No, no. We don't think so. There have been veritable sightings, proof, over the years. Whether or not it's the piasa, we are still not sure. But a long, scaled bird, or some other creature with wings, haunts this city."

"This is amazing," Sigrun said. Malse could tell the devil's amazement was fake, and he could see his roommate wanted to mock the alien. "Who has seen it?"

"I can share the record books with you later. We have sketches, drawings, all done by members of PHAT. But the details are consistent. A bearded face, glittering scales. Everything you heard in those tales as a child, there is some basis in reality. That's enough for now, though. Let's get started!"

The alien turned to address the rest of the room.

"No new sightings or data to report this month, unfortunately, but I was hoping a few of our members could share with us anything they found or encountered on their recent hunts. I believe some of you looked into the source of that red feather we found out on the edge of the forest last month, care to share more info?"

There was some murmuring amongst the PHAT members in response to this, but no one seemed to supply any interesting information. Malse was getting frustrated. This had to be a dead-end. These conspiracy theorists didn't seem to have any meaningful connection to the mothmen or to the death of Kevan Ares.

"The feather had to belong to something, right guys? We'll keep hunting, we'll find something eventually!" This was the alien speaking again. He sounded desperately hopeful.

The alien looked at some notes, and asked, "Did anyone happen to follow up at the factory?" Silence around the room, a few shakes of the head. "Jahat, you expressed interest in that last month, right?"

Malse was about to abandon this silly meeting, but upon hearing mention of the factory, he remained where he was. Jahat, who now had frosting on the edges of his mouth, seemed to stiffen at the mention of his name.

"Haven't been to the factory in a bit, busy month, ha." His look was apologetic, but forced. Was this ahool hiding something? His wings curled out and back, in a rhythmic pattern. Along the edge of Jahat's wings were sharp points, and each time he curled them in, the normally separated barbs clicked against each other.

"What about the factory?" Sigrun asked. He finally asked a good question.

"Ah, yes," the alien said. "Last month, there was a sighting of something flying over the abandoned factory on the outskirts of the city. A few of us went over there, and we found large claw marks in the bricks on one side. Now, claw marks alone don't necessarily point to the piasa, as nearly every creature in Turu has claws, but on the ground below the marks were more red feathers.

"They were old though, so we were unable to confirm that the red feathers at the factory were the same as the one found in the forest. We decided to leave further hunting to the rest of the PHAT members. Jahat was the only one who volunteered to go."

So not only was this ahool at a hunting club with the city's low-lives, but he was volunteering for hunts over at the factory. Something about Jahat was suspicious to Malse, but he couldn't put a hoof on what. Perhaps coming here wasn't a waste of time after all.

"The betting group isn't going to be happy about the results though," the alien continued. "They're meeting later today, out by the lakes in Royal Kire. I heard lots of them put money down on something being found at the factory."

And with that, Malse ran from church. He knew where he had to go next.

Jessica sat across from Orli, slumped in a rusting metal chair in a cramped room at the police station. She refused to look the bigfoot in the eye.

"Jessica. Took me a bit to realize it was you."

The girl remained still. Orli had been trying to get her to speak up, to say anything, for nearly an hour now. The most she got from her was a slight shift in her posture when she mentioned that Kevan had been murdered.

"Okay, you don't need to say anything if you don't want to yet. But I'm going to lay out what I know."

Orli rearranged her notes in front of her before continuing. "Last night was the full moon. I know that you, at some point before the moonrise, met up with your friends. Kevan, Jahat, Draak. What did you guys do? Pre-party? Drinking? Loosen yourselves up for a night on the town, right?

"I know that you met up with them. I know because I've already spoken to Jahat and Draak. At some point, you turned. I assume you then felt more comfortable being in public, having lost your human appearance.

"I haven't quite fit all the puzzle pieces together yet, but there was a fight. I know you tried to stand up to Elrong and his gang of mothmen, and I know you failed in that task."

Jessica grunted, a sly smile creeping across her face. Her first reaction since they arrived back at the station. Still no eye contact, though. Or words.

Orli sighed and shook her head. "If that's not what happened, Jessica, then tell me what did. I'm only trying to find the truth."

Jessica's head rose, her blue eyes resting on Orli, and she said, "Those mothmen were hurt. They ran away from us. Never got a chance to finish the damn job!"

Orli leaned back. She still didn't understand why they ran. This piece of information could be the key.

"Okay, the mothmen ran away. Then what?"

More silence from Jessica, but at least her head was raised now.

Orli took a gamble. "You all run, where? Back towards Pashimi's, right? Regroup before calling it a night?"

The pale skin on Jessica's forehead wrinkled and her eyebrows dropped. So that's not what happened.

"No? Did you all just scatter? Run home?"

Jessica slouched in the chair and looked back to Orli.

"Okay, yes, I ran towards the factory, found a spot to hide," the lycan-thrope said. "It's not the nicest place to crash, but I was desperate."

"Okay, good, good. And Kevan? He was with you?"

Jessica got defensive again. Angry. "What? No, I just told you we all scattered. No one was with me. I ran because we all ran. I passed out where you found me."

Orli sighed and thought back to what she'd heard from Kevan's friends earlier. Jahat said they regrouped before deciding to head home. All of the stories she's heard differ. Who was lying?

Orli stood in the lab with the lizardman medical examiner, looking down at the test results from the blood found on the door handle inside the Ares household.

"Give it to me straight," she demanded as she set aside the paper. "These numbers don't mean anything to me."

"Well, that blood belongs to a mothman."

Orli wasn't sure what she was expecting, but the blood of a mothman wasn't it. She ran back to her office, grabbing another shroom tea on the way, and flipped through her notes.

The mothmen were at the center of this case. They provoked and bullied the victim and his friends. Malse, since he nearly burst into Orli's home earlier that morning, was sure Elrong was involved.

She needed to hear his side. She needed to talk to Elrong.

Orli loaded up her utility belt, and was about to head back out to find the mothmen, when the doors to the station burst open. A tall, dark mngwa strode towards her. The low hum of the station paused, every monster around her stopping what they were doing to watch.

"I've come to submit a formal complaint against Draak and his family." The creature had a deep voice, that of an elder. The voice of a mngwa who has lived long and seen much.

Orli glanced around the room with raised eyes, before turning to address him. "How can I help, sir?"

"Draak, he runs with bad crowds. Bringing Kevan Ares around our youngest, into our neighborhood. Our quiet, friendly neighborhood. And also that troublemaker ahool, why won't those filthy monsters die off already?"

"Sir, Kevan Ares was found–"

"Oh I know he was murdered, just proves my point. Bad news, that Kevan. I'm sure he got what was coming to him, hanging around where he does. And Draak brings it home with him, ok? I don't need my kids seeing the discarded remnants of a night with those merwhores in my own neighborhood!"

Orli cringed at the insult before replying.

"Okay, let's slow down and start at the beginning. What happened?"

The mngwa sighed and began pacing, clearly upset that Orli couldn't read between the lines.

"This morning, I found scales. Glittery scales, all over the ground, right in front of my house. And do you know what my kids asked me? They wanted to know if they came from a mermaid. I did my best to explain it off as a fluke, but how else would those show up near our home? The closest mermaids live several blocks away." The mngwa took a breath and continued. "Clearly that Draak boy was out last night, out with merwhores. Bringing his leftover trash to our home."

It took a while, but Orli eventually managed to collect a coherent story from the mngwa. Each new detail of this story further confused Orli, rather than bringing her any clarity. She was frustrated.

Time for another trip to Royal Kire.

Malse

A Jersey devil strutting around Royal Kire isn't exactly uncommon—the Devil's Syndicate has a lot of hands in the wealth of the city, after all—so Malse just tried to act like he belonged. The colors assaulted his eyes as he wandered through the streets of the ritzy neighborhood.

He had never actually been in this part of Turu himself, so he had no idea what lakes the alien back at the PHAT meeting was talking about. His best chance, he figured, was wandering around until he found them. How hard can it be to find lakes, anyways?

The answer: far longer than it should have. He had to navigate nearly every street in Royal Kire before realizing that the lakes were outside the crumbling walls.

He could only hope he didn't miss this supposed meeting involving bets, as it could turn out to be incredibly useful.

At the back of the collection lakes was a small hut sitting half on land, half on water. A table ran through the middle of the hut, so monsters from both the water and the land could partake. Three merwomen floated along-side it, and a kraken was splashing nearby. On the land were even more creatures.

Malse stepped up to the hut, still pretending like he knew what he was doing, and took a seat at the table. A big cat, a mngwa he thought, sat to his left, dark gray fur standing on end. Across the table was a lizardman shuffling several decks of cards with his several hands at once. Aliens, owlmen, and chupacabras filled in the rest of table.

"When's this thing getting started, any-hoo?" said the kraken. He poked his tentacles through the surface of the water one by one in a repeating pattern, clearly annoyed at the delay.

The lizardman rolled his eyes and sighed. "Hold ya fins, I'm almost ready."

Malse watched the monsters around him fiddling with coins and dirty old bills while they waited. He pulled out several of his own coins and dropped them on the table, ready to make a few bets if he needed to. At this point, he'd empty his pockets if he could learn more about what happened last night.

A conversation carried on between the merwomen in the water to his right. "Well anyways, I ended up having Kadyn go over there to see what was going on. Their grass was untended and they were past due on other fines. And you will never believe what we saw through their window…"

Silly neighborhood gossip was of no interest to Malse. The mngwa to his left was now stooding, and paced along the length of the table. The beast seemed a bit unsettled.

"Will you calm down Draak?" the lizardman asked the cat, before turning to address the rest of the crowd. "Alright, everyone, let's get started."

Conversation hushed all around and the creatures in the water moved closer.

"We'll start by going through last week's PHAT bets."

The lizard man rattled off who won bets based on piasa clues that were found, and the subsequent hunts that took place.

"Nothing at the factory, you fuckin' kiddin' me?" It was a chupacabra that spoke, anger apparent in his voice. His long claws tittered on the table and a low growl came from deep in his chest.

"I only report what I know. Moving on."

The lizardman finished settling payouts and debts over the hunts, and then started with the traditional stuff. He lined up the many decks of cards and several games started up. Malse played, betting little here and there, never losing or winning too much. The mngwa, Draak he now knew, continued to drop coins over and over again, as if he was a bottomless pit of money. Spoiled little brat.

Out of nowhere, a jackalope shoved Draak aside as he made his way to the table, the stench of day-old ale from Pashimi's following behind. Without hesitation, the jackalope's long paw was on the table, near pounding, trying to get the lizardman's attention.

"So this is how ya grieve, huh, Banut?" The lizardman curved his scale lip in pure derision.

Banut threw down some coins. "Just deal me in, and throw the rest on my credit."

The lizardman laughed. "Ya damn fool, ya can't play on against credit if you never pay it off. I'm sick of your shit."

Banut slammed his massive jackalope antlers on the table. Everything scattered, coins rolling from the table, and a strained silence fell over the crowd.

"Deal. Me. In."

The lizardman's face fell into a neutral stare as he started dealing a new game. "Yes, sir."

The kraken splashed in the water, spinning to the merwomen beside her.

"Rumor has it he's lost the entire Ares fortune at these little get-to-gethers," she said, as her three eyes glimmered with excitement. "I heard he's so broke, he ain't gonna be able to even pay for his own son's funeral. Damn shame."

Maybe there was more to this Kevan Ares murder than he thought. Maybe something happened within the family? As revenge for debts held by his father?

Was Malse out of his league amongst this spoiled crowd?

The mngwa's eyes widened as he heard the kraken's rumor. He was unsure of himself, maybe scared? Draak caught Malse staring and moved far too quickly to pick up his cards and throw more coins to the middle of the table.

After another round of losing, the mngwa leaned over to Banut. He tried to stay quiet, but Malse's Jersey devil ears rarely failed him.

"Banut, if things are—"

"You fucking loser!" Banut was not quiet at all, once again interrupting the games. "You got my son killed!"

Banut shoved his antlers at Draak, pushing the cat to the corner of the hut. The other monsters scattered away from the conflict, but not too far that they missed watching what went down.

Draak used the full weight of all four of his paws to shove Banut back. The jackalope went careening across the table to the other side of the room, nearly falling into the water. Draak purred as he rounded the table and stared down at the father of the murdered monster.

Banut rose from the ground, and when he did, a murmur rippled through the crowd. There were deep scratches across the jackalope's face and chest, blood darkening his light brown fur. He hopped away quickly, not making eye contact with anyone, as he tried to escape his own shame.

It was time to involve Orli. Malse could no longer shoulder this on his own.

Orli

Orli gazed around the quiet mngwa subdivision in Royal Kire. The raving father she met at the station earlier was nowhere to be found, and she hoped it stayed like that.

The pieces were about to fall together, she just knew it.

The mngwa subdivision of Royal Kire was a large circle, with homes running along the outside and large, freshly manicured lawns in the middle. At the center was a beautiful statue of a leaping mngwa, the first to come to Turu.

All of the houses were large, and all were elaborate, typical of the Royal Kire aesthetic. A gentle breeze sent dandelion seeds into the air, and Orli breathed deep. Spring was her favorite time of the year, and it wasn't often she was able to enjoy the crisp air in such a green and vibrant space.

The house she stood in front of belonged to Draak's family, the grass in front glittering. It hadn't rained in several days, despite the season, so she was sure it wasn't dew that caused the glimmer.

She carefully placed her large, brown feet into the grass and knelt. Fine bits of something were scattered all over the grass. The substance was vaguely familiar, similar to what she saw at the crime scene. She brushed a small amount of the powder into a bag for comparison later.

Orli stepped off the grass and continued her way past the other homes. An older mngwa laid sprawled on the lawn in front of another house, a deep purr emanating from the creature. The mngwa really loved their sun time.

She almost missed it, but that same shimmer she saw at Draak's home surrounded the elderly mngwa that was sunbathing. She paused, considering her words so as to not sound crazy, and prompted the creature.

"Excuse me, ma'am. Do you have a quick moment?"

The mngwa eyed Orli suspiciously. "I'm kind of in the middle of something."

"I was just wondering…" Orli trailed off, unsure of how to best phrase her question. "Do you know why the grass glitters like that?"

The mngwa glanced around, annoyance creeping across her face. "Everyone has these fancy new water systems. They fine you if your grass ain't green, ya know?"

Orli sighed, knowing this didn't explain the powder, but this creature seemed completely clueless to her surroundings.

"Good point. Thanks."

Orli continued through the neighborhood, and realized the glitter was more prominent than she initially thought. It seemed to form a path, zig-zagging its way across the neighborhood, across the lawns. Her heart beat a little faster as she continued to follow the shimmering path out of the mngwa subdivision and into the center of Royal Kire.

The path wound its way chaotically throughout the prosperous neighborhood before jerking away towards a large house on her right. The Ares house.

Excitement rattled her bones as she made her way up the front walkway. The glittered path ran through the lawn and over a fence that surrounded the mansion. She wouldn't be able to access their property without explicit consent.

She pounded on the front door, anxious that her lack of answers would upset the family. Rayna opened the door, anxiety spreading across her face when she recognized Orli on her doorstep.

"Mrs. Ares, I'm so happy you're home. I was wondering if you'd let me into your back yard?"

"Surely there's no evidence here, why are you not over at the factory?" Rayna was annoyed that Orli did not come bearing answers. "Why are you wasting your time bothering us?"

The comment stung. For someone that used to be such a close friend, Rayna sure did look down on Orli now.

"I have to investigate all angles, Mrs. Ares. I don't believe you or your husband are involved."

That may have been a white lie, as she hadn't ruled out any suspects yet. The presence of the mothman blood inside the house in conjunction with this mysterious trail that led her here certainly raised a lot of questions.

Rayna eventually gave in, leading Orli through the home and out a wide door into the backyard. The property was impressive. The policefoot wondered how so much land could fit into the cramped Turu she grew up in. The amount of privilege held by some monsters in this Nessie-forsaken city was too much for her to bear at times.

As soon as Orli stepped onto the grass, she caught sight of the shine again. It continued on its haphazard way towards the back of the Ares property. Orli followed it until she cloaked in the shadows of tall trees lining the edge of the property, and the glimmer became harder to spot. The silence of the small forest she had entered was deafening. Each foot crunched on leaves underfoot, one in front of the other, and she narrowed her eyes.

"What ever could you be looking for out here?"

Orli nearly jumped out of her skin, spinning around defensively. She had no idea the jackalope had followed her.

Rayna recognized the passing fear on Orli's face and quickly apologized. "Oh, I'm so sorry. I just… We never come out this far. Banut sometimes, to keep the lawn trimmed, but not often, no…" She trailed off, confusion entering her eyes.

"I'm following a lead," Orli said.

The policefoot needed this investigation to continue without an audience.

She said, "Mrs. Ares, please, if you could just head back inside, it would be best if I continued this in private."

Rayna nodded, unsure of herself, before turning away and hopping back towards the house.

Orli continued through the murky forest, trying to find where the shimmer might lead. Eventually she reached a stone wall, which must be the edge of the Ares property.

The dust didn't carry on up the wall like it had at the front fence. Did it end here? She glanced around, hoping to find some clue as to what happened, when she saw an arm sprawling out from behind a tree.

She stepped towards it, slightly crouched in case of a surprise attack, and looked behind the tree. On the ground lay a dark gray creature, its body mangled and bloodied. A rotting stench had combined with the moist air of the forest which told Orli that this body had been here for at least twelve hours, maybe even longer.

This was the body of a mothman that had been through one hell of a fight. Its wings were spread wide, torn to shreds in places. Its face was pummeled, with one of its two eyes completely gone, long scarred over. The monster was gutted, its entrails spilling across the dried dirt ground. Its mouth hung open, a look of anger cemented on its face. It felt pain before its death.

There were large, deep claw marks on the sides and back of the creature, much larger than any she'd seen before. These were the claw marks of a creature that didn't belong in Turu, she was sure of it.

"I knew it," Rayna said, sobbing behind her.

Orli spun, once again surprised by the shifty jackalope.

"Do you know who this is?" Orli asked. This was her whole case. She knew the mothmen were at the center of all of this.

"No. But Banut..." Rayna broke down, collapsing to the ground. "I knew he owed them money."

Orli was going to need some backup, and fast. She led the jackalope away from the crime scene and into the house, where she would call for help and maybe get some answers from this trainwreck of a family.

Malse flew from the lakes at Royal Kire to the police station in the center of Turu as quickly as he could. He'd spent all day trying to find proof that the mothmen had committed murder, but instead he'd discovered more information than he knew what to do with.

He didn't need Orli's prying eyes and overactive imagination quizzing him on mafia business, but this was too important to keep from her.

Once he arrived at the station, he burst through the doors.

"Orli!" He bounced between desks and knocked steaming tea from a chupacabra's paws. "Sorry, have you seen Orli?"

The angry chupacabra barked at Malse. "She's investigating a murder."

"Where is she? I have information regarding the murder of Kevan Ares!"

A quiet fell over the station and Malse felt all eyes turn to him.

He continued, and lowered his voice. "I need to speak with her now."

The chupacabra nodded, wiping shroom tea from its chest and face.

"She went to Royal Kire, to the mngwa subdivision," the monster explained. "But it might be best if you waited here."

Malse was already shoving his way towards the door.

He should have known she'd be in Royal Kire.

First, he coasted over the mngwa subdivision, but it was quiet, just a sunbather and no policefoot in sight.

He headed towards the lakes on the opposite side of the neighborhood. The ahool jungle passed by underneath him and there was still no sight of Orli. Then, the rows of rainbow houses. The bigfoot would stand out here and yet she is nowhere to be seen.

He was about to give up and return to the station when he saw her brown, thick fur-lined body step out of a white mansion.

He plunged toward her, the excitement of the moment tingling his skin.

"Malse!" Orli said, confused. "What are you doing over here?"

He was panting as he landed, trying to catch his breath before speaking.

"So?" she demanded. "Spit it out!"

"Promise you won't be mad," he said, taking a deep breath. "Please."

"Oh Nessie, what've you done now?"

"Well, you know how the mothmen have been causing us trouble, right?" Malse asked. "I figured, maybe they were the ones that did this. Killed Kevan Ares, I mean."

Orli shook her head. "You'd make a terrible investigator, you know that?"

"Oh c'mon, Orli! You know it's possible!"

"Anything is possible, yes!" Orli replied. "But you can't go around making assumptions."

"I know, I know," Malse said, his face burning with embarrassment. "But because of that, I decided to follow around this other Syndicate guy, Sigrun. I overheard him say some things…"

Malse recounted his day, telling Orli all the details he could remember about PHAT, the gambling club, everything. When her eyes lit up, he knew he did good.

"Well, Malse," Orli said. "I've gotta admit, this is helpful, but you need to back off. Forget about this case. I've gotta go back inside and finish this thing." She gestured at the white mansion behind her.

She walked away, leaving him alone in a place he didn't belong. A place neither of them belonged. He was stunned. He knew his intel was good, he knew it. And she still brushed him off. Was she not grateful?

He would wait. Wait for her to step from that house, wait to help her finish this case. Mothmen or not, he was invested now.

Orli

Malse's surprise visit to Royal Kire was the key to this murder case she didn't know she needed. A club to hunt the *piasa*? She nearly couldn't believe it. Some monsters actually believe it existed. And the gambling.

The gambling element is a crucial part of the puzzle.

Orli sat down across from Rayna while the tears poured from the jackalope's eyes, soaking the peppered gray fur and catching in her whiskers. The inside of the Ares house was high and very open, the walls adorned with gaudy decorations that seemed to scream nothing more than "I'm rich!"

All this money spent while Orli's neighbors starved.

A chasm split Turu right down the middle, and it was getting worse every day.

"I knew he'd gotten all mixed up with the wrong crowd," Rayna said, choking each word out between sobs. "I knew there was something wrong."

"Who? Kevan?"

Rayna looked offended. "My boy? No, my boy is perfect. My husband, I always had suspicions."

Orli let the mother vent. If Banut Ares was getting involved with gangs—*the Devil's Syndicate or the mothmen?*—that raised a whole lot of possible motives for the murder of his son.

"What crowd, Mrs. Ares?" Thanks to Malse, Orli now knew that Banut was gambling down at the lakes, but she didn't know who else might be involved.

"Oh, I have no idea, don't you see?" The anger was coming through now. "He never told me shit! He hid it all."

"It seems like you might have a better idea than you're letting on. Please, Rayna."

"You want me to speculate? Fine! I'll speculate. My husband, that grimy monster, was probably down there where you creatures live. Sleeping with some merwhores, gambling away all his fucking money. *Our* fucking money." Her eyes had dried by now, and the jackalope rubbed her antlers, a nervous tick of some kind. "You know he's been restricting my spending lately? Like somehow we can't fucking afford another piece of owlmen art? So it all makes sense now."

Rayna's head shook violently as the pieces started to fall together for Orli.

"And he just leaves for hours on end, in the middle of the day. Like now, where is that loser? Which merwoman is he with today? What a low-class piece of…"

"Okay, okay, I get it," Orli said, cutting her off. "Slow down. How much of this do you know for certain?"

"I know he's gone right now. I know he left without telling me where he went. I know your people just dragged a…" Her voice trailed off. "Dragged a body…" Another round of sobs began.

Orli was impatient, but decided to hold firm. She'd stay here, partially to keep an eye on the jackalope, but mostly hoping her husband would decide to return home. Orli paced around the massive mansion, and eyed a collection of art depicting the deific Loch Ness monster. Nearby, there was a collection of owlmen feathers with a now nonexistent pattern of brown and gray.

Orli was on the opposite side of the spacious room when she noticed an uneven glimmering shape contained inside an elaborate stained wood frame. It almost looked like the scales on a merwomen, but the piece was much larger.

She lifted the frame carefully and carried it back towards Rayna. The woman cooled off when she saw Orli holding the piece of art, a slight smile finding its way onto her face through the tears.

"My Kevan," she said, a longing in her voice that Orli felt in her heart.

"Did this belong to him?"

"Yes, one of his friends gave it to him." Rayna reached for the frame and Orli passed it over to her. "The glittery appearance is so unique, so beautiful. It was such a thoughtful gift."

"Oh, this was a gift?"

"Yes, yes. His friend Jahat, you know him? The ahool, lives over in those jungle homes up the road." Rayna smiled the longer she gazed at the frame. The friends were so close.

"This may be an important piece of evidence in your son's murder," Orli said. "Did Jahat ever tell you where he found this, Mrs. Ares?"

"Oh, no, no, but I don't know that anyone ever asked. Why is this important, Orli?"

"That glimmer," Orli replied, gesturing at the frame in Rayna's hand. "That's what led me here today. That's what led me to the body on your property."

Rayna was stunned. She was about to question further when the door burst open, Banut striding into the room.

"Banut, what…" Rayna's voice cracked as she addressed her husband.

Banut's face was swollen and scratched, his snout and lips a single darkened mass, and his eyes half-closed.

"Banut, your face…" Rayna tried again. Her beady black eyes somehow grew even larger as she watched her husband limp-hop away from them.

"Stay here, okay?" Orli said, more of a command than a question. "I'll go speak with him."

Orli followed quickly behind Banut as he escaped into the yard, a long pipe of hashish hanging from his mouth. He was staring towards the trees at the back of the property. She could see the confusion in his posture. Or maybe that was from his injuries.

He spun, trying to growl something fierce, and then wincing in pain. His pipe fell to the ground.

"What's all this?" His voice was muffled as he raised himself to his hind legs, attempting to match Orli's towering height and gesturing at the investigators on his property.

"Mr. Ares, if you'd come inside, we can talk. I have a few questions."

"Absolutely not, you good for nothing animal." Banut's tired, inflamed eyes bore into Orli like daggers. "Get those dirty chupacabras off my property!"

"I can't do that, Mr. Ares. A dead body has been found on your property, and if you'd step back inside I'd like to ask you a few questions."

Banut laughed at this, disbelief coloring his words. "So what, now I'm a suspect?"

Orli corralled the blustering jackalope inside and sat him down with Rayna. His wife's eyes never rose from the ground in front of her.

"The body of a mothman was discovered at the back of your property. What do you know about that?"

Orli saw the ears on Banut shift ever so slightly. He knew something.

"I don't know any mothmen, so how would I know about that?" Banut was being careful with his words. "Right, dear?"

Rayna's gaze never moved from the floor.

"Rayna, back me up here," Banut said, as uncomfortable laughter spilled from his mouth.

"I know you're holding back on me, Mr. Ares," Orli said. "You've been lying to your wife. Disappearing for hours at a time without warning. And then there's the money–"

"What?" Banut's temper changed from one of fake confusion to anger quicker than she thought possible. "Who said there was anything to do with money?"

"You've been gambling it, haven't you? How much have you lost?" She knew this was true based on her earlier conversation with Malse, but was curious how he'd react to the accusation.

The jackalope stared at her, his resolve weakening. "It wasn't that bad!"

"Start from the beginning."

"Rayna always wants nice things. The house, you know, we could always use more money to keep things proper."

A storm raged inside of Orli. Sitting here, she was surrounded by elegance and wealth.

Banut continued. "I figured, what's the worst that can happen right? I have enough money, I can use that to make more. But those fucking losers, they cheat! I tell you, they cheat, and they steal, and they're out to get me! They've taken everything I have!"

"Who?"

"Who?? I don't know who…" Banut said, his posture crumbling further as he shook his head. "Someone behind the scenes finances the whole thing, the whole club. And the debt I owe them, oh no."

Orli watched as the realization spread through Banut, as he began to understand the impact his extracurriculars may have had on his son's murder.

"I'm going to need you both to join me down at the station while we sort this whole mess out. Mr. Ares, I want to hear everything you know about this gambling club."

Elrong

The night of the murder

Elrong shoved the owlman against the wall, leaning in so his one red eye nearly came in contact with its feathered face. A gang of mothmen stood guard for the shakedown.

"Your debts are high, bird. Your payments are behind. You know the consequences."

The owlman sputtered a reply.

Turu is all idiots filled with excuses.

He shoved his knee into the owlman's midsection, and the monster crumbled to the ground. Elrong backed away, waving at his goons to take care of the mess. The owlman's hoots echoed in the alley. No one messed with the mothmen.

When he'd heard enough from the creature that was now barely alive, he pulled back his goons and they moved into the streets. The drunken crowds parted to make room for them, afraid of the beatdowns handed out on the regular.

What he could really go for right now is a Jersey devil. If he caught even a glimpse of one of those deadbeats, it was off to the races. Nothing felt better under his curled fist than their long, soft faces.

As they approached the abandoned factory on the edge of the city, the rowdy crowds thinned, and Elrong set out to discuss business.

He addressed one of his comrades. "Make sure you grab a bag of coins for tomorrow's gambling circle. Drop it off with the lizardman first thing in the morning. He should have records for you."

"Yes, sir, can do, sir." His minions were all obedient fools, eager to please, but also too afraid to speak out of turn.

The street contained only the natural light the full moon above them provided. The silhouette of the factory loomed just ahead as they stepped into a large clearing between buildings.

"We got you just where we want you," a female voice behind Elrong said. He spun quickly, in a defensive stance, but was knocked to the ground before he could see anything.

Sharp claws dug into his chest and Elrong screamed, moving his wings to give him leverage over the beast that got the jump on him. He managed to get out from under the creature to get his first look at his attacker.

In front of him stood a monumental monster covered in thick gray fur, sharp teeth bared and long nails held at the ready for another attack.

A werewolf, he thought. *There hasn't been a werewolf in Turu for decades.*

Elrong and his goons stood back to back, at a disadvantage and surrounded. In addition to the werewolf, Elrong saw that idiot kid jackalope and understanding came crashing down. This was that little fucker's revenge for what he did to his dad, was it? Well not tonight. As they've seen time and time again, a stupid jackalope was no match for a mothman.

Elrong was blessed with the gift of partial premonition and knew that Kevan Ares was going to die tonight, and by Nessie he hoped it was by the hands of a mothman. This is what happens when daddy doesn't pay up!

"On my signal," Elrong said, his voice as hushed as he could make it. "Ready... go!"

All three mothmen beat their wings and rose into the air. Seemed like the rich kid had a plan for that too, as a fourth body flew into the air with them. The ahool was ready and threw his massive body at the mothman closest to him, in mid-air. The two of them struggled mid-flight, and then both collapsed to the ground.

Meanwhile, Elrong and his other thug got into position before dive-bombing their attackers from above. Apparently jackalopes weren't quite as quick as they thought. That or this one was just a little drunk. Either way, Elrong managed to get the jump on him and leaped on his back. While Elrong was trying to spin the jackalope around to face him, he was tackled by the strong paws of a mngwa.

The big cat forced down Elrong's wings so the mothman couldn't take flight again, and the werewolf came in for the kill. Elrong knew he was about to take a massive hit, until one of his goons plowed into the werewolf, taking it on alone. That gave Elrong the moment he needed, crushing his fist into the mngwa's side and knocking it down.

Elrong pounded on the crumpled cat until it stopped moving. He turned to find his next target, just in time to see the jackalope barreling at him, and knocking him down with those wide antlers. He wasn't down long, though, and realized the fight was now three versus two, as the cat was unable to bring himself up and the ahool was drunkenly missing his punches.

The three mothmen focused their attention on the werewolf, bringing themselves off the ground and surrounding the beast. They landed blow after blow, but the werewolf fought on despite being weakened.

A noise came from Elrong's right, echoes of scuffling, and a shadow bounced around the corner in that direction. He thought he saw the long face of a Jersey devil. He should've known these idiots would team up with the Syndicate!

Elrong abandoned his beatdown of the werewolf and flew towards the noise. The scuffling continued, as if the creature were running away. Just as his hidden attacker's small wings opened, Elrong came crashing down onto it.

He was happy to see it was in fact a Jersey devil, and the monster had nowhere to run.

It was easy for Elrong to assume control of the monster. He scratched and tore at the devil below until it stopped fighting back. He heard footsteps behind him and spun to see his two goons.

"What the hell are you doing here?"

They looked confused and one said, "We just followed you…"

"You idiot! We had them! I was just coming to take care of this devil they had hiding in the shadows!"

Elrong left the bloodied and unconscious devil in the dirt and strode back towards the clearing where they were attacked. When he got there, no one remained.

"They got away!" Elrong was seething. He was going to find Kevan Ares tonight, and he was going to kill him. He could still see the jackalope's bloodied, dead body.

Out of the corner of his eye, there was a shimmer in the sky above the factory. When he turned to look, something disappeared behind the smokestacks.

Probably that drunk ahool.

"They've gone into the factory, let's go!"

They flew up to the roof of the factory, investigating each possible hiding spot. The moonlight made the cement below them glimmer. As they passed by the smokestacks and approached the center of the roof, they found a large hole, cement crumbling into the endless dark below them.

"Wait here," Elrong said to his mates. "I don't need you fucking up anything else tonight. If you hear me scream, come help me finish those idiots off."

He slowly beat his wings so as to make as little noise as possible, and lowered himself down. Large unmoving mechanical beasts surrounded him.

There were muffled voices off to his left, and he was confident now that he had the jump on his enemies. As he stepped through pitch black factory, his single eye adjusted and he began to make out the shadows around him.

He stayed hidden as he moved closer, and the muted conversation slowly came into focus.

"I thought for sure Jessica would be stronger. And Jahat, oh no. He was so drunk!"

It was the jackalope, he thought. He was sure of it.

"You should be avoiding them, what you did tonight was silly," A rich, female voice said. "I mean, just look at the state of you!"

"I know, Debrania. I just..." Kevan paused, the deafening silence ringing in Elrong's ears. "I was hoping if we could conquer those mothmen, maybe they'd lay off my dad, you know?"

Elrong peered around the corner at the two voices, wondering if the others, the werewolf especially, were hiding here as well. His eyesight had sharpened even further, bringing into focus the source of the voice.

He stumbled back. It's not possible.

Huddled up in the corner of the factory, mere feet from where Elrong stood, the measly jackalope was wrapped up by a massive creature's long, scaly body. Beautiful red wings were spread open, and a bearded face gazed down at Kevan. The creature's skin glittered, and its pincer claws gently caressed the jackalope's body. The end of the monster's tail flopped casually almost ten feet from where they lay.

The creature was beautiful, and it was massive, bigger than anything else that lived in Turu.

It turned out the piasa was real.

Orli

Orli stepped out of the Ares household, still processing everything Banut had told her about the gambling club he was involved with. He managed to fill in many of the missing details from what Malse told her. But there was still something missing, something important.

As she stepped down onto the main road, she nearly bumped into someone.

"Malse? What are you still doing here?"

"Orli, I need to know." The Jersey devil had a pleading look in his eyes. "I spent all day trying to pin this on the mothmen, trying to put you on their tail, but I'm wrong. I can feel it. I need to know who killed him."

"Why do you care?"

Malse shook his head. "I know you won't understand…"

Orli walked past the Jersey devil and said, "Walk with me. Tell me what's going on."

She wanted to sympathize with her old friend, to understand what was going on, but with his involvement in the Syndicate, it was hard.

"It's been so long since we saw Rayna," Malse said. "I realized today how much I missed her. And you."

A silence fell between them then, as Orli considered this. Was she any better than Rayna? Was Malse? They all ran away to do different things. To meet different people. To live different lives. Why did she hold such a grudge against the two of them all these years?

"I miss you both, too," Orli said, stopping in the middle of Royal Kire, right in front of the rainbow houses. She turned to Malse and wrapped her arms around him for the first time in years. "I'm sorry, Malse."

The Jersey devil pushed away after a short time, his Syndicate toughness probably not allowing for too much emotion. He laughed and they continued walking.

"I kinda get why Rayna moved here," he said. "There are some cool looking creatures. Like the kraken and all those tentacles? And those ahools with the prongs on their wings. Kinda sucks we never really got to meet any of them over on the other side."

Orli stopped dead in her tracks and laid a huge kiss on Malse's face.

"Malse you beautiful fucking devil, you did it!"

There were some loose ends to tie up, but she had it. She knew who murdered Kevan Ares.

The body of the dead one-eyed mothman laid on a metal table in front of Orli and the medical examiner.

"The claw marks on Elrong's body are incredibly unique," the lizardman explained. "I don't believe they belong to any creature known to me, certainly not any living here in Turu."

This was the one piece of this crime that still confused Orli. She ran through the possibilities in her mind. The claw marks were different from those found on Kevan's body, much longer and wider, almost as if whatever caused them had grabbed the mothman and held him in a tight grip.

"Make sure you save extra pictures of these ones, and a mold if you can manage it," Orli said.

"Of course."

"What else have you learned? Cause of death?"

"I don't have a certain cause of death, no," he said with a frown. "He lost a lot of blood from whatever caused all this damage. I'll likely just mark the cause of death as blood loss leading to exsanguination."

The lizardman stepped over to his desk on the other side of the room and continued. "An interesting thing though, Elrong's blood matches the sample you obtained from the Ares household."

"That lines up with what I expected."

He nodded and handed Orli a folder containing all the details of all the tests that were run. She flipped through the pages, confirming for herself what he just shared.

Banut and Rayna Ares were currently sitting in her office, awaiting further questioning. She had sent one of the chupacabras to round up Kevan's friends as well. She had a lot of questions she still needed to ask.

"The mothman found on your property was Elrong." Orli stared at the stunned jackalopes in front of her. "He was one of the major suspects I've been trying to track down in connection with your son's death."

"I… No…" Rayna sputtered, trying to form words, but unable to. "We had no idea he was out there."

"And that isn't all. When I visited you earlier this morning to notify you of Kevan's death, I collected a sample of blood from the inside of your door. Turns out that blood belongs to Elrong. But I think I know how we can explain that, right, Banut?"

"Me? You think I brought him there?" Banut asked, scoffing at the notion. "No mothman has ever set foot in my home." He shifted uneasily on his long paws and his eyes darted frantically around the room.

Orli stayed silent, watching Banut's eyes.

Banut continued his restless dance, as if considering how much information to share.

He sighed and finally said, "Fine. Fine, ok, but we had nothing to do with his death, I swear!" He looked towards his wife. "I'm sorry Rayna, I'm so sorry. I owe the mothmen thousands, okay? I've lost nearly everything."

Rayna seemed numb to this further confirmation, drained of emotion.

Banut looked back at Orli and continued. "They were threatening me, okay? I ran into them yesterday, and Elrong was very much alive. Alive enough to shove me around at least. I defended myself, scratched him. That must be where the blood came from."

"But this morning, when I first saw you, you weren't beat up like this."

"No, this…" Banut shook his head. "This was… I saw Kevan's friend today. I'm sorry." His head hung, antlers rattling against the metal table.

Banut has so many enemies inside the crumbling walls of Turu.

"Mr. Ares, why wouldn't you share this information about the mothmen with us?" Orli was furious. This explained why the gang would be attacking Kevan.

Banut just continued to shake his head. The Ares family was now destitute, in debt to the mothmen gang.

"Look, I already told you everything, alright?" Jessica pleaded. "I don't know anything else!"

"I just want to go through a few more things with you. Kevan. Tell me why you befriended him."

"What?" Jessica went from annoyed to confused quickly, and a flicker of concern passed through her eyes. "Well, for one, he's fine with me when I'm in my human body. Why does this even matter?"

Orli didn't doubt this to be true, but she knew Jessica was holding back. She knew about Jessica's deal with the Syndicate. "How did you meet him?"

"Ran into him at one of my rare trips to Pashimi's. Him and his friends are hard to miss, they're loud drunks."

"Kevan grew up in Royal Kire," Orli said. "With Draak and Jahat. Those friendships run deep. It's odd to me that you'd suddenly join them, someone who seems to avoid interaction with the other creatures most of the time."

Jessica just stared at Orli, as if waiting for her to continue, so Orli did. "I guess I just wonder how well you know him?"

"I might not have grown up in that ritzy part of Turu, but that doesn't mean I don't know Kevan."

"Did you know why the mothmen constantly bothered him?"

"Troublemakers, I guess they saw a target in Kevan. They could be after Draak or Jahat, too?"

"Kevan Ares was poor. His father gambled away the family fortune. He was in debt to the mothmen."

Jessica's eye widened ever so slightly, before falling back into place as she tried to remain calm. That about confirms what Malse overheard, then.

"I don't know anything about that," Jessica said.

"Hello Draak," Orli said to the mngwa sitting calmly across from her. The jet black stripes down the side of the big cat reflected the neutral white light of the barren interrogation room. He nodded to Orli but otherwise stayed silent, waiting for her to start the conversation.

"You grew up with Kevan, right?"

Draak nodded, but stayed silent, his posture perfect and statuesque.

Orli placed the framed, glittering scale on the table in the center of the room. "Have you ever seen this?"

Draak moved forward and glanced at the frame briefly. "Yes, Jahat gave that to Kevan. I've no idea what it is."

"The glitter is fairly unique. Nothing like this is found in Turu, not that I've heard of at least."

Draak nodded, seeming to agree with her.

"Thing is, though. I followed a trail of glitter through Royal Kire. Led me straight onto the Ares property. I picked it up near your home."

Confusion spread across Draak's face. "What are you saying?"

"I certainly can't prove that it came from your home. In fact, I can't be certain it even started there, but I was hoping you'd be able to identify this scale here, in the frame."

Draak shook his head. "All I remember is when Jahat gave it to Kevan, months back. Was all secretive about it, weird, ya know? But Kevan loved it, you could see how much he admired the gift."

Orli considered this. It further cemented Orli's working theory. Kevan may have been familiar with the scale, with the glitter.

The ahool paced along the back of the interrogation room while Orli remained seated, the frame sitting on the table in front of her. Jahat was clicking his spurs on the tips of his wings together quickly.

"Just found it, you know? Just something I found, I don't even remember where." Orli knew that Jahat was lying. She knew he was a member of the Piasa Hunter Acquisition Team.

"Okay. What did Kevan think when you gave it to him?"

"Oh you know, he liked it fine. Put it on a shelf in his house, but there's so much stuff there, so many little things. Probably got lost."

"Do you know if Kevan knew what this was?" Orli asked.

Jahat frowned and shook his head. "No, no. None of us know what it is." Jahat chuckled nervously and avoided making eye contact with Orli.

Orli left the room, taking the frame with her, and considered the interviews. Despite not getting clear answers from any of the friends, Orli was beginning to form a picture of Kevan's last night in her head.

Kevan

The night of the murder

Kevan hopped around a corner, blood dripping into his eyes. The mothmen were stronger than he expected. He needed to escape before they found him again. He cut quickly through random streets, trying to make his path random and unpredictable. He had no idea who might be following him. After several minutes, he finally came to a halt, and listened.

The suffocating pitch black night folded around him. There was not a sound to be heard. He approached the edge of the building to his right and peered around the corner. If anything lurked in the shadows, Kevan could not see or hear it.

He re-oriented himself and realized he was somehow still only a few blocks from the abandoned factory. His zig-zagging escape didn't bring him very far. He didn't want to run into Elrong again so he stuck to alleyways and side streets, before approaching the factory from the side.

There was a hole in the back corner of the building, one he used frequently, and hopped through. Silhouettes formed quickly, his eyes used to the murkiness. He followed his usual path, winding through machinery and cobwebs, before coming upon the wide hole in the high ceiling. He knocked his antlers in a specific cadence against a nearby hunk of metal, causing a clanging noise that echoed in the silence, and then he waited.

Minutes later, a majestic beast, *his* majestic beast, glided through the hole above and into the factory. The air around Debrania shimmered as she landed next to him, and Kevan let it envelope him. They remained quiet, moving to a corner of the building, where they settled down.

His relationship with Debrania remained a secret for the past several months for so many reasons. If she was spotted out anywhere in Turu, she would be killed by the sheer number of creatures who wished her dead, that hunted her, that made money off of her. Not to mention his parents, they'd never allow him to continue a relationship with what they thought to be such a dangerous creature. Debrania was different though. She wasn't actually dangerous. Not to Kevan.

Debrania wrapped her large, red feathered wings around Kevan before he started rattling on about what happened that night.

"And I thought for sure Jessica would be stronger. And Jahat, oh no Jahat. He was so drunk!"

"You should be avoiding them, what you did tonight was silly," she said. "I mean, just look at the state of you!" Her beautiful brown eyes peered into his, pleading with him to leave things alone.

He was frustrated. He knew she was right, but he felt a need to somehow help his father. He never told his friends about his father's debt, but they were willing to help fight the mothmen gang regardless.

"I know, Debrania. I just…I was hoping if we could conquer those mothmen, maybe they'd lay off my dad, you know?"

Before Debrania could reply, a sound bounced from above, maybe in the catwalks. She held a firm paw on Kevan's back.

"Stay here. I will take care of this."

Kevan, feeling the weight of his injuries from earlier setting in, did not protest. He was scared, afraid that Elrong and his goons had tracked him down. If they did manage to find their way inside, Debrania would be able to take on three of them easily, shredding them to bits like she's done to so many others.

The stunning piasa flew high, close to the ceiling, and approached the catwalk that ran along the walls of the factory. From where he sat, Kevan could barely make out her silhouette as she rose. He heard her sharp claws land on the metal catwalk when suddenly she yelped. It was a scream unlike anything he'd ever heard, and he was sure something had happened to Debrania.

Kevan moved without thinking, and climbed up to the catwalks from behind, across the abandoned machinery, hoping to surprise Debrania's attacker.

When he was on the catwalk, he could see Debrania in the distance, and in between them those large, familiar wings.

Debrania yelped again, moving towards Kevan and her attacker. "Run, my love! Get out of here, I'm okay!"

She didn't sound okay, and Kevan braced his posture, ready to pounce on the creature from behind. Just as he was leaping, the monster turned, its wings curled in a defensive maneuver.

Kevan's body was on fire, gashed all over, as his head smashed on the edge of the window and he tumbled through glass, falling violently to the ground.

Elrong

The night of the murder

The piasa flew to the rafters in search of the loud noise from above. Something must have attacked the monster as it let out a high-pitched bellow, and the jackalope bound over the machines to catwalks to help.

Elrong stepped from his hidden position to get a clearer view of the seeming battle that raged near the ceiling, but could only make out shadows in struggle, backlit by the moon shining in through the window.

The jackalope stood on the left, and the piasa was on the right. In between them, the attacker was focused on the piasa.

"Run, my love! Get out of here, I'm okay," a female voice said, the sound barely making it to Elrong's ears. He continued to move closer, hoping to get a better view of the fight, and who might be attempting to fight this magnificent beast. He beat his wings softly, rising to a perch on top of one of the ancient pieces of machinery.

From this higher vantage point, he could better make out the struggle. Kevan was ready to attack the other monster from behind, when it turned, curling its wings in an attempt to defend itself. Kevan yelped, but Elrong was unable to see how the other beast had attacked the jackalope. And then suddenly, Kevan lost his balance, shattering a nearby glass window and falling from the building.

"Kevan, my love! No!"

For some odd reason, the attacker backed off, fluttering out and away, through the hole in the factory ceiling that Elrong had entered through. The piasa looked through the window at Kevan, and continued to wail.

Elrong remained crouched, unsure of what to do. He considered following the attacker, but he was keen to know where the piasa might run off to. His mouth watered at the thought of the money he could make, knowing where the beast lived.

At some point, the piasa spun around and must have seen Elrong, because the creature moved towards him violently. "You killed my Kevan!"

Elrong leapt from the machine, intending to fly through the ceiling and escape, but the long sharp claws of the piasa dug deep into his back. Elrong howled at the pain, pain so much greater than anything he had ever felt. Tears flowed down his face as he tried to shake himself from the pincer-like grip of the monstrous bird, but each movement, ever so slight, sent a bolt of pain through his body.

The piasa rose from the building, quieting the sobs that came. Even in a moment as horrible as this, it seemed she knew she was still in danger.

They flew, the piasa's glitter flowing freely from her body, as Elrong remained as still as possible. The bird would occasionally readjust her grip on his back and wings, which caused a fresh sting of pain. He was beginning to lose consciousness, but recognized the mansions of Royal Kire below him.

Spots of black formed in his eye and he felt the piasa mercifully release her grip on him. And then his body fell, his wings damaged and useless, slamming first into the trees, and eventually the ground.

"I know it was you," Orli said, as she stared across the interrogation table at the somber creature. "What I don't know is why, but I have a few guesses."

The creature stayed silent, downcast eyes refusing to make eye contact.

"You see, it was pretty easy for me to put most of it together after our last interview," Orli continued. "Your body language revealed so much.

"The glitter was a major clue. Where it led, to Elrong's body. He might've been a criminal, a punk, but he was innocent this time, wasn't he? Wrong place, wrong time?

"What do you think it was that caused the piasa to attack him?"

This got a reaction, the creature in front of her raising its eyes, looking at her for the first time.

Orli continued, "Oh yeah, I know all about the piasa. It's real, as far as I can tell. You see, I went over and talked to the leader of PHAT after our last chat. Showed him this," Orli said, gesturing to the framed, glittering scale. "He confirmed it was a major clue that led to some recent hunts. He was also kind enough to share some drawings with me, sketches of what the piasa might look like.

"I'll tell ya, those claws are pretty nasty huh? I know these sketches aren't necessarily the truth, but I'm willing to bet it's those claws that gashed Elrong to death."

"No." The creature finally spoke. "No, that's not possible. None of this is possible. We've been hunting the piasa for decades, it doesn't exist."

"Jahat, I think it does. And I think you almost killed it," Orli said. "Or at least, you certainly tried. But what happened? Why did you kill Kevan?"

"I didn't kill him. If your stupid piasa exists, wouldn't you think she'd have killed–"

"She?" Jahat had made a mistake, just as Orli knew he would. "Who said anything about a she?"

Jahat was stunned. "I... no... some theories predict it's female, but..."

"Save it. Let me continue. We'll see how close I get.

"Some struggle occurs between you and the piasa, is that true? The question is, why was Kevan a part of this? I think that all comes down to the framed scale. You loved Kevan, and you thought the gift of this scale would mean something to him, did you not?"

"Love? No, he was just my friend." Jahat chuckled. The ahool tapped his foot anxiously under the table.

"A friend you gave something meaningful to. You never gave anything like that to Draak. But what happened when you gave it to him? His reaction was more than you expected, wasn't it? His reaction was recognition, and you knew that."

Jahat continued to shake his head, mumbling obscenities under his breath.

"Okay, let's go with that assumption, that Kevan Ares knew about the piasa. He knew it was real, and he hid that from you. He hid that from all of you. Why? My thought? Kevan was in love with the piasa, and when you saw his face the day you gifted him that scale, you knew.

"Last night, after the fight with the mothmen, you all scattered. Maybe you're hiding, maybe you're trying to get home. But something catches your eye doesn't it? Something at the factory. Maybe that's where the piasa is, you think, and you go on an unofficial little hunt.

"You catch the jackalope you've loved your whole life, wrapped in the embrace of the beast you've spent your life hunting. Your rage at this point must have hit an all-time high, right? You engage with the piasa, but Kevan gets involved, trying to protect her. He falls from that window along the catwalk, cracking his skull into pieces. And those sharp prongs at the tips of your wings? They match the marks we found all over Kevan's body. You're the one who pushed him, Jahat. You killed your best friend."

Orli let her story set in. Jahat was tense, as if he was trying to hold an explosion inside of his chest.

After several silent, uneasy minutes, Jahat crumbled. His body collapsed forward, and tears streamed down his face. "It was only an accident, I swear. I wanted to kill that monster, just that awful monster."

Orli listened while Jahat rationalized and explained and cried. No doubt the ahool was deeply in love with his best friend, but his decision to attempt to kill that creature would hold consequences for the rest of his life. And she wondered if it might be time to disband the hunting and gambling collectives that profited off the existence of the piasa.

Orli stepped outside into the center of Turu and looked around at the bustling city she called home. It might be a city of monsters, but under it all, love still thrived. She felt for Kevan, for the piasa, for what they lost. She walked home, past the neverending shacks.

As ugly as it was, this was her home.

Malse knocked back a mug of ale and nodded at Pashimi for another.

She swam circles in the pool behind the bar, mixing drinks and pouring ale for the raucous crowd jammed into the small establishment.

An alien band played a popular tune, and the monsters danced wildly, bouncing into each other with little semblance of coordination. Malse admired the pulsing sound before turning back to his friends.

"This song was my favorite," Rayna yelled over the noise. "I can't believe I forgot about it!"

Orli laughed and sunk her teeth into a molding pus-filled donut. Malse didn't understand why she continued to eat those vile pastries. Just bigfoot things, he guessed.

He was happy the three of them could be together again. Nothing would be the same as all those years ago, though. Not since they grew up, since they lived different lives. But he thought having them here again, it might help him.

Tomorrow he was going to quit the Syndicate. Devils rarely did, but Orli promised she'd protect him from any attacks, and Rayna was ready to offer payment from the small amount she had hidden away from her husband.

They were finally friends again. He couldn't let them down.

Acknowledgments

This project was a special one for us because the Piasa cryptid was the founding stone of our friendship. No, seriously. That bizarre looking cliff painting brought us together. Since we've met, we've gone on a lot of adventures and shared many experiences. We owe so many thanks to our families for their support, our friends for their help, and to each other.

A call-out to Bill Brave who made us a squad and bound us together – he will forever be in our hearts.

And the biggest thanks to Laurel Hightower for our mutual cryptid love and for writing our foreword, Molly Halstead for all the formatting, Natalie Kovacs of Shapelessflame for her stunning cover artwork, and our amazing beta readers for sacrificing their time to help make our stories amazing. And to our families, who supported us as we cried and raged over our manuscripts, and our pets who are just adorable.

And thank you, fellow cryptid lover. May your journeys be ever suspenseful and full of mystery.

Authors

Bridget D. Brave
couples' therapist for Piasa

Bridget D. Brave is a writer and reluctant lawyer living at the edge of the Ozarks. A true Midwesterner by both birth and habit, her non-fiction and fiction can be found in various places, if one knows where to look.

Find her recent weird-ass stuff at: https://www.beedeebrave.com and nearly everywhere online @beedeebrave

P.L. McMillan
Mothman reanimator

P.L. McMillan is a writer whose works have been known to cause rifts in time and space itself…

Well, not quite. But writing often makes her feel that powerful.

P.L. McMillan is a Canadian expat living in the States, after having taught English for three years in Asia. With a passion for cosmic horror and sci-fi horror, P.L. McMillan sees every shadow as an entryway to a deeper look into the black heart of the world, meant to be discovered and explored. Infatuated with the works of Shirley Jackson, H.P. Lovecraft, and Ridley Scott, her dream is to create stories of adventure, of chills, of heartbreak, and thrills.

Visit her at her website at https://www.plmcmillan.com

Or follow her on Twitter or Instagram: @authorPLM

Ryan Marie Ketterer
head of HR for the Turu police force

Ryan Marie Ketterer is from Malden, Massachusetts. Her work can be found forthcoming in Clarkesworld, and currently in Dark Matter Magazine, Cosmic Horror Monthly, and several anthologies. She's a fan of the weird and uncanny, and her writing draws most of its influence from the works of Shirley Jackson and Thomas Ligotti. When she isn't writing stories, Ryan is writing code for a software startup in Boston, MA or training for another road race. You can find her on Twitter and Instagram at @RyanMarie47.

Check out all her weird stuff at: https://linktr.ee/ryanmarie47

Salt Heart Press

"Invention, it must be humbly admitted, does not consist in creating out of void but out of chaos." — Mary Shelley

We at Salt Heart Press seek the best in horror. We live for it, we crave it, we desire it — nothing gives us more pleasure than the thrills and chills found in the perfectly crafted dark tale. As such, it is our mission to seek out fresh voices in the genre, search out the new and unique, the brave and challenging. We want to be scared. We want to be haunted. And we want the same for you.

So take a look at the books we have and keep an eye out for those to come.

https://www.saltheartpress.com/

www.ingramcontent.com/pod-product-compliance
Lightning Source LLC
Chambersburg PA
CBHW060311260626
47160CB00007B/2571